FRINGE RUNNER

Book 1 in the Fringe Series

RACHEL AUKES

FRINGE RUNNER
Book 1 of the FRINGE SERIES

Surprisingly Adequate Publishing
Edited by Stephanie Riva, Riva Reading and
Laurel Kriegler, Kriegler Editing Services
Cover Design by EJR Digital Art

ALSO BY RACHEL AUKES

The Deadland Saga
100 Days in Deadland
Deadland's Harvest
Deadland Rising

Short Stories in the Deadland World
Fat Zombie
At Hell's Gates

Colliding Worlds Trilogy
Collision
Implosion
Explosion

Anthologies
Out of Tune, Vol. 2
Imagines
Never Fear
Stealing Fate
Tales from the SFR Brigade, Vol. 1
Stories on the Go

For the freedom fighters, everywhere.

CONTENTS

The Collective	viii
Acknowledgements	ix
Fringe Runner	1
Glossary of Terms	269

THE COLLECTIVE

The Collective is a collection of six planets within the Milky Way galaxy. The Collective is controlled by the dual leadership of Alluvia and Myr. Only those born on Alluvia and Myr are given legal status as citizens, while all others are considered colonists and receive fewer privileges. The Collective views colonists as means to achieve gain, and their pressure will drive the colonies—the fringe—to desperate actions.

MYR is a silver-rich, water-rich world with idyllic islands. Myr was the first settled planet in the Collective. Myrads have argyria and take great pride in their blue-hued skin.

ALLUVIA is a water-covered world and home to First City, the Collective's largest city. Alluvia was the second settled planet in the Collective and has the highest gravity of all Collective worlds. Alluvia has thick cloud cover and frequent storms.

DARIOS is the most naturally habitable world and provides much of the Collective's food supply. As such, it's heavily regulated by the Collective. Its fringe station is Sol Base.

PLAYA is the furthest world from Alluvia and Myr. It has low gravity and freezing temperatures. Its fringe station is Ice Port.

SPATE is a desert-like world and has the largest fringe station, Devil Town, known for its massive garden.

TERRA is a battle-scarred world, where much of the fringe Uprising took place. Its fringe station is Rebus Station. Terra, the planet nearest to Alluvia and Myr, is home to the Citadel, the Collective's high-security prison.

SPACE COAST is an asteroid belt outside Collective control and home to smugglers, pirates, and other outlaws. Its fringe station is Nova Colony and home to the infamous Uneven Bar.

ACKNOWLEDGEMENTS

With many thanks to my editors, Stephanie Riva and Laurel Kriegler, for their adept counsel and helping bring this story to life. A huge thanks goes out to Sarah Lyons Fleming, Michael Koogler, and Will Lenzen for reading the very ugly rough draft and generously offering your wisdom on how to turn a decent story into a great story. I'm fortunate enough to be a member of the Bards of Badassery, where I've often leaned on my good friends, Elle J Rossi, Cynthia Valero, and Beth Ciotta. And, I most certainly couldn't have done it without the support of my husband for putting up with long writing hours and plenty of craziness. Most of all, thank you, my readers, for your messages, cheers, and enthusiasm.

FRINGE
RUNNER

"Across the sea of space, the stars are other suns."

Carl Sagan

PROLOGUE

After the successful colonization of Mars and Europa, it took us fewer than five generations to reach beyond our solar system and discover a planet hospitable to human life. That world was Myr, and the single ship of three hundred and eleven colonists flourished as they created Earthlike ecosystems on the untouched world.

After that, it took less than a generation to reach Myr's water-covered neighbor, Alluvia. Colonization was nearly as swift on the temperate world, but friction between the two planets was even swifter. Within decades, Myrads stated that Alluvia was their colony, while Alluvians countered that both planets were Earth's colonies and thus, should follow Earth's interstellar directive—that all colonies were ordained to govern themselves.

The friction grew worse over the next two hundred years until the inevitable happened. The first interplanetary war erupted, a war so horrible that history came to refer to it simply as *the War*. After decades of carnage, Alluvia and Myr had pushed themselves to the brink of annihilation. To save themselves, the pair sacrificed their rivalry and created the Collective, an alliance that established the people of both worlds as citizens and equals in all ways.

Under the new order, each world governed itself, while their Collective oversaw such things as interplanetary trade, security, and exploration. Alluvians led interstellar commerce activities while Myrads commanded the newly-established joint navy—the Collective Unified Forces, or, CUF—created to protect the citizens of both worlds.

Hostilities faded as the Collective thrived.

Over the next few centuries, four additional planets were terraformed and colonized by the Collective. First came Terra, a black desert planet abundant with rilon—a durable yet lightweight metal. Second came Darios, the warmest of the planets, with lush fields and rich soil. Third came Spate, a bleak world with harsh storms and even harsher microorganisms. The most recent was Playa, a massive ice world in the farthest reaches of the Collective. These four colonies, far from the comforts of Myr and Alluvia, came to be known bluntly as the fringe.

Each colony had a single fringe station—a trading post with space docks—that made interplanetary travel and commerce affordable. The fringe's resources brought untold wealth and capabilities to Myrads and Alluvians, but the colonists reaped few benefits. Instead, the fringe was heavily regulated and taxed. To make matters worse, Myr and Alluvia, having long since forgotten that they had each started as simple colonies themselves, refused to grant citizenship to colonists across the fringe.

A new divide formed, and history seemed doomed to repeat itself.

When exports coming from fringe stations reached optimum levels for Myr and Alluvia's elite classes, the Collective began to lay additional laws upon the fringe. Of all these new laws, the one colonists hated most was mandatory service to the Collective for any able-bodied colonist upon reaching adulthood. The colonists had become little more than slaves to the Collective's ruling class.

Exhausted, hungry, and angry, the colonists stood up to their oppressors. Torrents—rebel colonists—across the fringe banded together and closed off fringe stations in demands for equality. Strikes and protests led to bloodshed.

The Uprising had begun.

Instead of listening to colonists' demands, Myr and Alluvia sent in the CUF's great warships and armies. Torrent rebels were slaughtered alongside hapless innocents. The Uprising was quelled, and the few remaining torrents faded back into the fringe.

That was twenty years ago.

Today, colonists labor under the watchful eye of the all-powerful CUF.

Unknown to the fringe, ancient tensions have sprung back to life. Alluvia's economy has now surpassed Myr's, and the Collective Parliament has staggered to a standstill under bipartisan leadership. The CUF has become fractured and segregated, with many warships operating with either all-Alluvian or all-Myrad crews.

Myrads crave control, and Alluvians have acquired a taste for power. As the two worlds face one another again, they fail to take into account one important factor, one that could bring the entire Collective crashing down...

The torrent spirit is very much alive, and has been waiting for the right time to strike.

THE PACKAGE

"Guys, just a friendly reminder that we have only seventeen minutes until the star swarm obliterates us." Throttle's words came through all too loud and clear in Aramis Reyne's and Jeyde Sixx's spacesuit headsets.

"Working on it," Reyne shot back as they continued to cut through the damn-near-indestructible rilon hull of Myrad hauler M4029LW, which was proving to be thicker than they'd estimated, throwing off their timetable.

"I think we should go with Plan B. Tell Genics Corp that we couldn't get to the ship in time, and let's clear out of here," their pilot countered.

"Not your call." Using a quick burst from his suit's propulsion system, Reyne moved to the side, giving the other man room to secure a pry bar that resembled a spindly, long-legged spider.

Sixx hit a button on his suit, and the tip of each pry bar leg thrust into the four-square-foot outline they'd burnt through the outer hull.

"Usually I enjoy a bit of excitement," Sixx said before hitting another button on his suit. The bar's legs slammed deep, and both the pry bar and the square section of the hauler's outer hull shot out into space. "But I'll be damned if star swarms don't scare the hell out of me."

Reyne gave him a wry look. "Worse than that woman you hooked up with on Sol Base?" he asked as he pressed through the hole and into the cargo bay of the dead hauler.

"Double-jointed Sally? Now, she was scary. The things she could do with—"

"Hey, you guys are still transmitting. And, we're down to sixteen minutes until bingo."

"We're inside." Reyne watched his arm display as he scanned the large, round room with rows of crates fastened onto every open wall space. His scanner was weak and wouldn't register the package unless he was within a dozen feet of it. As he completed a sweep of the cargo bay, his scanner flashed red.

He grimaced. "Package isn't in the cargo bay. Must be deeper in the ship."

"Hey, Reyne. Check this out. Those viggin' Myrads get all the best hauls."

He turned to see Sixx shining his light on crates strapped against the far wall. The words *Genics Corp Biome Kits* were emblazoned on each crate.

"These guys were hauling enough kits to jump-start a new colony. You know how many credits we could get for these?" Sixx asked.

Reyne frowned. "Why were they hauling so many kits? I

haven't heard of any new colonies being started."

Sixx shrugged. "It's not like they'll be able to salvage this hauler once the swarm hits it. What do you say, boss? Knowing that we're taking from Myrads feels just as good as seeing the credits we'll get for these kits."

Reyne held up a single finger. "One crate. You get it back to the *Gryphon*, and I'll grab the package." Reyne could see Sixx's wide grin through his helmet, so he tacked on, "We don't have time to mess around, got it?"

"Got it, boss."

Reyne turned, grabbed a railing, and thrust himself through the gravity-free bay toward the interior door. "Throttle, tell Boden to prepare for incoming cargo."

"*Already done. Fifteen minutes, gentlemen. Take your time.*" Her sarcasm made him chuckle though he quickly sobered. Anxious to be done with this job and back on his own ship, he hit the door with more momentum than planned, and the impact rattled his joints.

He wrapped a leg around the railing for leverage, reached for the manual gear below the panel, and cranked open the door. He grunted with each crank, frustrated that ten years earlier he could've done the same thing without so much as a bump in his heart rate.

With the last crank, the door swung outward, and a large object was sucked past Reyne and into the cargo bay. The object, which turned out to be a frozen crewmember, bounced off Sixx's back.

"Holy shit!" Sixx scrambled out of the way before shoving the body away. "How about a little warning next time?"

Reyne watched the body rebound off a wall and slow to float listlessly around the bay. He furrowed his brow after he noticed the dark stain on the body's chest. "He didn't die from exposure."

"Huh?"

"This man was shot. He didn't die from exposure."

"Maybe someone spaced out and killed the rest of the crew?" Throttle asked.

"Maybe," Reyne said before pushing into the now fully-depressurized hallway. The ship had suffered a cat fail—a catastrophic failure. They happened from time to time on fringe junkers, but they were unheard of on modern, high-tech Myrad haulers.

As he floated down the hallway as quickly as he safely could in zero-g, he reported in. "You were right about the systems, Throttle. No life support of any kind. Even the emergency backup failed."

"Why do you ever doubt me?" she replied. *"And you're down to fourteen minutes."*

"I'll be there. Just be ready." He pressed through the hallway. Something had clearly happened beyond a standard cat fail. That fact became more and more clear as he passed the crew quarters, counting five more crewmembers, each staring out into nothingness with frozen, glassy eyes. More importantly, each bore a dark gunshot stain on his torso or head.

Mercy kills, or something else?

Throttle's earlier comment made the most sense. Someone on the crew must've spaced out, killed the crew, and busted the ship. Space psychoses sometimes happened to crewmembers who spent too many years in the scalar void. It wasn't uncommon to hear of ships where one or more crewmembers went into full-out psychotic rage.

"May you find peace in the eversea," he said softly.

"Thirteen minutes. Please tell me you've found that viggin' box and

are on your way back."

"Working on it." He stopped at the captain's quarters and peered inside to find the room empty. He held his scanner up. Still nothing. "Shit."

"What's wrong?"

"I thought the package would be in the captain's safe." Reyne looked around. "I'm running out of places to search." He pushed off the wall and flew toward the open entrance to the bridge, his mind racing, along with his heart rate.

In the case of a breach or electrical malfunction, even in a cat fail, all doors were set to close automatically, sealing off non-critical areas to buy time for the crew to hail for assistance. Standard protocol on all ships. An open door meant someone had to manually override the system. That the bridge door stood wide open was an ominous sign.

He had no doubt now the cat fail had been intentional. If someone hadn't spaced out, someone had definitely done *something* to the ship and crew.

"I'm dropping off the cargo now," Sixx reported. *"Then, I'll head back over for one more crate."*

"Negative," Reyne said. "There's not enough time."

He was already holding his ship and crew too damn close to a swarm, but they desperately needed the money. The Collective kept lowering its run rates while increasing taxes, making it near impossible to break even, let alone make a profit.

And so he pushed himself to keep going, adrenaline surging through his muscles.

"Twelve minutes," Throttle said. *"Don't make me come and get you."*

"Don't even think about it," he snapped back.

When Reyne reached the bridge, he found the remaining two

9

crewmembers. The pilot was still strapped in at his seat. He sported a sizable hole in his head, and the ship had frozen his corpse in a slumped position. Where the pilot's death would have been instantaneous, the captain was likely the last of the crew to succumb to her injuries. Her body lingered near the ceiling, with a single shot to her abdomen. She would've died from freezing hypoxia long before internal bleeding took her.

His scanner beeped green. Good news. He'd found the package. Only one small problem. The gray box with a Genics Corp logo on it was lodged smack dab in the middle of the fractured view panel, with nothing but the blackness of space on the other side. The panel looked like it could shatter under any pressure, leaving nowhere for Reyne to place his feet for leverage.

He blew out a breath of frustration. "I've acquired the package."

"About viggin' time," Throttle said. *"Grab it and hurry the hell back here."*

"Trust me. That's the plan."

"Oh, and you have eleven minutes until bingo."

Reyne focused on how to get the package free from the view panel. It didn't make sense for something so important not to be secured in an encrypted safe. Yet, there was the small crate, stuck halfway out of the view panel, space sucking at it with her cold breath. Multiple shots dotted the pane around the box, and cracks webbed across the panel. Instead of smashing through, the package had crashed into the panel in such a way that it had somewhat sealed the breach, keeping the pane from fully shattering back when the ship still had pressure.

"Ten minutes. Reyne, we're getting nervous over here."

The pieces of what had happened on this ship started to fall into place, but Reyne shook them off, not having the commodity of time to dwell on the crew's story. He pushed off and bumped against the view panel. New cracks formed. Fearful that it would float into space, he grasped for the package, his thick gloves sliding right off the securely wedged box.

A twinkle in the distance caught Reyne's eye. Through the pane, he watched more and more glimmers appear as starlight reflected off the millions of space debris entangled in the asteroid's gravitational pull. Star swarms were basically space tsunamis on an orbital schedule. No one saw swarms up close like this. No one was that stupid.

The *Gryphon* was about to become slivers in this swarm if it didn't get out ahead of it.

"Throttle," he began. "You'd better be ready for jump speed by the time the counter hits zero."

"I'm ready to go now. You keep lollygagging, and I might decide to leave you behind, old man."

"I knew I could count on you," he said drily, tugging at the box. His fingers slipped, but he kept pulling.

"That's an interesting place to put a valuable thingamajig."

Reyne glanced over his shoulder to see Sixx fly onto the bridge and grab an instrument panel to slow his speed, nearly dropping the armful of biome kits he held.

"Nine minutes. Are you on your way back?"

Reyne motioned to Sixx. "Get your sticky fingers over here. This thing's wedged tight in here. I need leverage. I can't operate my jets and hold onto it at the same time."

Sixx gave a longing look at the biome kits in his arms before letting out a drawn-out sigh. He released his prizes, flew over, and wrapped his hands around the package. "Ready," he said with the biome kits floating around them. "Did I mention how much I dislike star swarms? Watching one coming right at me isn't

11

exactly reassuring."

Twinkling reflections from the swarm's debris spread across much of the view panel's width now.

"Then, we'd better grab this and get out of here," Reyne said.

Wrapping an arm around Sixx, Reyne used his free hand to control his propulsion system. As soon as the package moved, cracks filled the panel before it shattered, creating an opening from the bridge into space. Shards of panel floated around biome kits. Sixx scrambled and grabbed for a kit.

"Leave 'em," Reyne ordered.

"Just one," he said as he tucked a biome kit atop the package and began to strap them to his suit. "Consider it my bonus for saving the day."

"Three minutes. Did you hear me, guys? Three minutes."

Reyne shot Sixx a harried glance before responding. "What happened to four through eight?"

"I may have forgotten to take into account the star swarm's leading buffer impact on our acceleration. Don't mess around, guys. I'm not joking on this. Get back here now."

Reyne's mind rushed through options. He grabbed onto Sixx. "We'll go faster using our propulsion tanks together." He pulled out a carabiner and hooked their suits together. "You hold the package. I'll run both our jets."

"Faster is good."

They kicked off from the bridge and flew through the shattered pane and out into space. Clear plastic pieces from the view panel scraped against their helmets.

With Sixx clutching their payday and Reyne holding onto him, Reyne shot alternating full bursts from their suits to propel forward. Unfortunately, even with both at max output, their civilian-grade pressure suits were designed for slow, safe travel through space. As they moved through the blackness between the dead ship and the *Gryphon*, the star swarm closed the distance in a terrifyingly deadly sort of way—like a huge, sparkling chimera coming to swallow them.

"Two minutes. I'm running through the pre-jump protocols now."

"We're on our way," Reyne said, trying not to sound like his heart wasn't pounding out of his chest. He wished their suits to go faster, but wishing didn't seem to help.

Every second was too slow as the distance between them and the star swarm disappeared faster than the distance between them and the *Gryphon*, which floated like a rilon angel waiting for them.

"Sixty seconds."

"Can't these things go any viggin' faster?" Sixx complained.

Reyne racked his brain for ideas, but nothing would get them back to the ship in time. As they moved through space, his muscles shook with adrenaline and fear.

"We're at bingo."

The *Gryphon*'s Flux Whisper engine roared to life. A second later, the airlock door began to close.

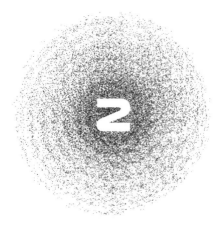

A SHIP CAUGHT IN THE SWARM

Even with both suits blasting at full propulsion, Reyne figured they needed at least ten seconds more than what they had to reach the *Gryphon*. He continually hit their thrust buttons, only to have the suits chime negative responses at his attempts.

"Ah, shit." He grimaced before giving the order he dreaded. "Get out of here, Throttle. You've got to leave us."

"Don't you dare leave us, Throttle," Sixx countered.

"Like hell I'm leaving, you idiots."

Through the window on the other side of the airlock, Reyne noticed the ship's mechanic. Boden had stopped the door once it reached halfway down, and was now motioning wildly with his hands. Unfortunately, Reyne couldn't speak to him through his comm link, since the channel at that chamber had fried months ago and he didn't have the credits to fix it.

"I can't make out what he's—oh." A retention cable shot out from the chamber and straight toward them. Reyne had only an instant to comprehend Boden's intent and prepare for the incoming object. "Hold on."

Reyne collided with—more so than caught—the heavy tow hook. The impact knocked the air from his lungs, and sharp pain stabbed where the hook had hit his chest. His suit blasted an alarm. Their forward movement instantly reversed. A single carabiner held the two men's suits together, and Sixx was yanked along like a raggedy doll. The cable jerked to a stop, and it felt like Reyne's arms were snapped from their sockets as their now-backward propulsion was halted.

The cable began to retract, the metal line sliding through Reyne's hands, and he scrambled to get a grip. He wrapped his hand around the hook just as the cable picked up speed. A lot of speed.

Reyne tried to find his breath as they were dragged to the ship. "Tell me you still have the package."

"I have it, plus a nasty case of whiplash."

"Good. Keep hanging on because we're coming in hard."

It took them only a couple seconds to close the remaining distance. They flew into the airlock and slammed into the door on the far side of the small pressurization chamber.

The outer door clanged shut behind them, and with a low hum, the ship's EM field cycled up the gravity in the room. The men dropped to the floor with grunts.

Reyne pulled himself to his knees, seeing stars through the pain. "*Hell*," he ground out.

Sixx sat up. "That wasn't so—"

The *Gryphon* shot into jump speed with no warm-up. Reyne

and Sixx were lifted off the ground for a tiny instant before smashing against the back wall.

Reyne couldn't breathe for several long seconds before he realized Sixx was lying on top of him. He managed to unhook their suits and roll the other man off.

The red light by the door switched to green. He twisted off his helmet and sucked in cool, fresh air. "You...were saying?"

Sixx came up on his elbows and tossed his helmet. "Now, that was a wild ride. *Shit*. That hurt."

Reyne dragged himself into a sitting position and leaned against the wall. "What are you complaining about? You used me to cushion your fall."

"Yeah? Try having a biome kit smash through your helmet."

Reyne looked to see Sixx gingerly touching his bloody, broken nose. Dark circles were already forming under his eyes. "You good?"

Sixx touched his forefinger and thumb tips together to form an O, for *Okay*.

Reyne continued. "How's the package?"

Sixx set aside his biome kit and rolled over the metal box. "A few scratches, but still sealed."

"Let's hope the contents are secure and that they survived a scalar freeze, or else we won't be seeing a paycheck. It'd be a whole lot easier if I knew what was in there."

"As long as they pay us, I don't care," Sixx said.

"Agreed."

Reyne winced, tentatively rubbing his tender chest. "Hell, it feels like I've bruised or broken half the bones in my body."

"Only half?" Sixx asked as he climbed to his feet and helped Reyne up. "We pulled out pretty good, then."

They kicked out of their suits and hooked them up to charging stations.

Sixx bent over and picked up the single biome kit. "This baby's all mine. I've already got a nice piece of property on Spate picked out for it."

"You about got yourself killed for it." Reyne shot his friend a hard look. "I ordered you to stay put on the *Gryphon.*"

"What? And let you have all the fun?"

"There are several women who would be very sad if you died in a swarm."

Sixx smirked. "How right you are."

The inner door to the pressurization chamber opened, and Boden stepped inside. The sandy-haired Alluvian took a quick look at each of them and gave a reassuring nod. "I was beginning to think you two weren't going to give up your front row seats to the star swarm."

"Nah. That show's overrated," Sixx replied.

Reyne nodded to the mechanic. "Quick thinking with the cable. You saved our asses back there."

"Throttle would kill me if I left her father out there to die," Boden said.

"Hey," Sixx chimed in. "Don't I count, too?"

Something clanged against the outer hull, quickly followed by another something that sounded like it tore a hole through the ship.

Boden spun on his heels and sprinted away.

Reyne pointed at the box in Sixx's arms. "Get that package secure." Then, he took off at a run, or at least as fast as a battered, arthritic man could move.

"Status," he called out as soon as he reached the bridge.

Throttle didn't look up from her instrument panel. "We were too late going to jump speed. We're getting dinged up by the leading edges of the swarm, but the jump shields are holding. We'll get through it in time." She paused. "I hope."

"You *hope*?"

She didn't reply.

He turned his attention to the view panel. A cacophony of tiny collisions sparked against the jump shield and chewed at his raw nerves. Glimpses of debris lit up space like tiny stars. Many chunks were smaller than an inch in diameter, but each was capable of piercing a view panel without jump shields as easily as a knife tip through a sheet of paper.

A larger metallic shard skidded off the jump shield, and he instinctively ducked. "How close are we to the leading edge?"

"Close. I'm trying to get us a little closer."

He spun around "You're what?"

"We're too close to outrun the asteroid's gravitational pull, so I'm skimming across the leading edge like I would with a planet's orbit. If we hit it at just the right angle, we should skip right off the buffer, instead of getting sucked into the swarm. At least, that's my guess."

Turbulence sent Reyne collapsing into his seat, and he buckled in.

Throttle, even with her wheelchair locked in, held onto the instrument panel with one hand while punching in commands with her other. "Just a few more seconds." Her voice trailed off in a small shriek when something that looked eerily like a chunk of Myrad hauler M4029LW collided with the bow, and the ship pitched.

Then, as quickly as the star swarm began, the space outside became blissfully silent.

"Damage report?" he asked.

The petite blonde blew out a breath, leaning over her panel. "It will take some time to run diagnostics, but the engine isn't running at full capacity, and I'm showing a thirty-four percent vulnerability in our jump shield."

He grimaced. "That's not going to be a cheap bill." He pulled up the quadrant map. "If we maintain jump, we can be to Ice Port in seventy-four hours, still well before our deadline."

She shook her head. "If we lose any more of the jump shield, we'll have to drop to sub speed."

Reyne tapped the comm on his panel. "Boden, you there?"

"Yep."

"We need to boost the jump shield. Divert any extra power you can find."

"That's a big viggin' negative. We have a five-foot-long chunk of rilon sticking through our stern right now. Damn thing skittered right across our jump shield to nail us in the ass."

Reyne winced. "Shit."

"We're bleeding out. I need us to shut down as soon as possible to plug the leak in the stern, or else we'll never make it home."

Reyne watched his pilot before he replied, to make sure she was listening. "Throttle will drop us out of jump speed as soon as we're a safe distance from the swarm."

"Give me ten minutes," she chimed in.

"Can you work on the hull with the solar sails out?" Reyne asked.

A pause. *"I'll make it work."*

"Good." He released the comm, unbuckled his belt, and pushed from his seat with a groan.

"One more thing," Throttle said. She abruptly unlocked her wheelchair and spun around to give Reyne a hard look. She wagged a finger at him. "Don't you *ever* order me to leave you behind again. That was an asshole move."

He stiffened. "The safety of the crew always comes first."

"Oh, so you and Sixx aren't part of the crew now?"

He pursed his lips. "We knew the risk when we went out there. You should've—"

She held up her hand to stop him. "You can be such an idiot sometimes." She blew out a breath. "For a moment, I thought you weren't coming back."

He strode over to her and squeezed her shoulder, using the physical contact to convey things he never had a knack at saying right.

After a lengthy moment, emotion softened her features, and she placed her hand over his. "I couldn't imagine being on the *Gryphon* without you."

"I know," he said softly, before adding on a bit louder, "You might not be my daughter by birth, but you'll always be my daughter in all the ways that matter. As long as there's the barest hint of a chance, I'll make it back. That's one promise I can make."

She eyed him. "I'll settle for that. For now."

He patted her back and stepped away, pausing at the doorway. "By the way, where in the galaxy did you ever pick up a term like 'lollygagging'?"

She shrugged. "Probably from you, old man."

He grinned and left the bridge.

The hallway's soft neutral lights brightened to signal the dawn of the thirty-hour standard day. His bunk was the nearest room to the bridge. He pressed the manual switch to open the door—the retinal scans had long since stopped working—and stumbled inside.

Not bothering to kick off his boots, he collapsed onto his bed and closed his eyes. The constant hum of the *Gryphon*'s systems soothed his frayed nerves, and he felt himself relax. Here, he was home. The only place in the Collective he ever truly felt safe.

He inhaled deeply and winced at the pain in his chest, a familiar ache of broken or badly bruised ribs. Grudgingly, he pushed off from his bunk and shuffled down to the medical bay. There, he found Sixx lying on the single table and illuminated by overhead bioscanner's amethyst light.

Doc glanced up. "I should've known that you'd manage to get yourself injured, too." Sixx raised his head, and Doc swatted him. "Lie still."

"You know, I've been thinking about that hauler," Sixx began while lying on his back. "It didn't have the psychotic feel of a spaced out crew."

"What's a psychotic feel?" Reyne asked.

"No blood on the walls, things busted and thrown around, you know, that kind of psychotic feel," Sixx answered.

Reyne leaned against the wall. "What do you think happened?"

"My guess?" Sixx asked. "I think the ship suffered a cat fail. The captain drifted her crew with mercy shots before turning her pistol on herself."

Reyne thought back to the two pistols he'd seen floating on the bridge. He shook his head. "No."

"No?" Sixx asked.

"The captain had a gut shot. Not a pleasant way to die. And, I don't think there was anything merciful with what went down with the crew. I'd lay my bets that the captain initiated the cat fail. She was planning to get the crew off her ship while she stayed behind under the pretense that she'd call for help and stay with their cargo."

The bioscanner turned off, and Sixx sat up while Doc analyzed the results.

"So," Sixx began. "The captain wanted the ship and a shitload of biome kits for herself. It'd make for a nice golden parachute."

Reyne cocked his head. "It would. And, I bet the pilot got a whiff of the captain's plans and confronted her. There was an exchange of gunfire, leaving the pilot dead and the captain with a bad injury. The captain, figuring the gig was up, took out each of the remaining crew one by one so no one would ever know she tried to pull off a heist."

"That's a hell of a tale, but it makes sense," Sixx said.

Reyne sighed. "That's the thing. The pieces don't all fit together yet. There's more to the story, and I'll be damned if it's not related to that package."

"With all the gunshots in the view panel," Sixx said. "It looked like she was trying hard to get rid of the package. It's like she didn't want anyone to have it, not that she needed to bother, with the star swarm headed her way."

Reyne snapped his fingers, and he pushed off the wall. "What are the odds a brand new Myrad hauler would suffer a cat fail in the path of a star swarm?"

Sixx shrugged. "Pretty damn low."

"More like impossible," Doc chimed in. "Star swarms are rare. There is only one documented case of a ship running into a swarm, and that ship was in jump speed at the time."

"Exactly," Reyne said. "The captain intentionally planned a cat fail at that exact location. No one would want to stay on a ship that was in the path of a star swarm. Once the crew was off the ship, she was going to drop the package and cut out of there with her ship and cargo all to herself. The star swarm would've obliterated any evidence that package ever existed."

"A perfect plan until someone got in her way," Sixx said.

Reyne nodded. "Which then forced her to improvise and take

out the crew. By the time she drifted them, she was too weak to drop the package and run. When she realized she wasn't going to make it, she tried to decompress the ship to have space suck the package out for her. My guess is she lost consciousness before she could blow out the view panel."

"Good for us she didn't succeed," Sixx said. "Or, else that contract would turn into a zero paycheck."

Reyne thought hard for a long moment. Then he pinged the bridge on the comm. "Throttle."

"Yeah?"

"I want you to plot out the fastest course for Ice Port. I want that damn Genics Corp package off this ship yesterday."

"Consider it done."

Reyne turned to find Sixx and Doc watching him.

"What's your gut telling you?" Sixx asked.

"My gut is telling me that we never should've taken this contract," he answered.

"You've always had a good instinct," Doc said. "There's a reason the CUF assigned you as a chaser."

"You think we should drop the package and run?" Sixx asked.

"I think we should've left the blasted thing back on the Myrad hauler and let the star swarm have it," Reyne answered. "Except that we need the credits too damn much. Its paycheck is more than the ten months' pay we earn as runners."

"Well, I'm sure the credits will help soothe your conscience." Sixx blew out a breath. "This whole mess is giving me a headache. How about some painkillers, Doc?"

"You're lucky you have only a headache," she answered before she read from the tablet she held. "You've broken your nose. Again. Fortunately, you have no broken bones and no signs of internal injuries. However, you have torn ligaments in your knee and have a hairline fracture in your left wrist. I'll wrap your wrist, and I'll put you on a three-day cycle of injections for your knee."

The blonde medic grabbed a syringe off the table and pressed it against his swollen knee.

He sucked in air. "Damn, that hurts."

"That should teach you not to treat your body like a battering ram."

"Yeah, yeah," Sixx said. "What I need are some painkillers, Doc."

She swapped the syringe for a small bottle, and placed a single pill into Sixx's palm.

He stared at her, incredulous. "Only one? Seriously, Doc. That won't even take the edge off. I need at least three."

She gave a tut. "You're in your prime. You'll be at one hundred percent in no time."

Reyne smirked as he watched the pair hold a battle of the wills, knowing full well Sixx didn't stand a chance. After lasting longer than Reyne expected, the man relented and swallowed the single pill without any water. He climbed to his feet, towering a foot over her. "You're brutal, Doc."

He limped away from the table. As he passed Reyne, he said softly, "She's in a mood today. Good luck."

"I heard that," she called out.

With a sly grin, Sixx scurried away to leave Reyne alone with Doc.

She patted the table. "Your turn, Captain."

He winced as he pulled himself onto the slab.

"Where do you feel pain?" she asked.

"Everywhere."

Her gaze narrowed.

So he added, "My chest hurts the most."

With no further acknowledgement, she helped him lie back before moving to her control panel.

The overhead scanner lit the small room with its ambient glow. Beginning at his head, the bioscanner's silent line of light progressed slowly toward his feet.

When the light finally shut off, Doc read the results on her tablet. "You got off easier than Sixx. Your chest hurts because you have three bruised ribs. You also have some tearing in your shoulder. A single injection and some sleep should have you recharged in no time."

She pursed her lips. "You need to be careful. You're twice Sixx's age. Your body isn't going to snap back after every new abuse you subject it to."

"Trust me," he said, sitting up. "It reminds me every minute of every day."

Her voice softened. "How's the arthritis?"

He didn't respond.

She motioned to the man-sized booth in the corner. "You've got to start spending more time in the gravity chamber. Too many years in ships' point-seven gravity factor has added decades to your bones and joints."

His upper lip curled into a snarl at the booth, finding it difficult to breathe as his mind painted an all-too-real picture of the cramped space inside.

Doc cocked her head. "I know it isn't easy, but it's important."

"I'll log an hour in it tomorrow."

Her brows rose. "Promise?"

"No."

She sighed. "Have you tried watching a movie in there to take your mind off your claustrophobia?"

"Doesn't help. Nothing relaxes me in there."

She placed a hand on his chest and pressed him back down on the table. "I know something that can help relax you," she said in a sultry voice.

"Later," he said, brushing her off. "I need rack time. Go find Sixx."

Her lips thinned. "I thought I lost both of you today. I couldn't bear it."

Reyne's gaze softened, and he allowed her to press him back onto the table. They'd never had a romantic relationship, but they'd been friends for over two decades. Besides, everyone needed companionship on long space runs.

She straddled him, her pale skin against his dark skin. He knew he had no more chance of swaying Doc when it came to her sexual needs than Sixx had earlier in asking for painkillers.

Some time later, Reyne finally pushed off from the table. Doc began tidying up the med bay.

"Where's my pill?" he asked.

"Your injuries don't warrant a painkiller," she replied as a matter of fact.

"Come on, I'm the captain. Doesn't that warrant any special privileges?"

"All the more reason not to have drugs clouding your mind."

"Oh, but it's okay for Sixx?"

Doc shot him a wry look. "Do you really think Sixx's decision-making abilities could get any worse?"

"Good point."

She shooed him away. "Now, off with you. I'm starving and need some breakfast."

Doc didn't have to tell Reyne twice. He headed straight back to his bunk, collapsing onto the mattress. He felt himself swirl into sleep.

Then his viggin' comm chimed.

He muttered out a long string of cusswords before answering. "What now?"

"*Hello, grumpy,*" Throttle replied. "*You should take a nap.*"

"Brilliant idea," he gritted out.

"*Except it'll have to come later. Kason's pinging you.*"

He groaned. "I'll be right there."

He dragged himself up and made a detour through the commons to grab some food and drink. When he reached the bridge, he tossed Throttle a food bar and drink bag, and she caught both.

"How's Boden coming along with repairs?" he asked as he tore into his own food.

"He needs a couple more hours. Then we'll be good to go as long as we keep running on solar sails. I've plugged in our scalar plan to Ice Port. We should arrive in eighty-seven hours." She yawned. "Oh, and Kason's on channel Four."

"Eighty-seven hours is cutting it close."

"We'll make it."

He sat down and took a long drink before opening the comm channel. Unable to get a live video feed this deep in the fringe, Kason's picture showed on the screen. Clean-cut and generally well-behaved, he was one of the few guys in the Collective that Reyne would trust to date Throttle.

"Tell me you've got the package," Kason said without any sort of salutation.

"I've got the package. I'll reach Ice Port on day one-twenty-six around time—" he looked to Throttle.

She flashed her fingers in a quick succession of movements.

"—twenty-six-forty-five common time," he finished. "If we

28

can drop it off at the stationhouse, all the better. That package puts us behind schedule on our mail delivery."

Audio relays were delayed by a couple seconds per every ten light years or so. Kason's response came faster than Reyne expected, meaning the Alluvian was in the fringe rather than back on his home world. "Genics Corp gave specific instructions. You are to hand deliver the package to Vym Patel. They won't transmit the credits until you verify she's personally signed for it."

Reyne frowned. Vym was Ice Port's stationmaster. The old woman's vocal opinions against Collective companies were no secret. "Genics Corp must be paying her a hefty sum to get her involved."

After a delay, Kason's answer came. "No idea. Anyway, I need to sign off. I'll be at Ice Port by the time you get there. Report in when you land."

Reyne closed the channel, put his feet up, and looked out the view panel. He could see nothing but infinite space before them. The cosmic solitude was a stark difference from the star swarm they'd escaped barely two hours earlier.

This particular solar system had hundreds of large asteroids in orbit. Generations of using space as a dumping ground for satellites, stations, and other waste had led a few of the larger asteroids to suck up space junk into their destructive mass. As an asteroid accumulated junk, its path widened, shooting through anything unfortunate enough to be caught in it. The four largest swarms had even been given names. The particular one they'd escaped was called Hugo. By now, anything left of hauler M4029LW would be a part of Hugo's gravitational pull, flying forever in an orbital path.

A loud beep broke his concentration. "What now?"

"That's strange," Throttle said. "We're being hailed, but I

didn't pick up anyone on radar."

Reyne's feet dropped to the floor with a thud, and his hands flew over his console. "Stealth."

"They sent a message." Her voice bore a nervous tinge.

"Speakers," he commanded.

"Hauler Playa-Seven-Five-Five-One-Bravo, this is the Collective Unified Forces warship Arcadia. *You have been flagged for a standard dock check. You are hereby ordered to dock onto the* Arcadia *at port number Two. You have five minutes to comply. If you show any signs of noncompliance, you will be fired upon. Respond within sixty seconds of your confirmation of receipt. Convey ship logs and crew list with response."*

"Shit," Reyne said. After taking a deep breath, he hit the transmit switch. *"Arcadia,* this is Playa-Seven-Five-Five-One-Bravo. Received instructions and will comply. We've been doing some maintenance and are running slow. It may take us a bit longer to dock."

"Hauler Playa-One-Bravo, you have five minutes to comply."

Reyne glanced at Throttle. "You can always count on the CUF to be consistent," he said.

"Yeah, consistently be assholes," she muttered.

"Language," he added before broadcasting an alert to the crew. "Red alert, guys. We've been invited to tea with our CUF friends. Check your bunks. Make sure you hide anything less than perfectly legal, because we're about to be boarded."

COLLECTIVE CAGES

Collective Unified Forces ships stopped and searched fringe haulers all the time—sometimes out of boredom, sometimes after being tipped off that a particular hauler carried contraband, most of the time just to make life harder for colonists.

Throttle's brows furrowed. "Why do you think they used stealth on us?"

Reyne shook his head. "Don't know, but I bet we're about to find out."

It was unheard of for CUF ships to burn the extra juice needed for stealth, instead using the advanced tech only when they needed to make sure their prey wouldn't see them coming and run. In Reyne's twenty years as a runner, he'd been dock checked every few months by a CUF patrol, but he'd always been careful.

With a past like his, he had to be. He played by their rules, and every single time he'd left with his cargo intact, often with a frivolous citation or two as a memento.

In all that time, he'd never been tracked by a warship, let alone a warship in stealth mode.

Whatever the reason for this stop, Reyne knew it didn't bode well for him and his crew. His sore body was quickly forgotten while he watched in trepidation as Throttle brought the *Gryphon* alongside the massive, gray warship. He stared at the ship's name—ARCADIA—emblazoned on its hull as the *Gryphon* glided to its docking bay.

"I see they've rolled out the welcome mat," Throttle said, and he then noticed the opened doors a couple hundred meters down from their current position. The number 2 was painted in iridescent white near the opening.

"Slowing to point three. Setting thruster for sixty-degree turn," Throttle voiced her maneuvers aloud, a habit she picked up at the age of eight. She effortlessly negotiated the docking procedures, and claw-like rilon mooring bars clamped onto the *Gryphon* with a metallic clang.

Reyne took a deep breath, suddenly feeling trapped, much like that Myrad hauler had been just before being destroyed by the star swarm.

"Well, I guess we're in their hands now," she said. "At least they were gentler grabbing onto us this time. We still have a shimmy in the gear after the last dock check."

"It's on the fix list."

A pressurized tube shot out from the dock wall and fastened over their port. The comm panel beeped.

"Hauler Playa-One-Bravo, we read green on docking sequence. Power down your ship immediately. The entire crew must proceed

through the tube for decontamination and interviews. No weapons or hostility of any kind will be tolerated."

Throttle unlocked her seat and wheeled back. "I suppose we shouldn't keep our gracious hosts waiting," she said with her usual dash of sarcasm.

"No, I suppose we shouldn't," he echoed.

He followed her down the narrow hallway. The rest of the crew stood waiting for them at the small port door. When Reyne approached, Sixx cranked open the door. He then took a step back and waved in an exaggerated motion. "After you, boss."

Reyne chortled and entered the tube that was no more than four feet in diameter. He walked in a crouch through the tunnel, his bruised ribs crying out against the constrictive stance.

"Viggin' CUF," Boden grumbled as he crammed his muscular body into the tunnel.

"Careful. If they hear you, you'll be issued a citation," Reyne warned over his shoulder.

Throttle followed Boden into the confined docking tube that was too round and too narrow for her to ride her wheelchair. The sounds of her legs dragging behind her echoed through the confined space.

Reyne reached the other end and dropped down into the decontamination chamber. Boden landed heavily on his feet, turned around, and caught Throttle. Doc followed, with Sixx covering the rear.

As soon as Sixx was clear of the tube, a door snapped shut, sealing them in the small chamber.

"Decontamination commencing."

Mist shot out from the walls, encapsulating them in a damp spray. Reyne didn't mind this part, but he hated what came next. After several seconds of the spray soaking their skin, the wind shot out, nearly knocking him down. The wind—what was commonly called the rinse cycle—burned his eyes and etched his skin raw.

All CUF ships and space docks had decontamination chambers to prevent the spread of disease, and Reyne was convinced they cranked up the rinse cycle on anyone from the fringe just to be assholes.

When the fog cleared and Reyne could see again, he turned to his crew to see them all red-skinned and with tears streaming down their faces. "You all good?" he gritted out.

He received nods and rough affirmations.

Boden jostled Throttle, and she smacked his chest. "Damn it, you big lug. I'm not a viggin' doll."

"My eye itches," he replied, sounding hopeless.

She grumbled something Reyne couldn't make out.

Sixx grinned. "Oh, quit your moaning, Throttle. You know you like it."

She flipped him off before sulking in Boden's arms.

The entire wall shot up into the ceiling with a whoosh, and Reyne found himself face to face with a dozen armed dromadiers. Each soldier held a photon gun and had stun sticks strapped to his legs. They wore blue chimesuits, a nickname earned for the sounds that emitted from the copious number of alarms and warnings built into the smart suits.

"Form a line, facing us," a dromadier ordered, consistent with the same protocols they'd experienced during every CUF dock check before. Without hesitation, Reyne and his crew did as they were instructed.

An officer emerged, followed by an assistant carrying a DNA scanner.

The pair stopped in front of Reyne. The officer's skin had the bluish tint that all citizens who'd spent a lifetime on the silver-rich planet of Myr had. "I'm First Officer Laciam of the *Arcadia*, serving under Commandant Heid, and you've been stopped for a standard dock check."

Reyne's brows rose, not believing for an instant that there was anything "standard" about this dock check. Instead of saying what he really thought about the officer and their current situation, he said, "I'm Aramis Reyne, and this is my crew. We're happy to be of service."

The officer's eyes narrowed as though he'd bit into something sour. "I know who you are, *torrent*. Now, bare your left forearms for identification. Do not make any sudden moves, or you will be arrested."

Laciam's assistant—a pale, scrawny fellow who didn't look a day over seventeen—pressed a dark rectangular instrument against Reyne's forearm. Reyne winced at the quick prick as the instrument drew a sample of his blood. The young man looked at the screen and announced, "Identity confirmed. Aramis Reyne, Playa colonist."

Laciam didn't acknowledge the results as he'd become engrossed with Throttle. He cocked his head as though he was looking at a three-eyed dog. "What's wrong with you?"

"My legs don't work," she answered simply.

Laciam frowned. "I don't understand."

"I'm paralyzed," she said with a deadpan expression. "My legs don't work." She'd spoken her last statement slowly as though speaking to a child.

He took an obvious step back as if she were contagious. "I've heard about such things, but have never seen one in real life. You know, if you were a citizen, your faults would've been repaired."

Reyne chimed in. "Too bad colonists don't have those kinds of luxuries."

Laciam ignored him, still staring at Throttle. "You wouldn't be bad looking—for a colonist, that is—if you weren't broken."

She clenched her fists, but said nothing.

Reyne bit back the urge to rip out the officer's throat. "I'm sure you're busy, officer. What can we do to help you process us so we can get out of your hair?"

Laciam snapped around to face him. "You don't speak until spoken to, got it? One more unsolicited word from you, you get to spend a week in the brig. You want that?"

"Not especially," Reyne answered drily.

The CUF officer glared at Reyne for an endless moment before finally breaking eye contact and nodding to his assistant to resume the task at hand.

Boden had to jostle Throttle again to reveal his forearm to the assistant.

"Confirmed. Tren Boden. Alluvian non-citizen," the assistant read from his monitor before moving onto Throttle. "Confirmed. Halit Herley. Terra colonist."

Then came Doc. "Confirmed. Aila Chapei. Terra colonist."

Finally, Sixx held out his arm. "Confirmed. Jeyde Sixx. Spate colonist."

Laciam scrutinized Reyne and his crew. "It's your lucky day. It seems you match up with your crew list." Laciam motioned, and the dromadiers closed in around Reyne and his crew as though they'd try to make a run for it. Even if they wanted to— and Reyne certainly did—it wasn't as though any of them could escape while deep in the bowels of a CUF warship.

"Follow me to your holding rooms for interviews," Laciam ordered, and took off ahead without waiting for a response.

"We know the routine," Reyne said under his breath.

Laciam led them down a large hallway until they reached a line of doors along one wall. He punched keys on his wrist comm, and several doors opened.

"One per room. Get moving," the officer commanded.

Reyne's crew split into their cells. The dromadiers were none too patient as Boden carried Throttle into a room and set her down. They yanked him back and shoved him into a cell next to hers. "Lay off," Boden snapped. "I'm going, I'm going."

After his crew was in their individual cells, Reyne entered the last open room. Even though he had no control over what the CUF did to his people, he still felt responsible for them and would damn well do everything in his power to see that they were treated as well as colonists could expect to be treated.

His tiny room was made of bright white walls saturated in a near-blinding light. Inside sat a bench, the only furnishing. Spotlessly clean and exactly like every other CUF holding cell he'd ever been in. With nowhere to go, he took a seat, covered his eyes, and tried to catch some sleep.

No such luck.

The sound of powered movement alerted Reyne. Scowling, he opened his eyes and squinted against the dark shape emerging through the brightness. As his eyes adjusted, he noticed that a table and a cushioned bench had come out from the wall. He didn't need to look around to know that there was also an automatic gun leveled at him from the ceiling.

"Good day, Captain Reyne," a female voice said as the newcomer's features sharpened in the light. "I am Commandant Heid. Welcome to the *Arcadia*. I hope my first officer was not overzealous in processing you and your crew."

Reyne pushed to his feet to meet the senior officer at eye level. "In all my years as a runner, this is the first time a commandant has come down to talk to me. Adding that to the fact you burned juice on stealth, I'm guessing this is no ordinary dock check."

"Perhaps. Or, perhaps I'm simply bored." She smiled. "But I'm not the first commandant you've spoken to, am I?"

He didn't answer.

Heid took a seat across the table from him. "Today is a standard dock check, more or less."

"If it's a standard check, then we should be wrapped up in no time. As you should be able to read in my records, I'm a legit runner, and I hold my crew to the same high standards."

She chuckled. "'High standards' is not a term I'd apply to your crew."

Reyne realized just how young the officer was—in her mid-thirties or so—which meant she'd earned her rank from money—or was very, very good at her job. As he watched her, he supposed she could've also gotten promotions the old-fashioned way—from sleeping with the right officers. She had the curves of a fit woman, a model's face, and eyes twinkling with keen intelligence. He doubted anyone ever told her no.

He watched her, but she was busy scrolling through whatever information she was perusing on her wrist comm. Her dark hair was pulled into a tight bun, and he suspected she never let it down — figuratively speaking, that was.

"When it comes to your crew, I think 'miscreants' may be a better term, don't you think?" she continued, without looking up.

He didn't answer.

"One of your crewmembers has seventy-eight open misdemeanors filed against him."

"Ah, but the CUF doesn't deal with misdemeanors," he countered, trying not to grin. Sixx must've scored another one in between their most recent runs.

"Another one has been in and out of rehab three times for sweet soy addiction."

"Boden's clean now. That's ancient history."

"Last rehab was only eleven months ago." She glowered. "Sweet soy is a terrible plague on Alluvia. I saw it everywhere, growing up. I'm from First City, on the other side of town from where Tren would've grown up in the tenured district. Life isn't easy for tenured. Nearly all of them are addicts by the age of ten. He never stood a chance, really. I can't imagine how much he must hate every citizen he sees." She paused. "Though, I imagine your other two crewmembers hold even more hatred in their hearts against my people. Tell me, Captain Reyne. Do you still hate citizens as zealously as you did in the Uprising?"

He shook his head. "I never hated citizens. I was just against the unfair treatment of colonists."

"Ah, but the two lines can become blurred. I imagine many of your torrents in the Uprising couldn't differentiate between the two." She paused. "Speaking of the Uprising, I was too young to participate, but I read about how you inspired rebellion. You were never afraid take the lead in battles. It was almost as though you weren't afraid to die."

He shrugged. "None of us get out of life alive."

"No, I suppose not. However, while you had a reputation for taking dangerous risks, I also saw that you were never foolish. I studied your style. You led with your head and not your heart. I consider us kindred spirits in that."

He guffawed. "A citizen comparing herself to a colonist? Now, I've heard it all."

Her lips curled upward. "We're more alike than you think. You know what else I think?"

"What's that?"

"I think you're still a torrent. Just like your entire crew are still torrents."

"You're chasing ghosts. There are no torrents left," he said simply. "They all died at Broken Mountain."

"Ah, yes. Broken Mountain." She gave him a sympathetic look. He fought to hold himself back from strangling her.

"The entire Collective equates the name Aramis Reyne with Traitor," she said. "What impresses me is how you've managed to stay alive this long. You didn't change your identity. You still fly the *Gryphon*. You're basically spitting in the eye of the torrent spirit. How, in twenty years, did you not end up with a photon blast to the brain?"

Reyne forced himself to breathe slowly in and out. "Just lucky, I guess."

She cocked her head. "Lucky is one thing you most definitely are not." She leaned forward. "Will you tell me the story?"

His jaw tightened. "I'm guessing you've heard it already."

"I've read your records, but they lack the flavor of what really happened. They speak of how a torrent marshal and a medic were at a farm, helping an injured little girl, when they were attacked. The marshal held off the dromadiers so that the medic could escape with her patient. The marshal was badly injured, but instead of killing him, the dromadiers brought the marshal to a nearby CUF base. It was at that base, while he was shackled to a gurney, that a commandant placed a radio in the marshal's room so he could listen to the attack on Broken Mountain as it happened.

"But, rather than breaking the marshal's spirit as intended, it sent him into a berserker rage. Somehow, he managed to break free from his bonds and take the officer hostage. The marshal would've gotten free, too, except an adjutant showed up with two dromadiers, each one holding a gun to the head of the medic and little girl. They threatened tit for tat, so to speak. The commandant's life in exchange for the two females. The marshal hadn't realized that the pair had also been captured, and he surrendered rather than escape and live with their deaths on his conscience. The marshal was held on that base until after the torrents within Broken Mountain surrendered."

She held up a finger. "Surprisingly, rather than send him to the Citadel for prison or execution, the officer granted the marshal's freedom. The *Gryphon* was disarmed, and all three fringe prisoners were released without further delay."

Reyne's heart pounded as he relived in his head the weeks he spent at the CUF base. "Nice story, but I don't see where you're going with this."

She frowned. "The records have too many gaps, especially between the time of your attempted escape and your eventual freedom."

He leaned forward. "Is this why you stopped my ship? To fill in some gaps for your war story?"

The side of her lip curled upward. "No. I have other business, but I've always found your story fascinating. Will you tell me why the officer expunged your record?"

"Why don't you ask him yourself?"

She tapped a finger on the table. "I have two theories. My first theory is that when you found that small, broken girl, surrounded by death, she tugged at the last shreds of humanity you had left. Unable to let her die, you betrayed the torrents to save her life." She cocked her head. "Or, you were a scapegoat. You remained true to the torrent cause, despite all risks to yourself and to the two females. Whether it was by calculation or by generosity, the officer released you. His actions set you up to take the fall, especially when all the other torrent marshals were sent to the Citadel or escaped to the edges of the fringe."

Reyne stared at her, teeth and fists clenched. "You don't know me."

She shrugged. "You're right. I don't know you, but I bet one of my theories is close to being right."

He pushed off from his bench. "Are we done here?"

"No, we're not finished. Sit down."

He didn't move. After an interminable silence, he relented and sat down.

"Now that we've had a chance to talk, I think I know which theory is correct."

"And which one might that be?"

Her wrist comm chimed, and she glanced down. She sighed deeply. "Our time together is growing short, and so we must talk about your cargo."

"Your men will find nothing," he said coldly. "I've never smuggled contraband."

"It's not illegal cargo I'm interested in," she replied. "Tell me about the Genics Corp contract."

His eyes narrowed as she confirmed his suspicions regarding the reason they'd been stopped. "There's nothing to tell. Standard salvage contract. A hauler ended up stranded in the path of a star swarm. We were sent in to retrieve a high-priority package. I have all the paperwork."

"I've read the paperwork. You didn't find it suspicious that a modern hauler would have a level one catastrophic failure—one where not a single crewmember could reach an escape pod in time—exactly in the path of a star swarm only a few hours away?"

"You tell me. I'm a runner, not a detective."

"Ah, but you were a chaser when a conscript in the CUF, were you not? You were paid to solve mysteries and hunt down criminals." She tilted her head. "What did you find on the hauler? What was the state of the crew?"

"Standard cat fail. All crew dead from exposure. Nothing out of the ordinary."

"Really?" Heid watched Reyne for an uncomfortably long moment, and he began to suspect that she knew more than she was letting on. "How convenient for you that we'll never know, now that the ship has been destroyed by a star swarm."

Her comm chimed again, and she read the message. "I have what I need. My apologies for detaining you and your crew, and my apologies for having to seize the package you salvaged from the hauler."

Reyne's hands hit the table. "Why? That was a legal contract. You can't do that."

She ignored his question. "My men also removed twenty units of biome kits, as you did not have proper paperwork for those."

"We found them on the hauler," he gritted out. "Code Eighty-Four-Bravo-Twenty-Six. It's fully legal to salvage supplies from ships facing imminent destruction if the owners cannot retrieve them in time. Paperwork is not required as long as the goods are logged in to the system, which I did. I'm a licensed runner. You can't take legal cargo without a warrant."

"I'm a commandant in the Collective Unified Forces. I will do anything I please to preserve the Collective's well-being."

"Including stealing from colonists?" he snapped back.

"I'm not stealing. I'm *reappropriating* those biome kits to where they can be better served."

His eyes narrowed. "Sure you are. And the package?"

She stood and headed to the door. "I believe we're done for today, Captain. Thank you for the conversation."

"Wait." He jumped to his feet. "What's in the package?"

She stood in the doorway as though thinking. "You ever wonder about the decision you made while imprisoned on Terra? That you made the wrong decision?"

The abrupt subject change made him take a second or two for her question to process in his head. "Never."

Heid gave a small nod and an almost-smile. "Don't be glum. You should be thanking me. After all, I just saved Ice Port."

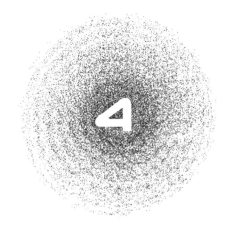

UNFINISHED BUSINESS

Heid

Commandant Gabriela Heid stood before the monitor in her quarters and watched the *Gryphon* detach from the docking bay. The wheelchair-bound Terran's skills were impressive, especially considering the colonist's disability and lack of professional training. Heid was half-tempted to offer the pilot a job on the *Arcadia*. Heid could see to the repair of the colonist's spine, but she wasn't convinced that would be enough to sway the pilot to join the *Arcadia*'s crew without conscripting the Terran into service. Still, she made a note to have Sebin add the pilot to her personal watch list.

Heid turned her attention back to the package resting on her table. Knowledge of its contents made her nauseous. When she first heard of its existence from sources far too reliable to be wrong, she knew it needed to be destroyed. Yet, despite the actions she and her counterparts had taken to ensure its demise on the Myrad hauler, it continued its path against everything Heid worked for.

She reached for the small tablet and entered her credentials. Once the machine ran through its series of encryption protocols, she fired off a message.

Mason ~
The cake is ready for delivery.
~ Baker

Within minutes, she received an encrypted response.

Baker ~
Driver will pick up the cake from you and deliver it to the party. Ensure he has it ten hours before the event.
~ Mason

She committed the message to memory and then deleted it. As she slid the tablet into her pocket, her door chimed, and her adjutant's image appeared on the monitor.

"Enter," she commanded.

The tall, well-built Alluvian strode into her quarters. "All biome kits retrieved from the fringe runner have been secured in cold storage, sir."

Heid nodded. "Let's pray the kits can be used for new settlements rather than to rebuild existing ones."

Sebin glanced at the wall panel.

She motioned to the same panel. "I already have the dampener on. The room is secure. You may speak freely."

"Any references to the package have been removed from the ship logs, Baker." He intentionally called her by the code name no one else on the *Arcadia* knew—a code name that would spell their deaths if it became known to the wrong person.

She sighed in relief. "Excellent work, Sebin. Today, we saved the life of Seamstress as well as the lives of thirty thousand Playans."

"Have you received instructions on what we are to do with the package?"

"I have. We'll be heading home to Alluvia. I imagine the crew is in need of some R&R."

His brows rose. "Alluvia? Isn't that too dangerous? What if the package breaks open?"

She shook her head. "It'll never touch Alluvia's surface. As soon as we reach orbit, Driver will relieve you of the package and see to the remainder of its journey back to its creator."

A smile crept up his face, but Heid didn't smile. Instead, she added, "We can only hope that our luck holds and that we're able to prevent the delivery of other packages."

He frowned. "Why would there be more? I thought Mason said this was an attack aimed at Vym Patel for her slander against the Collective."

She shook her head. "I believe that was merely an excuse for Myr's elite to initiate their efforts to take over the fringe. With the colonies under Myr's control, Alluvia wouldn't stand a chance."

Sebin thought for a moment before nodding. "Now is the perfect time for them to make their move. Anyone would be blind to not see the separatist attitudes spreading like floodwater across Myr."

She held up a finger. "And Alluvia." She sighed. "I'm afraid the time is here where people will be forced to choose sides. Those for Myr, those for Alluvia and the Collective, or those for entirely something else."

"The fringe will never support Alluvia, even if it means the Collective will fall. And, Alluvia will certainly never align with the fringe to bring about a new Collective."

Her jaw tightened. "Then, Myr will win." She took a deep breath. "But, let's leave that discussion for another time. Right now, we need to focus on the immediate mission of searching for other packages."

"Mason will find out if there are more," Sebin offered hopefully. "He has to."

"Let's hope he does so in time." She paused. "I'll secure the package in my personal safe along with further instructions. You know the access code. Retrieve the package the moment we reach Alluvian orbit. I'll count on you to handle it from there."

"I'll see it done." His gaze softened. "Is there anything you need?"

"No. Get some rest. You'll need it. I worry the CUF will be busier after United Day. And, as will you..."

He frowned. "How so?"

She smiled warmly. "Mason said your training is near completion."

His lips parted before curling upward into a smile. Then, he stood taller and clicked his boots together. "For the free."

She clicked her boots in response. "For the Founders."

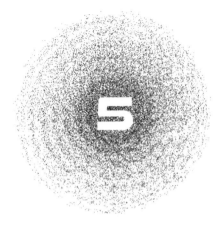

INFINITE PROBLEMS

E ven after Boden worked miracles in patching the hull, the *Gryphon* docked at Ice Port on Playa three hours after their delivery deadline. No matter how fast Reyne hustled from the docks, he knew he was in for a penalty. He hadn't even stepped through Kason's door before his usually stoic handler jumped to his feet.

"You're late. In all the years we've worked together, you've never missed a deadline. Not once. Please tell me it's not what I think it is."

"Well," Reyne drawled. "If you're thinking I no longer have the package, then yeah, it's exactly what you're thinking."

Kason fell back into his seat and dropped his head into his hands. After a string of curses, he leaned back and sighed. "What happened?"

"Our friends in the CUF are what happened," Reyne said before taking a seat across from Kason. "What I've been trying to figure out is how they even knew about the package. The contract was privately negotiated through Genics Corp, wasn't it?"

"Yeah. Nobody knew about the contract except for us. Genics put out feelers for anyone who had a hauler in that sector, and I signed us up. You sure the CUF stopped you for the package? After all, they had no reason to care about a private package, let alone have it show up on their radar."

"Oh, they cared all right. They cared enough to divert a warship to intercept it."

Kason's jaw loosened as he stared at Reyne.

Reyne's lips thinned. "Tell me what was in that crate, Kason."

The Alluvian shrugged. "I have no idea. It was no-questions-asked contract. A simple grab-and-go." After a moment, he sighed. "But I guess it's out of our hands now. The CUF never returns anything they take. I'll tell Genics Corp that you weren't able to reach the hauler before the star swarm hit. Better they think their property was destroyed than sitting in a CUF cargo hold. Best-case scenario, we don't get paid. Worst-case scenario, they blacklist us."

Reyne winked. "I'm sure you can sweet-talk Genics Corp into giving us another shot. After all, you're a citizen."

His handler chortled. "I'm an *Alluvian* citizen. Genics Corp is a *Myrad* corporation. In case you haven't gotten the memo, Myrads think Alluvians are beneath them."

"They think everyone's beneath them. At least you have your citizenship. Colonists rank lower than the mud on their boots."

Kason smirked. "A proper Myrad would never have mud on their boots. They'd ride the backs of tenured across anything not paved with silver."

Reyne chuckled. "Good point." He pushed to his feet. "Now, back to business. Tell me you got an after-hours pass for me. I need to get my regular cargo dropped off before a penalty kicks in."

Kason held up a hand. "Sorry, mate. You'll have to unload in the morning."

"But that'll put me at a thirty percent penalty. I'll be taking a loss."

"I know. I tried everything I could to get you in tonight, but Vym called me personally. She said in no uncertain terms that the stationhouse would not reopen for—and I quote— 'some ne'er-do-well who thinks the rules don't apply to him'."

Reyne gave a crooked grin. "Sounds like she missed me."

"I was paraphrasing." Kason's gaze narrowed. "You're not thinking about talking to her tonight to get her to change her mind, are you? She'll put your nuts into a vise just for knocking on her door at this hour."

"I've got a broken ship and not nearly enough credits to fix it. Vym is the only one who can waive the penalty fee, and—if she's in a really good mood—loan me some credits."

"You are an idiot, Aramis Reyne."

"Desperate," Reyne corrected, holding up a finger. "That's an entirely different thing than being an idiot."

"Sounds awfully close in my book. Go right ahead. It's your gonads. Enjoy the torture."

"Ah, Kason. You always say the sweetest things."

The man waved him away. "Now, shoo. I've got contracts to line up before I head back home for United Day. Tell Boden if he wants me to bring anything back from Alluvia, he needs to stop by before morning."

"Will do."

Reyne left Kason's office and took the long way back to the *Gryphon* to delay sharing the bad news. The bitterly cold wind seeped through the seams between his goggles and hood. Everything else was covered by his puffy, thick anorak, its length covering his entire body, all the way down over his hefty boots.

Playa was the Collective's ice world, far from the temperate planets of Myr and Alluvia. Without the right gear, a man could face hypothermia in fewer than five minutes standing outside in its freezing temperatures.

His goggles iced up, and he walked alongside a wall to not lose his way. What little sunlight Playa days brought was long gone. His headlamp pierced bare inches of the icy slivers tearing through the wind. A blur of tall green anorak plowed into him, and he found himself slammed against the wall.

"Watch where you're going, fella," Reyne said as he pushed himself off the wall.

The eight-foot-tall stretch put his hands on his hips, indignant. "Wat you talk 'bout? Ain't no man."

"Oh. Sorry, ma'am. I couldn't tell through your coat."

She shoved past him. "Outto my way, viggin' out-worlda."

"Hey, I'm no off-worlder," he snapped back. "I'm a Playan, like you."

She ignored him and ran off.

"Viggin' rude stretches," he muttered as he watched the rail-thin woman run into the wind. Playa's gravity was so low that colonists who couldn't afford gravity suits mutated over the generations. Folks called them stretches because they grew so tall and thin. After a couple decades in Playa's low-g without gravity suits, those colonists could never travel to another planet without their lungs collapsing and their hearts giving out under the pressure. They'd become fated to never leave their home world. Reyne imagined stretches would reach ten feet tall within a few more generations.

Even though Playa was one of the few Collective worlds to contain breathable air before terraforming, it had been more expensive and took more time to prepare the ice world to sustain life. After nearly two hundred years, there were still only three cities, the smallest population of any of the Collective planets.

Most citizens found no pleasure in making the long trip to the cold, dark planet. Kason was one of a few citizens to have ever stepped foot on Playa. A wanderer at heart, he spread his time equally across all the Collective worlds.

The CUF was also an exception. A CUF ship docked at Ice Port every month for one very important resource—conscripts. By law, the CUF could enlist any able-bodied colonist into five-year service. Stretches were excluded from service, and fringe doctors could be paid to mark a person down as unfit for service. But Reyne wasn't a stretch, and had no money. He'd left Playa a week after his eighteenth birthday to serve a government he'd never seen or benefitted from.

Collective law required only five years of service, but colonists who performed well rarely received their dismissal papers in fewer than twenty years without having connections or money. He had served eleven years on a CUF warship as a chaser before he'd earned enough money on the side to expedite his dismissal papers.

That was a lifetime ago.

A lifetime he'd rather forget.

When the space docks came into view, Reyne blew out a frosty sigh of relief. He flashed his pass-card to enter the massive building, and jogged down the ramp to where the *Gryphon* waited. She was smaller than most haulers. Scratches and dents marred her rilon hull, and he noticed the new, six-foot-long dented slice she'd acquired from the star swarm. Still, she looked good considering the rough life she'd had. He found an uptick in his mood as he walked up the steps to her port.

Inside, he found everyone in the commons. Doc was reading a book to the crew—with Throttle in her wheelchair, Sixx on the floor with his eyes closed and hugging the biome kit he'd managed to hide from the CUF, and Boden leaning against the wall. When Reyne entered, Doc stopped reading.

Sixx sat up. The bruising under his eyes accentuated his Asian heritage. "Are we getting paid tonight?"

"Still working on it." Reyne nodded to the mechanic. "Gear up, Boden. You're with me."

"Where are we going?" Boden asked.

"We're off to pay Vym a little visit."

He grimaced. "I hate going there. She always touches me."

"Maybe she won't this time."

"I'll go," Sixx volunteered.

"Hell, no," Reyne retorted. "She said she'd shoot you if you came within eyesight of her."

"What'd Sixx do now?" Throttle asked.

Reyne tossed a sideways glance. "He slept with Vym's niece."

She rolled her eyes. "Smooth move, Sixx."

Sixx leaned back down and waved a hand in the air. "What was I to do? She threw herself at me. I didn't want to hurt her feelings."

"She was eighteen."

"She knew *plenty* for an eighteen-year-old." Sixx pouted and blew out a breath. "It's not like I have anywhere else to go. I had an appointment scheduled for later tonight, but unless you get me my paycheck, I'm going to have to cancel on Naughty Naomi. Too bad, too, because she is a *very* naughty lady."

"Ew," Throttle said.

"You, you, and you, behave." Reyne pointed to each crewmember staying behind. "Boden and I will be back in no time. We'll unload the cargo then." He turned to Boden. "Let's go."

None of them were happy about sitting in the docks with a ship full of cargo and empty pockets. With equal parts hope and doubt, Reyne and Boden headed to Vym's. Ice Port's stationmaster had shown a fondness for the Alluvian mechanic the moment she'd met him. If anyone could help sway the old woman's mind, it'd be Boden.

For negotiations involving any other woman, Reyne would bring Sixx. He had a body built for fantasies, a smile to melt hearts, and renowned sexual prowess to make even the most resilient woman weak in the knees. Women flocked to the thief like mice to philoseed. But not Vym. Most definitely not Vym. He could only hope that seeing Boden would improve her mood tonight.

The stationhouse, which was located within the fringe station's center, was only a couple hundred meters from the docks. Even then, the winds had doubled in intensity during the minutes Reyne had spent on the *Gryphon*. The winds would continue to pick up speed throughout the night. Anyone caught outside during the four "dead hours," as the Playans called them, would be blown into the frozen abyss. Reyne and Boden had nearly three hours before that time.

When the men reached the stationmaster's office, Reyne chipped ice from the comm on the door and spoke loudly into the panel. "Aramis Reyne here to see Stationmaster Patel."

55

They waited outside for several freezing seconds before the door opened and one of Vym's overly muscular lackeys motioned them inside. "No weapons," he mumbled in a baritone voice.

"We're clean," Reyne said, though between him and Boden, they had two photon guns and several knives. It was an unspoken rule on any fringe world. A colonist without weapons was either stupid or dead, with one usually following the other. Vym would be disappointed in Reyne if he showed up unarmed. After all, the woman had practically raised him after his mother was caught outside in the dead hours. His father had been killed while in conscripted service two months before that. Reyne had been only eight at the time.

The lackey—one of Vym's regulars—led them down a stark hallway to Vym's office and living quarters. Unlike her fellow stationmasters on the other fringe worlds, Vym showed no interest in luxuries or formalities. She looked hard, spoke hard, and was an even harder negotiator.

Reyne and Boden entered to find Vym honing one of her many knives, a sharp contrast to her thin, grandmotherly looks.

"Hello, Vym," Reyne said.

Her response was the rough sound of her blade against the whetstone.

Reyne glanced over at Boden, who shrugged.

She spoke after a lengthy moment. "Kason said you had a package for me."

"His statement was a bit premature," Reyne replied, "as said package is no longer in my possession."

"And just where might said package be now?"

"On a CUF warship."

"On exactly which CUF warship?"

Reyne frowned in surprise at why she would care. CUF was

CUF in his mind. "On board the *Arcadia*, the last I knew. It's captained by Commandant—"

"Gabriela Heid," she finished. "Yes, I'm aware of the *Arcadia* and her crew. I keep myself apprised of all the Collective's senior dromadiers."

Vym Patel didn't speak like a Playan. She spoke like a citizen, even though she was born on Playa. She looked like she drank tea in dainty cups, but Reyne knew she could drink any man under the table when it came to whiskey. No one knew her history, but it was obvious she'd served a length of time off world. Reyne had often wondered under which CUF division she'd served, and in what capacity. To become a stationmaster took a long reach with the Collective's powers that be, a reach longer than any fringe money could buy. Vym had clearly made an impression somewhere along the way.

"I find it bothersome," she continued. "That I have no knowledge of whatever gift someone sent me. Tell me more."

"I don't have much to tell. Kason got the contract from Genics Corp. There was a Myrad hauler cat fail in the path of a star swarm, and they needed someone to grab a package and deliver it straight to you."

"A single package? None of its other cargo?"

He shook his head. "Just the one."

She began sharpening a different blade. "What was in this package?"

He shrugged. "I have no idea. Kason doesn't seem to know, either."

"What did it look like?"

He held out his hands. "About this big." When she didn't look up, he continued. "A small metal box, each side no more than a half-meter."

"Intriguing," she said. "But we both know you didn't come here to talk about my secret admirer."

"It's about the delivery penalty," he began. "We docked this evening. We're ready to unload now. Waive the penalty fee and let us unload tonight."

She looked up. "You know I can't do that. If I did that for you, every runner would ask for the same leniency. Before you know it, the runners' union will demand no fees. Every runner will get lazy, and Ice Port won't get its deliveries on time. When deliveries are late, people starve. You unload in the morning, and you get a thirty percent penalty."

Reyne swallowed. "With that penalty, I don't break-even. I need to pay my crew."

"You also need to pay your rent and docking fees. You're two months late on both. One more week, and I'm renting your place out to someone else."

"Vym, come on."

"I hear you also need to repair your ship." She walked around her desk and headed straight toward Boden. Reyne's tall mechanic visibly tensed.

She ran her hands over Boden's biceps before letting them settle on his hips. Reyne winced at Boden's obvious discomfort.

She smiled. "Tell me, Tren. Who's your favorite stationmaster?"

"You are, Lady Patel," he replied glumly.

She slapped his butt and smiled. "I always love how you address me as though I were a citizen."

She took a step back, and her smile faded. "But I'm not a citizen and never will be. We're colonists. A simple label that makes us less worthy than a privileged few because of the land on which we were born."

She returned to her desk and took a seat. "Tren, what repairs are needed?"

Boden began counting on his fingers. "The stern has a breach. One of the nav engines is shot. The gear for the solar sails is sticking. The air converter overheated because I had to run it at max all the way back. Those are the critical issues, for starters. I have a long list on non-critical repairs needed."

"Those are costly repairs, and any single one of them grounds you." She looked at Reyne. "I've seen your bank accounts. After all, I am your banker. You're not going anywhere anytime soon."

Reyne clenched his jaw shut to not snap back a retort.

She resumed sharpening her blades. "I'm feeling generous. I'll fix your ship, Reyne. Not only that, but I'll also have it ready for you in three days."

Reyne's eyes narrowed. "Whatever your deal is, I doubt I can afford it."

She smirked. "We both know that you can't afford to *not* accept my deal, regardless of what it is. I'm not even asking you to do anything illegal. In fact, I'm giving you and your crew the chance to help the fringe in a way you've always wanted."

He cocked his head. "What's the deal?"

"I want you to speak with someone."

He laughed aloud. "You'll fix the *Gryphon* in exchange for me to talk to someone? That's all?"

She gave a thin smile and nodded. "That's all."

His eyes narrowed. "Who?"

"An old friend of yours."

"*Who?*"

Her smile grew wide. "Critch."

All expression leeched from his face. "*No.*"

"Consider it an opportunity to reconnect with an old friend."

He shook his head. "No way, Vym. We both know I'm a dead man the second I walk through his door."

She shook her head. "He and I have an understanding. Besides, you are kindred spirits. You've both always been after the same thing. You remember what that is, don't you?"

Reyne swallowed. "I remember, but that was a long time ago."

"Not so long ago, and things haven't changed."

"I know things have changed enough for Critch to want me dead. I guaran-damn-tee he's not changing his mind anytime soon."

She smiled. "Trust me." Then she shrugged. "Or, don't trust me. But if you want your ship repaired, you'll take the deal."

Reyne looked at Boden, who was watching him with an inquisitive expression. Without Vym, he couldn't get a loan on Playa. If he couldn't get the *Gryphon* repaired, they couldn't make deliveries. Even after working for the infamous Aramis Reyne, Boden, Sixx, and Doc could find new jobs, but Throttle didn't stand a chance. No one would hire her with her disability.

He gave Vym a hard look. "If I don't make it back, I need your word that my crew will be taken care of."

"Always," she said without hesitation.

"Then, you've got yourself a deal." Reyne turned abruptly and strode from Vym's office, with Boden's heavy bootsteps behind him. He suspected the game Vym was playing. There could be only one reason she'd want him to reconnect with Critch.

After twenty years, he'd given up hope for the Uprising. He'd thought everyone else had given up on the Uprising.

He was wrong.

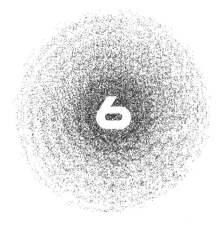

DANGEROUS DISCOVERIES

Three days later, the *Gryphon* broke free from Playa's atmosphere and cruised into the smooth blackness of space, where Reyne could usually find some semblance of peace. Only this time, their current run weighed heavily on his mind.

"I can't believe we're going to the Space Coast," Throttle said, not even trying to hide the excitement in her voice. "I've never been in a real asteroid belt before. Is it as dangerous as they say?"

He reined himself in from his thoughts. "Worse, and it's not because of the asteroids. The rocks move slowly. They're easy to miss. The danger with asteroid belts is what they hide. Once you enter the Coast, you have to keep one eye on the lookout for asteroids, and the other on the lookout for pirates."

She rubbed her hands together. "I can handle that."

Reyne smiled. "I know you can, but rest up. I want you at the top of your game when we enter the Coast. There's a reason even the CUF won't go near there."

"The ship's running better than ever," she said. "Flight plan shows we'll reach Nova Colony in twenty-six hours."

"Good," he said, unbuckling from his seat and crossing the bridge. "I want to get this deal over with. Keep running diagnostics. Vym didn't repair the *Gryphon* out of the goodness of her heart. She's got something up her sleeve."

He headed down the hallway to the commons to find Boden, Doc, and Sixx snacking from a bowl of raisins.

"Taking a break already?" Reyne asked.

"We've searched the ship," Sixx said. "We didn't find anything."

Reyne rubbed his neck. "There's no way Vym fixed the ship without leaving her grubby prints somewhere on it. Keep searching."

"We were thorough," Doc said. "We've scoured the cargo bay and went through every cabinet. If she's smuggling something, we're not going to find it without taking the ship apart piece by piece."

Reyne grabbed a handful of raisins from the bowl. "Then, you need to start taking it apart piece by piece."

Her jaw dropped. "You can't possibly want us to open every panel."

"That's exactly what I want. I need to know what she's having us smuggle for her before we get to Nova Colony."

The crew in the room let out a collective groan.

"Sure thing, boss. We'll get started on finding that needle in a haystack...right after break, of course." Sixx popped a raisin in his mouth. "So, fill us in. Who's this mysterious contact Vym is having you meet at Nova Colony?"

"Some man by the name of Critch," Boden offered, before digging out a handful of raisins.

Reyne glared at his mechanic, but it was already too late. By the look of Doc's blanched face, she remembered that name all too well.

"We're going to Nova Colony to see Critch?" she asked softly.

"No, we're going to Nova Colony, where *I'm* going to see Critch. You're all staying on the ship," Reyne replied.

"That's a suicide mission," she countered.

"Maybe. Maybe not." Reyne chewed on his raisins.

"Who's Critch?" Sixx asked.

"He's a pirate," Doc said, narrowing her eyes in a sideways glance directed at Reyne. "A very dangerous pirate."

"Psh," Sixx said. "Pirates are overrated."

"He captains the *Honorless,*" she added.

"Oh." Sixx's eyes widened, and he turned to Reyne. "Doc's right. It's a suicide mission. Why aren't we running the other way?"

Finding his stomach suddenly without appetite, Reyne threw his remaining raisins back into the bowl. As he strode from the commons, he heard Doc begin a tale he had no desire to hear again.

"Critch is more than a pirate," Doc continued. "You know the story that Reyne was one of the two torrent marshals at the Siege of Terra during the Uprising. You've also heard how Reyne disappeared just before the Battle of Broken Mountain, leaving behind an inexperienced marshal half his age?"

"Of course," Sixx said. "Everyone's heard that story, but anyone who's ever met Reyne wouldn't believe it for a minute."

"Well, Critch was that other marshal."

Reyne picked up his pace back to the bridge so that he could no longer hear the crew's conversation.

"Hey," Throttle said. "I was just going to ping you."

Relieved for the distraction, he headed over to her. "What'd you find?"

"I don't know yet, but Vym has definitely put something on the ship. I've been running the numbers against our power usage. We're running heavier."

He frowned. "How much heavier?"

"It's significant. If I'm reading this right, we're carrying a few hundred extra kilograms."

"Show me."

Her fingers flew over the instrument panel until the list of weight-and-balance calculations were brought to the forefront. He ran his finger down each line item until he came to the variance.

"Four hundred and twenty-nine kilos. It can't be." A shiver climbed his spine, and he found himself lightheaded. He grabbed ahold of the panel's edge.

"What is it?" she asked.

He took a deep breath. "The *Gryphon* used to weigh a bit more in her early days. Four hundred and twenty-nine extra kilos, to be exact."

He had to see the truth for himself. He hustled to his seat and ran through the menus.

"Reyne?"

He watched as a series of green lights came to life. Lines of text began to scroll.

"Reyne, seriously. What the hell's going on?"

Without looking up, he pointed in her direction. "Language."

She let out an exasperated sigh, but he read the text repeatedly before he believed it wasn't some error.

"That can't be right."

Reyne jerked around to find that Throttle had rolled up next to him and was reading the screen.

She pointed to the text. "Tell me that can't be right."

He read the seven lines one more time.

Phase Cannon: Operational and Armed.

Photon Gun One: Operational and Armed.

Photon Gun Two: Operational and Armed.

Photon Gun Three: Operational and Armed.

Photon Gun Four: Operational and Armed.

Photon Gun Five: Operational and Armed.

Photon Gun Six: Operational and Armed.

"Why would Vym arm the *Gryphon*?" she asked.

He took a deep breath. "My guess? Vym never gave up hope on the Uprising, and she's pulling us into her torrent army, whether we volunteer or not."

After a moment, Throttle's lips curled upward. "It's about viggin' time."

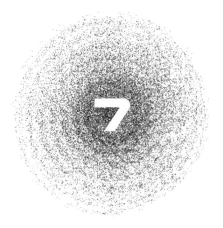

THE TROUBLE WITH PIRATES

Reyne woke the following morning with a hard reminder that with whiskey came hangovers. He still had all the memories he'd attempted to drown, except now he had a hell of a pounding headache to go along with them.

He gently lifted the arm draped across his chest and climbed out of bed. Doc mumbled something incoherent before rolling onto her other side. He didn't need to dress since he hadn't bothered to undress the night before. He buckled his pants and stumbled from his quarters and to the commons. There, he went straight for a juice bag and chugged the entire contents.

"Rough night?"

Reyne turned to find Sixx eating breakfast, realizing the other man had been sitting there the entire time. Reyne tossed the empty bag and grabbed a second juice bag before pulling out a chair and plopping down.

"Throttle told me about our upgrades." Sixx whistled. "That's some serious armament. Any theories?"

"Working on it."

"Hopefully, we don't run into a CUF cruiser. They'll be in for one hell of a surprise when they scan us. We'll spend the rest of our about-to-become incredibly short lives munching on vigs and cockroaches in the Citadel."

Reyne shook his head slowly, wincing at the movement. "The *Gryphon* might be a hauler now, but she's got the heart of a gunship. Her hull's been reinforced with rilon, with a couple extra layers covering the gun bays. No ramp scan would pick them up, and Vym knows this."

"Well, aren't we lucky?"

Reyne grunted. "Now, if the CUF did a manual search of the gun bays—"

"We'd be screwed," Sixx finished for him.

"Yeah, we'd be screwed."

With a sigh, he pushed to his feet. Now that he could string together semi-rational thoughts through the sledge hammer pounding a staccato rhythm in his brain, he headed toward the bridge. It was empty—Throttle would still be in bed after they spent most of the night hailing Ice Port. To no surprise, Vym hadn't responded to any of his pings.

The old woman wasn't dumb. She had to have known they would discover the armaments. Why hadn't she said something back on Ice Port? More importantly, what the hell was she planning?

He had a sinking feeling he'd been set up to deliver a gunship to a torrent crew of Vym's choosing at Nova Colony, and Critch would be there to clean up loose ends—namely, Reyne and his crew. If that were the case, Vym would quickly learn that Reyne wouldn't give up his ship without a fight. He'd have no problem using his new phase cannon to protect his ship and his crew.

A bell chimed, and Reyne checked the notification. He pinged Throttle's comm. "You'd better get up here if you want to fly through an asteroid belt."

After a delay, she grumbled, *"Coming."*

Moments later, Throttle wheeled onto the bridge—her eyes still half-closed—and locked in at her panel.

He watched her. "You sure you're up to this?"

She yawned and stretched. "Oh, yeah. Definitely." She pulled her mussed-up hair into a ponytail before turning her focus to the instruments. She cracked her knuckles. And, just like that, she was all business. "All right. Switching to manual controls. Maintaining speed until we hit the edge of the Coast. Then we'll drop down to half-speed to avoid any big, ugly rocks."

"And pirates," Reyne added, but she didn't acknowledge him, already deep into her own world.

He grabbed the comm and announced to the ship, "We're coming up on the Space Coast in ten minutes. Lock down anything that can be locked down, and strap in. Get ready for a bumpy ride."

In an asteroid belt, the larger asteroids were easy to avoid. It was the much smaller meteoroids—called mosquitoes—that wreaked havoc on hulls. Throttle's jagged flight plan appeared on Reyne's screen, and he began running scans for bogeys along the grid.

"I'm pulling in the solar sails now and switching on the Flux engine," she announced.

A moment later, Reyne felt the ship slow down.

"I'm starting the run-up sequence for the jump shields," she continued.

When Throttle was a little girl and first took the controls of the *Gryphon,* Reyne had made her talk through every single thing she needed to do to pilot the ship. It was a habit that helped her learn faster, and a habit she'd never given up. Thankfully, she no longer voiced each and every keystroke as she used to be so keen on doing.

"Jump shields are active at one hundred percent," she said before adding, "Bring on the rocks."

The Space Coast filled the view screen, a majestic expanse that was both awe striking and ominous. Reyne found it surreal—a three-dimensional black beach of rocks, some large enough to hold the entire CUF fleet, others small pebbles. The belt moved slowly. One would have to watch the asteroids for some time to discern any hint of movement. However, the devils would sneak up on a pilot if he weren't paying attention.

The Space Coast was a dangerous beauty.

It'd been too long since he'd been out there. When he returned from CUF service, he practically lived on the Coast. He honed his skills on the Coast, constantly pushing himself to fly faster and turn harder as he made the annual Coastal Run. He never won, but he always placed in the top ten, and—more importantly—he always survived.

Seeing the Coast made Reyne regret that he'd been too protective of Throttle. She would love flying the Coastal Run, and, unlike him, she'd win.

An alarm beeped, warning them they'd broken the Space Coast barrier. Autopilot would no longer be available, because the Coastal grid was constantly changing, not that Throttle would ever dream of using autopilot out here.

"Looks like I'm just in time."

Reyne turned around to see Sixx take a seat and strap in. "Damn, the Coast sure is a sight. It's been too long."

"Yeah." Reyne's nostalgia disappeared when the *Gryphon* veered a hard left. With his attention back on the view panel, he watched as Throttle maneuvered around a cluster of mid-sized rocks, making sharp turns...on purpose.

His eyes widened as a brown rock became a bull's-eye on the view panel. "Throttle, I assume you see the ship-killer at our twelve o'clock."

"Relax, I've got it," she said, before banking right and narrowly missing the boulder.

"Cutting it a little close, are we?" Sixx asked.

Throttle grinned.

The rocks became fewer and larger, and Reyne relaxed in his seat and began to zoom in on the larger asteroids.

"Hm," Throttle said.

Reyne looked up. "What's wrong?"

"This is nothing compared to outrunning a star swarm," she replied.

"Think of it this way," Sixx began. "The life expectancy of a pilot in a swarm is roughly eight point two seconds. Then, compare that to the Coast where people choose to live out nice, semi-long lives. So yeah, the two are nothing alike."

Her shoulders slumped. "I know, but I didn't expect flying the Coast to be so *boring*."

"Boring is good when it comes to flying," Reyne said. "It's the high-adrenaline moments when a pilot has to worry."

She straightened. "Ooh, I have an idea. Can we try out the phase cannon on a few rocks?"

"I think firing the phase cannon is a great idea," Sixx added.

"No," Reyne answered.

"How about the photon guns?" she asked.

"I think firing the photon guns is a great idea," Sixx tacked on.

"No." Reyne pointed at Sixx. "And you're not helping."

"Old guy's a real party pooper," Sixx grumbled.

"I'm not old," Reyne defended.

Throttle chortled. "You're old. You even walk like an old guy."

"It's called arthritis. You'd better be careful. Young space jockeys can get it, too."

Sixx joined in. "Keep telling yourself that, old guy."

As Sixx and Throttle continued bantering at Reyne's expense, he focused on his panel. His eyes narrowed on a large rock in their path. He zoomed in as far as the camera would go, to where the image became pixelated. The rock was dark, nearly pure black, with specks of brown pockmarking its surface. At its edge, something the color of dark gray peeked out.

The color of rilon.

"Throttle, you might get that excitement you were looking for," he said.

"What do you mean?" she asked.

"We have a tail," he announced. "But I can't get an ID."

"Where?" Sixx's seat buckle clinked as the man hustled to peer over Reyne's shoulder.

"I'm marking the rock in quadrant one-seven-four," Reyne said.

"Firing the phase cannon is sounding better every minute," Sixx said.

He glanced back at the other man. "Let's hope it doesn't have to come to that." He returned to his console. "The bogey hasn't moved, and sensors show no sign of their engines firing up."

"Maybe they haven't seen us," Throttle offered.

Sixx chuckled. "You're one hell of an optimist."

"Shut off all nav lights," Reyne commanded. "On the off chance your optimism turns out to be reality, we don't need to be lit up like a Spaten whore."

He then clenched the comm in his hand and broadcast his next words to the entire crew. "Heads up, everyone. Seems we have a player waiting on the sidelines who might try to jump into the game."

He turned to Throttle. "We've got a Flux Whisper. Chances are, they don't have anything near that caliber. Problem is, we don't know the Coast like the back of our hands, and I'd lay bets that they do. If they try to take us, do you want to outrun them? It's your call."

"Hell yes," she replied far too quickly.

"Okay, then. It's your party. We'll cover you." He nodded to Sixx. "You take the forward guns. I'll take the aft."

"Aye, aye, boss." Sixx buckled back into his seat.

"You won't need the guns," Throttle said with confidence.

"Let's hope that's the case," Reyne cautioned as he opened the weapons console. "Give them a wide berth, Throttle. Make it clear we know they're out there."

"Wilco," she said.

Tension built up within Reyne's shoulders as they closed the distance. He didn't take his eyes off the bogey. "We might get lucky. The scans haven't picked up any signs of it powering up yet."

Throttle angled the *Gryphon* to place a mid-sized rock between the two ships.

He held his breath as they passed the bogey. "Still no change."

As soon as they were beyond the ship, its engine flared to life and it shot out from its cover.

"He's out and on our ass," Reyne called out. "Looks like we've got ourselves some pirates. Find us some distance, Throttle."

The *Gryphon's* engine set the entire ship in a tooth-rattling, humming vibration. The next instant, Reyne found himself pressed against the back of his seat. He opened the gun bays and started sighting in each of the aft photon guns.

Throttle took the ship in aggressive twists and sharp turns, nearly skimming rocks. As expected, the pirate ship didn't have the speed of the *Gryphon*, and the distance grew between them. Reyne lost visual with the bogey when Throttle banked around a large rock.

"I think we lost them," she said.

Just then, a larger ship popped out from a cavern within the rock directly in front of them and shot out an EMP net.

"Shit!" Throttle yanked the ship at a hard angle to avoid hitting the net.

"It's a tag team," Reyne started. "Sixx!"

"Got 'em." Sixx fired off several bursts.

The first ship somehow managed to catch up and was tailing them again. Without taking time for automated targeting, Reyne manually fired at it, narrowly missing.

"I clipped mine," Sixx exclaimed. "Big bird's heading off. Doesn't look like he wants to play with us."

Reyne watched his target slow and peel away. "Other bogey is bugging out."

He scanned the quadrants, finding nothing but the two departing ships. "Everything looks clear, but keep your eyes peeled."

After closing the gun bays, Reyne turned to Throttle. "Was that exciting enough for you?"

She tried not to smile, but then broke into a wide grin. "That was crazy. But seriously, who would live out here if they had to fly past that every time?"

Reyne looked at the Coast before them. "Pirates don't attack their own. I'm guessing this pair was the welcome party, and I wouldn't be surprised if they were out here waiting for us. My guess is they wanted to strip us of our ship and weapons before bringing us into Nova Colony. I should warn you. I'm not the most popular guy out here."

"They're idiots then," she said simply.

His console chimed, and he let out a deep breath. He broadcast his words to the entire crew so that Doc and Boden would also hear. "We're coming up on Nova Colony. Prepare for landing."

Throttle contacted the port control and initiated the approach and landing sequence, switching from the powerful Flux engine to the two small navigational engines. Reyne watched as they approached the asteroid known as Nova Colony. From space, it looked like any other gargantuan asteroid. No lights or manmade architecture dotted its surface, as asteroids tended to be pelted regularly by rock showers.

Sometime in Nova Colony's distant history the asteroid had an abundance of frozen water that hollowed out a maze of underground caverns. Those now-empty caverns made perfect shelters, making Nova Colony the only official settlement on the Space Coast—and the only colony outside Collective control.

Life on Nova Colony wasn't easy. Inhabited by pirates, convicts, and anyone else who desired to live outside the Collective's reach, its residents weren't exactly friendly to newcomers. Nova Colony had its own police force, but they were as likely to kill you as to help you.

As Throttle lowered the *Gryphon* into the wide cavern leading to the landing docks, apprehension tightened Reyne's already tense shoulders. There were ten thousand reasons why he avoided coming here, and he began to have more doubts about taking Vym's deal.

The ship settled into a landing slot. Magnetized mooring cables shot out and attached to the *Gryphon* to secure it in place. Throttle powered down the engines, and Reyne jumped from his seat, anxious to put the whole mess behind him.

"That was an interesting ride," Doc said as she and Boden hustled onto the bridge.

"Listen up," Reyne said. "No one leaves the ship. And that includes you, Sixx."

"Like hell. I'm not letting you go into that viper's nest alone," Sixx said. "Besides, they have the best beer in the system."

Reyne's hard expression quelled any more dissent. "I need you all here to guard the ship. This asteroid is the worst place in the system for shipjackings. And we just gave away the *Gryphon's* secret, which makes her a hot commodity. Trust no one, and don't let anyone except me on board, especially anyone who looks official. If I'm not back in three hours, you leave. Got it?"

Throttle let out a *hmph*. "We're not leaving you."

"You won't be. If I'm not back, I'm already dead."

She sobered.

"That's why I need to come with you," Sixx said with no hint of humor this time.

Reyne shook his head. "If they want to kill me, it's not going to make a lick of difference if I'm alone or if I have an army with me. Anyone at my side will be just as dead."

"Maybe, but I'll sure as hell take out a few before I go."

"I know you would, but I need you here, with Throttle and the rest of the crew." Reyne attempted a smile. "Hey Throttle, it's not so bad. If I don't make it back, the *Gryphon*'s yours."

She sneered. "Oh. If that's the case, enjoy yourself out there."

He gave a weak smile. "Okay then. See you by…" He checked the panel.

"Thirteen-twenty," she said before he could speak.

"Thirteen-twenty," he repeated, then rushed from the bridge so he didn't have to see the worry in her eyes.

He headed straight for the airlock and hustled into his suit. Just as he was about to open the outer door, he heard Throttle's voice in his speakers.

"Hey, Reyne."

"Yeah?"

Throttle's tone was dead serious. *"Promise me you're coming back."*

He flipped off his speakers without responding.

On her tenth birthday, he'd had no gift for her. Instead, he'd promised her that he would never, ever lie to her. He'd kept his word, which meant he couldn't make her this new promise. He swallowed, opened the airlock, pushed himself out of the safety of the ship, and grabbed one of the many zip lines strung across the docks.

He pulled himself down the line until he reached a motorized handle, which then zoomed him into the deepest interior of the dock, just outside Nova Colony's airlock. He hit a switch on the wall. A second later, a light turned green and the door opened. He entered, immediately feeling the stronger gravity that was bolstered by EM fields, much like what the *Gryphon* used. A moment after the door behind him closed, a screen flashed the words *Pressurization Complete. Welcome to Nova Colony. Obey all Coastal laws or forfeit your life.*

Reyne tugged off his helmet and crossed through the internal door. The caverns inside smelled of human sweat and sounded like bustling activity. There was no atmosphere on Nova Colony, requiring the caverns to be tightly sealed and the air constantly recycled. It didn't smell pleasant, but there were far worse smells in the universe.

Everyone stared at Reyne, and he fought the urge to reach for his photon gun. Taking a deep breath, he began walking. It took him several long steps before he found his stride in the stronger gravity. Several more steps and he reached his destination. A neon sign that read UNEVEN BAR flashed above its door. The sign was askew, fitting for its namesake. The bar was the first commercial establishment in Nova Colony, having been built even before the EM fields were in place. Everyone who'd ever passed through the Space Coast ended up at this bar at some point or another.

Reyne entered the bar to find it hadn't changed much. It was still dark and dirty, and reeked of alcohol and sex. The tables were filled, as they were every hour of every day. The only things that had changed were that the bar was completely silent and everyone was watching him.

He could cut the tension with the blade he had strapped on his boot. He found it surprising he was still alive, considering how many faces he recognized—and knowing that every single one of them wanted him dead.

Yet he was still alive. Hell, maybe his luck was changing.

A man who'd been sitting at the bar turned and stood to face Reyne.

Like the bar, the man had changed startlingly little. He still had scars covering his face, still had the same brown hair, though the streaks of gray were new.

"Hello, Critch," Reyne said.

A smile tugged at the corners of Critch's mouth.

Reyne's eyes widened. He spun around, but was too late. Blinding pain erupted in the back of his head. He fell as blackness claimed him.

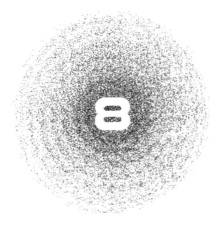

A HAZARDOUS PROPOSITION

Reyne came awake with his head throbbing twice as hard as it had that morning. He gingerly touched the back of his head. "Son of a bitch."

"I'm surprised you showed up."

Reyne cracked open his eyes to find two Critches standing in front of him. As Reyne's vision came into focus, the shape solidified into a single man. He hadn't seen the pirate in twenty years, but he'd seen his picture on the news plenty—each time, the bounty higher than the time before.

"And miss the chance to see your ugly mug again?" Reyne responded. "I never would've taken you for a nostalgic man, but the Uneven Bar? Choosing the place we first met makes me feel all warm and tingly inside."

Critch grunted. "I didn't want to make it too hard for you to find me, especially considering you don't come out this way often."

"Knowing that damn near everyone on the Coast wants me dead tends to put a damper on my travel plans." Reyne looked the room over. They were alone, but he didn't miss noticing that the familiar weight of his guns and knives was absent.

"Not true," Critch said. "*Everyone* on the Coast wants you dead."

"I see you still have that silver tongue of yours."

"And I see you're still damn lucky to have that head of yours."

"'Luck' is not the word that comes to mind with the pounding headache I have right now. Oh, and thanks for the welcome committee out on the Coast. That was real nice of you."

"You're still alive, aren't you?" Critch smirked, a crooked tug of his lips that in no way reflected humor. When he scowled, you didn't have much to worry about. When he smiled, you were screwed.

Reyne motioned to the pirate. "Tell me, buddy. You invite me all the way out here just to catch up on old times?"

"You're the last man I want to converse with."

"Setting the bar a little high considering your chosen profession, aren't you?"

"I may be a pirate, but I've never been a traitor."

"That makes two of us." Reyne gritted his teeth. "I'd tell you I had nothing to do with what happened at Broken Mountain, but I'm guessing you wouldn't care."

Critch leveled a hard gaze at Reyne. "Damn straight."

This Critch had colder eyes than the young man Reyne remembered, but his face had otherwise remained unchanged. He still had the familiar scars crisscrossing his cheeks. Reyne had been there when the pirate had gotten those scars. They'd been searching for survivors after a particularly bloody battle during the Uprising, and an unexploded grenade went off. Critch had still been a fresh recruit under Reyne's command then, not yet twenty years old, headstrong, and full of passion.

Reyne gingerly touched the bump on his head. "I think I liked you better back when you were Drake Fender."

"Well, not all of us marshals were able to have our torrent records cleared, like you. When there's a death sentence tied to your name, you're better off starting over."

"From what I hear, you've earned several more death sentences with the new name."

He shrugged.

"Speaking of death sentences," Reyne said, holding out his hands. "I'm still breathing, which means you need me alive, at least for now. Why don't you tell me what the hell I'm doing here?"

The pirate gave Reyne his back as he walked over to a table and poured himself a glass from a glass decanter that looked like it was worth more credits than what most colonists made in a year, including Reyne.

"For the record, Vym wanted to bring you in," Critch began. "Not me."

"I promised Vym I'd come out here and meet you. I did that. You don't want me here, so how about I make it easy for you." Reyne pushed to his feet and started heading toward the door. "See you around. Though, hopefully not in this lifetime."

He heard a glass set onto a table, and prepared for an attack.

Instead of attacking Reyne from behind, Critch said simply, "The Uprising isn't over."

Reyne turned slowly around to face the other man. "The

Uprising ended twenty years ago."

Critch shook his head. "The battles that took place there may be over, but the spirit of the Uprising, the *need* for an Uprising, is stronger than ever."

Reyne's brows rose. "You're thinking about starting a full-out Uprising again? Then you'll get yourself killed along with every fool who follows you. The CUF is stronger than they were when we ran the first Uprising. Myr and Alluvia will squash any rebellion—"

"You're wrong. Relations between Myr and Alluvia have fallen apart during Myr's recession. Myrads are jealous of Alluvians because they're thriving. The two are butting heads, and the fringe is stuck in the middle."

Reyne brushed the air. "Nothing's changed. They've always used us—first, to satisfy their greed for our resources, then, for our labor. As every year passes, they take away more and more of our rights. There's a reason the Uprising happened, but there's also a reason no one's instigated one since. We don't have the resources to fight them."

"This time is different. We don't have a choice. They're moving from oversight to outright ownership. Vym believes Myr is making a move to seize control of all the fringe stations."

The runner chortled. "That's impossible. The CUF would never let that happen."

"The CUF is splitting apart from the inside. Most warships and military units are now either all-Alluvian or all-Myrad. We're on the road to another war between Alluvia and Myr. Only, this time around, there are colonies in the mix. Imagine what would happen if Myr managed to gain control of all the fringe stations."

"They'd have control over all space ports in the fringe," Reyne said.

84

"Meaning…"

"Meaning they would own anything going to or coming from a fringe planet," Reyne finished.

Critch nodded. "If they take control of our space docks, the colonists are out of this fight before we even have a chance to throw a punch."

"Myr may be powerful, but you're talking about fringe stations. These are large cities. Myr would have a rebellion on their hands at the first station they made a play for."

"Not if all the colonists there are already dead."

Reyne sobered. "They'd never go that far."

"You underestimate the situation. If Myr and Alluvia start a war, we all know where the battlefields will be."

After a pause, Reyne spoke. "On the colonies."

Critch nodded.

Reyne eyed Critch a long moment before he frowned. "Why are you telling me this?"

"Because Vym wants you to join the cause."

"What?" He almost choked on the word.

"That was my first reaction, too," Critch said drily. "Somehow, you've conned her into trusting you. That don't mean shit to me, but she made a valid argument. Out of every runner in the fringe, you are the only captain who could go anywhere, anytime, without suspicion. You can run all four fringe stations and the Coast, and the CUF would never bat an eye. All my crews are on watch lists, but no one would ever suspect the traitor of Terra to have any involvement in a new Uprising."

"How reassuring," Reyne said with a hefty hint of sarcasm in his voice.

"It's not my job to hand out hugs."

"Tell me, exactly what is your job? Because Vym could've told me everything you just did. What am I doing here?"

Critch took a drink. "We're laying the groundwork for the new Uprising right here, from Nova Colony. Right now, I need runners to transport recruiters from the Coast to the colonies."

"The *Gryphon's* not designed to be a passenger ship. Besides, I have contracts on the books that I can't just drop."

"Not anymore. Vym is having your handler reassign any contracts you have on the books and set up new contracts as we speak."

Reyne's jaw loosened. "It's taken me years to build those relationships." The upgrades Vym made to the *Gryphon* were beginning to make sense, and he wasn't the least bit happy about her scheming. He shot Critch a hard look. "Without contracts, how am I going to feed my crew?"

"Vym will cover your crew's expenses under the guise of the new contracts. Everything will look legit in case the CUF gets curious."

Reyne paced the room as he thought through his options. "Vym sent me here to talk with you in case I said no, so she wouldn't have to deal with me."

Critch shook his head. "Contrary to popular belief, pirates don't kill everyone they meet, though I'd consider an exception in your case."

Reyne growled. "Watch yourself, pirate."

"I have crews and employees all over the fringe. If I wanted you dead, you don't think I could've had your throat slit in your sleep any damn time I felt like it?"

"You could try."

"You're here because we need a fast runner, and we need a captain who can get into places without questions. We've got recruiters ready to ship out. I need to know if you and your crew are in or out. You just need to know that as soon as any of them choose to make the first run with you, they're all torrents. There's no going back."

Reyne clenched his fists. "You don't even think about laying a finger on my crew."

"Then, make a choice. They're safe right now. No harm will come to them. If you'd like to keep any of them out of this arrangement, now's the time. Because once they're in, they're in." Critch held up a finger. "All the colonies are at risk if this Uprising fails. I warn you, if I get even a hint of you doing anything stupid, like running out to tell the CUF about our plans, none of your crew is safe. Not even your adopted daughter."

Reyne breathed in and exhaled slowly. "I wonder what a direct phase cannon blast would do to Nova Colony."

Critch narrowed his eyes.

"Because that's exactly what will happen if you threaten me or my crew again."

"You'd kill every person in this place? Women, children, and families?"

Reyne chuckled drily. "I'm the traitor of Terra, remember?"

Critch's lips thinned.

"Or," Reyne drawled out. "We can save plenty of headache on both sides and quit screwing around and work together through trust rather than threats. I owe Vym, and truth be told, I don't hate you. I'll work with you, but not under duress. Do we have a deal?"

Critch gave a slow, tight nod.

"So, when is this first run?" Reyne asked.

After a long moment of silence, the pirate tossed him a comm. "Soon. I'll call you once they get packed and ready. Until then, you and your crew can enjoy everything Nova Colony has to offer. My treat. One more thing." Critch opened a locked drawer in his desk and counted out several chains. He walked over and dropped them into Reyne's open hand.

Reyne held one up to examine the black chain with a single lump of rilon shaped like a raindrop hanging from the end. "What's this?"

"Every torrent gets one to identify those loyal to the cause. It's your access pass into any torrent base or safe house. There's one for each of your crew, should they decide to join up." He wagged a finger. "But don't invite them in unless you know they'll join. We can't afford rumors of an Uprising raising the CUF's suspicion."

Reyne slid one over his head and pocketed the other chains. Made of rilon, it was nearly weightless, and long, making it easy to conceal. Strangely, it felt like both a shield and a noose at the same time.

He strolled over to the table and poured himself a glass. Critch scowled, but said nothing. He held it up in Critch's direction. "Here's to the Uprising. Again."

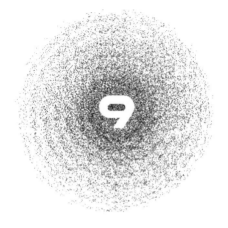

SHADOWED SECRETS

Heid

Gabriela and Sebin spent a picture-perfect day strolling around their home town of First City and concluding with a dinner cruise on the Great Sea. Everything worked out exactly as she'd planned. She wanted Sebin to remember every detail of his life-changing day.

She knew they looked like a couple to passersby. However, as long as she was Sebin's commanding officer, it was a line she didn't dare cross. She had worked tirelessly her entire life to make Commandant. She'd never risk it for something as selfish as love.

She guided him off the busy sidewalk and into the dark alley.

Sebin threw a furtive glance over his shoulder at the commotion of the city they were leaving behind. "Where are we going?"

Her smile grew wider. "You'll see soon enough."

They had to walk around a dumpster before the door came into view.

Very few Alluvians knew of the pub with no name at the end of the alley. Even fewer knew the role it played in shaping the Collective—both past and future. Heid hadn't yet joined the CUF when her father brought her here for the first time, a girl of barely fifteen years. Up until that moment, her father had overseen her training to become a Founder, like his father had done before him. She remembered every vivid detail of the alley and the pub, just as Sebin was taking it all in now.

She led Sebin into the dingy establishment. The pub smelled of fermented sea reeds and long-since outlawed cigars. Any proper citizen would turn around at the door and leave, which made the pub all the safer for the Founders' activities. Inside, the tables and barstools sat empty like lonely customers to the jukebox as it crooned a soulful song. The only person in the bar was the barkeep, who glanced up from washing glasses. The man, a Founder known simply as Bartender, gave the smallest nod to Heid, and she returned the gesture with the slightest smile.

"This way." She motioned Sebin to follow her past the bar and down a dark hallway, where she continued past the bathrooms until they reached the end. On the wall hung an oil painting. It was classic Alluvian artwork, portraying a schooner caught on a wave in a torrential storm.

Giving the painting little notice, she slid her hand behind the frame and felt the wall until she brushed the fingerprint scanner hidden within it. The technology was ancient, but foolproof. When the lock clicked, she stepped back and let go of the painting.

She pressed her hands against the wall and pushed. The wall

moved inward, revealing a staircase leading down into darkness. She glanced back at Sebin to see his eyes wide and jaw lax. She reached over and squeezed his hand. "Don't worry. We're nearly there."

He didn't let go for a long moment. When he did, he took a tentative first step through the wall space, and she followed. She pushed the wall back into its original arrangement, not moving until the locks clicked back into place.

Dim lights came on with each step, illuminating their way. There were one-hundred-forty-five steps. She'd counted them once. They were so far below the water table that they were deep into the planet's bedrock. A battle could be waged down here and no sensors on the surface would pick up any hint of a sound or vibration.

The original Founders had built this facility for secrecy and seclusion not long after First City was colonized and Myr made it clear they owned the new settlement. The leader of the Alluvian settlement, Jacob Mason, believed that more colonies would be formed in the future, and rejected the idea of a Myrad empire. At a time when Alluvia was still in its infancy, the visionary pulled together a group of powerful, like-minded individuals to help shape a "collective" of worlds. Mason's group eventually came to be called the Founders.

It took the organization eighty-seven years to instigate the War that would gain Alluvia's independence and form the Collective. Unfortunately, many Founders were killed during the War, and not enough survived to maintain full control of the government. They were outnumbered in the new Parliament, which quickly created a joint military force — the Collective Unified Forces.

By that time, the first Mason had long since died from old age. The new Mason knew the threat the Founders posed to an inexperienced government structure. Sure enough, the CUF's first directive was to hunt down and arrest all Founders, citing them as dangerous dissenters to the Collective. Many died, but Mason had gone to great lengths to ensure the Founders weren't completely lost.

The Founders had become the stuff of legends.

Where they had taken public stands before, their success now depended on the Collective believing they didn't exist. Shadow games became their new modus operandi.

As more and more colonies were established, the Founders grew to include a select few members from these new worlds. Despite the group's actions to bring about the Uprising, the group failed in achieving the Collective the original Mason had envisioned hundreds of years earlier.

Heid still believed in the vision of the first Mason, but she knew not all Founders followed that path. Still, she'd never stop working to see that vision made a reality...with or without the Founders at her side.

Sebin and Heid reached the final stair step to find a trio of Founders waiting for them.

The man in the center spoke. "Sebin Reinhardt, I am Mason. We are the Three who oversee the Founders. We have been looking forward to your initiation. Since I represent the Alluvian Founders, I've been especially looking forward to meeting you and adding you to my branch."

Sebin froze and glanced back at Heid. He mouthed *your father?* She nodded tightly.

He grinned, snapped around, and shook the man's hand. "It's an honor, sir, truly."

Mason then looked at Heid. "It's been far too long, Baker." His words were hard and cold.

Heid forced a smile. "Yes, it has," she replied just as coldly.

Mason turned his attention back to Sebin. "Sebin Reinhardt, you have been in training for seven years. You have progressed from neophyte to acolyte. Now, it is time for you to become a Founder. Are you ready?"

Sebin straightened. "I am ready."

Mason regarded Heid. "Baker, do you vouch for this candidate?"

She stepped behind Sebin. "I do."

"Remove your shirt, candidate." Mason commanded.

Sebin obeyed without question and Heid took his shirt.

Mason motioned to the two with him, and the three formed a semicircle around Sebin.

Heid took a hold of Sebin's wrist and lifted his arm.

Mason began. "Sebin Reinhardt, you have been deemed worthy. Once you are marked as a member, your legal name will never exist on the tongues of Founders. To the worlds, you remain Sebin Reinhardt, but to the Founders, you will be only known as Painter."

Mason held up a small metal device. "I, Mason of Alluvia, hereby induct you, Sebin Reinhardt, into the Order of the Collective Founders as Painter. Your role will be to bring to life the Founders' plans, using the six worlds of the Collective as your canvas. Do you accept this role?"

"I accept," Sebin replied quickly.

"Then I anoint you Painter." With that, Mason pressed the metal device against the upper inner part of Sebin's bicep, and the skin sizzled. Sebin winced, but didn't pull from Heid's grasp.

Mason stepped back and handed the branding iron to the woman to his right. She stepped forward. "I, Mariner of Myr, anoint you Painter." She pressed the iron near the spot Mason had branded seconds earlier.

Sebin's skin sizzled again, and this time he let out a hiss before clamping his mouth shut. Heid grabbed his forearm with her other hand to support him—and to make sure he didn't pull away.

Mariner handed the iron to the man to Mason's left, who then stepped up to Sebin. "I, Aeronaut of the colonies, anoint you Painter." He branded Sebin a third time.

Aeronaut stepped back, and Mason spoke. "Painter, what are you?"

Sebin held his head high, and he began to chant.

I am a raindrop in a storm.

I am a bubble in a waterfall.

I am a tear in the eversea.

I am water.

I am a Founder.

Everyone chanted the second verse together.

We are the storm.

We are the waterfall.

We are the eversea.

We are the Founders.

We are the free.

Mason clicked his boots together. "For the free."

Everyone clicked their boots in response. "For the Founders."

Heid touched Sebin's shoulder and spoke softly. "Welcome, Painter."

He embraced her and spun them around. He grinned widely before releasing her to examine his brands. Three runes stood bright white on reddened skin. Each mark represented an equal branch of the Founders—towers for Alluvia, waves for Myr, and wings for the colonies.

Heid warned him. "No one except a Founder can ever lay their eyes on those brands, do you understand? No men in the showers, no woman you sleep with, no one."

He gave her a sly grin. "No problem."

Mason said, "To all the worlds, we must not exist, or else we'll fail."

Heid found herself filled with pride as she watched Sebin in his accomplishment. She tugged his hand. "Now, let's go upstairs and celebrate."

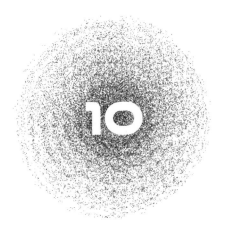

10

BUILDING A REBELLION

"What do you mean, 'we're not leaving the Coast'?" Throttle asked. "Two hours ago, you couldn't wait to leave."

"Change of plans. We've got to talk," Reyne said and plopped down on a seat in the commons. He looked around. "Where's Sixx?"

Throttle fidgeted. "He…"

"He stepped out to see someone," Doc said. "He said he'd be back before thirteen-twenty."

Reyne muttered a string of curses.

Boden, who lounged in his chair across the table from Reyne, nodded to the doorway. "Speak of the devil."

Reyne turned to see Sixx walk in. Reyne kicked out of his chair and pointed. "You can't keep it in your pants long enough to look after the crew?"

Sixx scowled. "Boden had things covered. I had to see someone." He paused. "It won't happen again."

"Damn it, Sixx. If something had happened, it'd be on you."

Sixx held up his hands in defeat. "I know, I know. I'm sorry. I made a mistake."

Reyne froze, shocked at Sixx's words. "Whoa. Hold on. You never apologize."

Sixx grabbed a drink. Everyone watched as he took a long swig in silence. When he finally spoke, his words were barely above a whisper. "I heard a rumor that Qelle was here."

Reyne's jaw dropped. "Your wife?"

Boden frowned. "I thought she was dead."

"She is," Reyne said. "She was on a CUF hauler when it went off-grid. Neither that ship nor any of its crew has ever been recovered." He turned back to his friend. "Sixx, she's gone."

"I know." He pulled out his comm. "Kason still runs searches across all video channels for me. He sent me a feed from Nova Colony's hallways. The picture is grainy and dark, but it came back as a seventy-nine percent match. It's Qelle. I know it."

He handed his comm to Reyne, who examined the lo-res video. "It's too poor quality to make out anyone. If it was Qelle, why didn't she contact you?"

Sixx slumped into a chair. "I don't know, but I can't shake the feeling that she's still out there, somewhere."

Reyne made a mental note to tell Kason not to send any more videos to Sixx. It did no good to get the man's hopes up when his wife had been lost to the abyss over ten years earlier.

No one spoke for a long moment. Sixx looked up. "What are we sitting around for? Let's get the hell out of here."

"Change of plans," Throttle said, echoing Reyne's earlier words.

"Shit. That's never a good sign." Sixx eyed Reyne. "How dangerous is it?"

Reyne sighed and pulled his torrent pendant out from under his shirt. "As dangerous as it gets."

Two days later

"How long do we have to sit around on our asses and wait for our next run? So far, being a torrent runner is boring," Throttle said as she organized the cabinets in the commons for the umpteenth time.

"Remember how I said that boring is good when it comes to flying?"

"Yeah?"

"It's also good when it comes to being a torrent."

She blew out a sigh. Reyne ignored her and kept reading.

"Look at the bright side," Sixx said, not taking his eyes off the news. "As long as we're sitting in a dock, we're not doing anything that would get us locked up in the Citadel."

"Fine," she said glumly. "I still wish Reyne would let us take the *Gryphon* out for some flying around the Coast. Now that we're torrents, the pirates will lay off us."

"Note to Throttle," Sixx countered. "Most pirates are *not* torrents. Most pirates are scum who find pleasure in stealing, raping, and killing. Not always in that order. Whoa." Sixx swung his feet off the table with a thud. "Reyne, you'd better see this."

Reyne did bother looking. "What is it?"

Sixx motioned to the screen. "I think I just found your package."

That got Reyne's attention.

"Replay most recent news clip," Sixx said.

The screen froze and played a news clip showing satellite shots of a city covered in a gray haze.

What was first believed to be a tragic accident on United Day has now been confirmed as a terrorist attack.

"There," Sixx pointed. "Freeze video. Continue audio."

It took a moment for Reyne to make out what Sixx had seen, but once he did, he could see nothing else. He came to his feet and stared.

Dr. Willem Song, a senior scientist at Genics Corp, died as a result of suffocation. Dr. Song was the botanist behind blue tea, which has been credited with saving hundreds of thousands of lives by helping people survive on less water than normally possible. His death is a tragic loss to the Collective. At the time of his death, he was at Genics Corp's highest security lab on Myr's Moon, overseeing their gene-editing program. In the attack, twelve civilians and over eight hundred tenured were killed.

It is believed that a fungal agent was released within the laboratory. Government officials have determined that the fungus, when exposed to air, produced a mass of spores. Once inhaled, these spores adhered to the lining of the lungs and quickly multiplied, suffocating the victims. There is no cure at this time, and government officials have quarantined the infected lab until further notice.

Dr. Zara Wintsel, president of Genics Corp, has offered her condolences to the families of those who've been lost to what she calls the "blight." Dr. Wintsel has pledged that Genics Corp will continue operations, and that her top priority is to develop a fungicide for the blight. Myr has pledged one billion credits to support Genics Corp's efforts. In addition, Corp General Michel Ausyar of the Collective Unified Forces has promised a swift response to this abhorrent form of bioterrorism.

Genics Corp, the worlds-renowned pharmaceutical organization, is headquartered in the Smithton province on Myr. This is Lina Tao reporting for DZ-Five, your Collective news source.

Reyne never took his eyes off the frozen video. He didn't know how it got there, but he did know that he was looking at the package he and Sixx had retrieved off that Myrad hauler. An icy chill climbed his spine. He'd transported a weapon of mass destruction.

What the hell had Vym been planning to do with it?

"Did you see it?" Sixx asked. "Sounds like the old doctor might have gotten a taste of his own medicine."

Without responding, Reyne left the room, put on his suit, and headed straight to the Uneven Bar.

People still glared, some threw out names and colorful descriptions of what they thought of Reyne, but no one attacked him. Critch had made it clear the crew of the *Gryphon* was now under his protection, and Reyne imagined how much it must've pained the pirate to make that declaration.

He found Critch sitting alone and eating a meal. He was easy to spot, with his telltale scars. Reyne knew the man had more than enough credits to have his skin repaired, but he also knew Critch wasn't the type of man who was into superficial improvements. He was a man who could never be bought, blackmailed, or tricked. It made him a stalwart ally...and a dangerous opponent.

Reyne grabbed a chair at Critch's table and sat down. "I thought torrents were above bioterrorism."

The pirate tossed his napkin over his half-full plate. "Ah, so you saw the blight."

Reyne rubbed his chin. "I'm still trying to put the pieces together, but they're not fitting. My guess is Myr had Genics Corp create the blight. They're the only corporation out there with the brainpower to create something like that, and they're based on Myr. That part was easy. Hell, their name was even on the crate. What I don't understand is why this package traveled all the way out to edge of the fringe only to be brought back to its home."

"Think about it. Why would Vym have the package brought out to her?"

Reyne stared at Critch for a long moment. His jaw slackened when the pieces fell into place. "Vym was the target, except the package was intercepted."

Critch nodded. "I think Ice Port was the target, not just Vym. You saw the blight. If they hit Ice Port, Playa's only space dock would be out of commission, essentially taking an entire planet out of the game. Some Myrad number cruncher must've decided that Playa's exports weren't worth the benefit of eliminating them. It was an easy plan. Release the blight on Ice Port using a good cover story. Every fringe station will be terrified that they're next. Myr announces they've created a fungicide, and every colony would pledge full support to Myr without any bloodshed."

Reyne considered Critch's words. "It's vicious, but it makes sense. Playa has always brought more hassle than profit to the Collective. Sacrificing Playa would make it easy for Myr to take control of the other fringe stations."

Reyne frowned and shook his head. "But the CUF grabbed the package. I can't believe the CUF would attack a Myrad location. That seems low, even for them."

"We don't believe it was the CUF."

"Then who was it?"

"There's obviously another player in the game."

"Alluvia?"

Critch shrugged. "Makes the most sense."

Reyne leaned back. "So, the package was intercepted not once but twice? That makes it a game of hot potato."

"Near as I can tell, yes." The pirate came to his feet.

"Done eating already?"

"Lost my appetite."

Reyne sighed. "If we're going to work together, you're going to have talk to me sometime."

Critch held up a finger. "First, you work *for* me. You're not working *with* me." He held up two fingers. "Second, a lot of good people died on Terra because of you. I don't have to talk to you if I don't feel like it."

Reyne rolled his eyes. "You know, maybe one day you'll believe me that I didn't betray the cause."

"Maybe, but I doubt it." Then he left.

After sampling Critch's leftovers, Reyne returned to his ship with a sinking feeling that he'd gotten himself and his crew into a bigger spider web of danger than he'd ever imagined.

The Uprising had been pure and simple—a fight for the colonies to gain equal rights in Parliament, citizenship for all. It was a belief he still held to fervently, despite every blasted colonist in the fringe thinking him a traitor.

This new Uprising was complicated. Now, it was a bid for survival, with the colonies standing in the middle of the ring between two heavyweight fighters. Myr and Alluvia were dangerous enough, but there was possibly a fourth contender standing in the corner, and he had a hell of a right hook.

His comm chimed, and he read the message. Once he climbed back onto the *Gryphon* and out of his suit, he leaned against a comm on the wall. He took a deep breath and broadcast to the crew. "To your stations. Cargo is on its way. We're heading out in one hour."

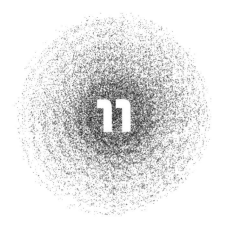

FALLEN WORLDS

Throttle huffed. "Quit looking at me," she said for the third time that hour.

Demes pouted. "But I like looking at you," the pirate said for the third time that hour.

She glanced at Reyne. "Please make him leave."

Reyne sighed and glanced back at Critch's young envoy, who was riding along on their first torrent run.

"How about you go hang out in your bunk," Reyne offered. "We'll ping you when we reach Darios' orbit."

"Nah," Demes said simply. "I like it here."

Throttle glared in response.

Reyne's comm beeped. "What is it?"

"I need you in Mech," came Boden's voice.

"Be right there." Relieved for the interruption, Reyne stood. Before leaving the bridge, he pointed to Demes. "You, behave." Then, he pointed to Throttle. "You, don't kill him."

He headed down the hallway, past the crew quarters, commons, and medical bay, and stopped at the cargo bay—where the passengers were staying—to find the door closed and locked. Reyne frowned.

He'd assigned Sixx to watch over the passengers—a full load of torrent recruiters. It was a job Sixx loathed, and Reyne had noticed that his friend's nerves had frayed more and more with each passing hour on this run. Reyne turned and headed to Sixx's quarters. There he found Sixx on his bed, a very naked Doc strung across his chest. Just as Reyne suspected, Sixx had taken a break to blow off some steam.

Reyne didn't turn away. "I thought you were supposed to be on cargo watch."

Sixx cracked an eye open. He gave a dramatic sigh, then nudged Doc none too gently. "Move. Play time's over, sweets."

She swatted him before rolling off. "You don't have to be so bossy."

"Funny. You weren't complaining a few minutes ago," Sixx said drily.

She tugged on her clothes and grabbed her boots. As she strolled out of the room, she put extra swing in her hips for the benefit of both men, who were obviously enjoying watching her.

After she left, Sixx turned to Reyne and gave him a look of exasperation as he pulled on his shirt. "They're driving me nuts. For torrents, they're viggin' high-maintenance. *I'm hungry. I'm thirsty. I need to use the bathroom. I'm spacesick,*" he mimicked in a high-pitched voice. "I needed a break or else I was going to shoot one of them. I locked them in. They'll be fine."

Reyne tried not to chuckle, and forced his grin down. "It's generally considered bad manners to lock passengers in the cargo bay."

Sixx didn't seem bothered.

"I'm surprised they annoy you so much," Reyne said. "Especially since half of them are voiceless."

The other man shook his head. "The voiceless are the worse ones. They have voice implants, which are *so* much more annoying than regular human voices."

"Go on. Get back there," Reyne ordered. "See to our passengers. I want them under supervision at all times. I won't want them messing around with anything on this ship."

Sixx grumbled as he strapped his weapons on. The pair walked together back to the cargo bay. When they reached the door, Reyne squeezed Sixx's shoulder. "Be patient with them. Most of them were tenured on Myr or Alluvia, like Boden. They've likely suffered under some pretty shitty citizens to have their voices removed."

Sixx scowled. "I'll stay patient as long as my sanity holds. No guarantees beyond that."

"Then, you have my permission to kick their asses when they piss you off. Just don't kill any of them. That would reflect badly on our hospitality."

"That I can handle."

Reyne gave him a quick smile and finally made it to the mechanicals room at the far end of the ship, where he found Boden standing with his forehead pressed against the wall.

Reyne winced. "That bad, huh?"

The mechanic shot him a quick glance before settling down on a large duct running in between the walls. "The *Gryphon* supports a crew of fourteen. We're flying with twenty-one right now. It's stressing the air exchanger."

"Are we running a risk of it failing?"

"Probably not, but the exchanger is overloaded. It's running hotter every hour. I need to turn it down to minimum support for a while to let it cool down."

"We only have enough oxygen cans for the crew."

Boden calculated for a moment. "I'll do it during the sleep hours, so they won't notice anything. Anyone awake may experience some mild hypoxia."

"Sixx will enjoy that." Reyne slapped Boden's shoulder. "Do what you have to do. I'll give the crew a heads up. Ping us when you reduce the air levels, so we can switch over to our portables."

"Sure thing," the mechanic replied.

Reyne made his way back to the bridge to find Throttle and Demes bantering. He leaned against the doorway and shook his head, feeling that all he'd done the past few days was lasso chaos.

"The *Honorless* could kick the *Gryphon*'s ass on the Coastal Run," Demes said.

"In your dreams," Throttle snapped back. "The *Gryphon*'s smaller, plus it has a Flux Whisper engine. Take that, pirate."

"Ouch." Demes smirked. "Impressive, but the *Honorless* has *two* Flux Whispers. I'll take that kiss now."

Throttle's jaw dropped before she clamped it shut and became instantly focused on her instrument panel.

Demes chuckled and strode over to her. Reyne felt suddenly more protective of Throttle, but forced himself to stay put.

She glared at Demes, then gave him a quick peck on the cheek.

He leaned back. "That most certainly is not a kiss."

He cupped her cheeks and swooped in, kissing her long and firmly on the lips.

Reyne cleared his throat and crossed his arms over his chest.

Demes pulled away with a grin, and Reyne relaxed.

Throttle swatted his arm. "Happy now?"

"Yep. For now." Demes walked cockily back to his seat, crossing paths with Reyne on the way. He paused and shrugged. "She lost a bet."

Reyne couldn't miss the smile Throttle was trying too hard to hide, and he suspected she wasn't feeling too badly about losing the bet. "I should've warned you," he said. "Never make a bet with a pirate." He nodded in Demes' general direction. "Any bet that one makes is guaranteed to be rigged in his favor."

"Lesson learned." She pouted dramatically before focusing wholly on her instrument panel.

Reyne took a seat and broadcast to Doc and Sixx's quarters, "Heads up, crew. In a bit, Boden will be reducing the air exchanger to let it cool down. He'll let you know when you need to switch to portables. No need to alert our passengers. Just keep an eye out for signs of hypoxia."

"What kind of junker are we flying in?" Demes asked.

"I thought pirates were a hardy lot," Reyne replied. "From what I hear, they don't even need air to breathe."

"It's a fact, but we sometimes like to pretend we need it. We don't want to intimidate the ladies too much," Demes said, tossing a glance in Throttle's direction.

She rolled her eyes.

Reyne ignored him and began to review the approach plates for Sol Base, the fringe station on Darios and the busiest space docks in the Collective. The planet produced a huge portion of the Collective's food supply, including all the Collective's philoseed and cavote, two bean-like staples in every civilian and colonist's diet. Alluvia and Myr depended on Darios, making that fringe station the CUF's most closely guarded colony.

Darios was also the most highly regulated, with over eighty percent income tax on its exports. Even with that penalty, Darions were the wealthiest colonists, making it clear just how much food they produced. However, Darions had been growing more and more agitated at the Collective's greed and had begun staging strikes, delaying shipments to Myr and Alluvia while bypassing their citizen middlemen to sell food directly to the other colonies. Their actions were a slap in the face to the Collective's two leaders.

Sol Base was a thermite trip wire that could be triggered at any time. It was the perfect time to send in torrent recruiters.

"Whoa. You have a phase cannon?" Demes asked.

Reyne shot around to see Demes running his fingers across the panel at his station. Reyne jumped to his feet and rushed over. "How'd you get access to the ship's systems?"

"I'm a pirate. It's my job."

"Stop that." Reyne pushed Demes to the side and ran commands to lock out the young man. Finished, he took a step back. "Listen here, pup. You're on my ship, but you are not one of my crew. If you put my crew or my ship at risk, I won't hesitate to drift you. Do you understand that?"

Demes leaned back in his seat and held up his hands in surrender. "I was just bored and looking around. No harm intended, I swear. I was running scans to make sure we didn't have a bigger problem than the air exchanger to worry about."

"I have everything under control. The next time you get bored and want to know something, ask." Reyne turned to Throttle. "If he pisses you off, shoot him."

Throttle grinned. "Aye, aye, Captain."

Reyne returned to his panel and hit the comm. "Boden, run diagnostics on the systems. Make sure no command lines were changed during this run."

"Why?"

"Just do it."

"I didn't change anything," Demes said. "I could have, but I didn't."

Reyne sighed. Why couldn't just one person behave and do their job and not give him a headache? He shook his head and tried to focus on preparing for Sol Base. He had some success until Demes continued.

"I'm not trying to butt into your business, but when I was in your systems, I couldn't help but notice that the *Gryphon* has fortified skins. Very impressive. She'd make a good pirate ship."

Reyne put his elbows on the panel and lowered his head into his hands. "How the hell did you see that?"

"I ran temp checks throughout the ship. The hull's insulation factor is much higher than normal. My guess is you have a full second layer of rilon inside the outer layer. It's an old pirate trick. The rilon fortifies a ship's hull without any suspicious onlookers being the wiser. The CUF would have to cut into the hull to even see it." He whistled. "That's not a cheap add-on."

"It's an old torrent trick. The pirates learned from the torrents," Reyne corrected.

Demes paused. "All in all, she's not a bad ship. I'd take her off your hands if you ever decide to sell her. Especially if the pilot comes with her."

Throttle flipped her middle finger at Demes.

"You'd have to pry this ship out of my cold, dead hands," Reyne said. "As for Throttle, she'd eat you alive."

He grinned. "Sounds like a challenge."

"Which part? The part about prying the ship out of my cold, dead hands? Or, the part about Throttle?"

"The part about Throttle. No offense, Captain, but you're old.

I think I could take you in a fair fight."

Reyne unbuckled his holster and pulled out his gun.

"Not that I'd ever consider it," Demes quickly added. "Especially now that we're friends."

Reyne slowly slid the gun back into his holster. "We're friends now?"

"Sure," the younger pirate said. "To prove it to you, I'll even tell you what else I found in your systems."

Reyne took in a breath. "What else did you find?" he asked, taking the bait.

"You have a tracking device on the ship. Looks like it's tucked into the gear for the solar sails. High-tech. My guess is it's Alluvian-made."

Reyne spun around to his panel and punched commands to pull up the ship's grid. Looking at the solar sails, he found nothing. He walked to Demes. "Show me."

He shrugged. "I'll need access to your systems."

Reyne grunted and unlocked the panel, not doubting for an instant that the pirate could've hacked into the system in seconds.

The man's fingers flew over the panel so fast that Reyne had a hard time following what he was doing. Soon, Demes leaned back and pointed.

Reyne leaned closer. Sure enough, whatever system scan Demes had run had caught the transmitter. "*Son of a bitch.*"

"If I were to play the devil's advocate—or Critch's advocate, in this case," Demes began. "That tracker has a CUF signature. Did you know that tracker was there? Critch warned me that you might try to rendezvous with your old CUF buddies. Or, did the CUF get a wild hair up its ass and decide to track a run-of-the-mill fringe runner for no particular reason? I'd hate to say it, but the first is a far more rational explanation."

Reyne took a step back to see that Demes had a gun leveled at his chest.

"Are you nuts, Demes?" Throttle called out. "Put that gun away."

"Just doing my job, sweets. It's nothing personal."

Reyne held out his hands. "I have no idea how that tracker got there. You have my word on that. And, I sure as shit don't have any CUF buddies."

"You shoot him, I shoot you," Throttle said, and Reyne saw she had a gun aimed at Demes.

Reyne waved his fingers in the air. "Enough. Both of you, put away your guns." When neither complied, he continued. "Demes, if you shoot me, Throttle will shoot you. Critch won't be happy, and he'll come after Throttle. Instead of wasting our lives and energy on being enemies, we need to focus on the job. Right now, that job is getting those recruiters sitting in my cargo bay safely to Sol Base so they can begin rallying the colonists. I give you my word, I'll find out who put that tracker on my ship. Until then, how about you give me the benefit of the doubt and help me figure out how to jam that signal? How about it, *friend*? Consider yourself a part of my crew while you're on board the *Gryphon*."

Demes eyed Reyne for a long second before sliding his gun back into its holster. He cracked his knuckles and smiled. "See? I told you we were friends."

Reyne nodded at Throttle, who then holstered her gun. Then, Reyne swung around and punched Demes. The younger man went tumbling to the floor.

Reyne stood over him, then held out a hand. "Now, we're friends."

Demes rubbed his chin and spat out blood. He eyed Reyne for a moment, then grabbed the outstretched hand, and Reyne pulled him to his feet.

He took a seat. "You've got a pretty solid right hook for an old man."

Reyne headed back to his seat. After he sat down, he fought the urge to shake the adrenaline from his trembling hands. He stared at his panel. "Hey, Demes, what's your job on Critch's crew?"

"I'm a tech."

"A tech," Reyne echoed. "Great."

Great. Reyne had assumed Demes was a hired gun to watch over the torrent recruiters, but Critch had put a hacker on board, which meant Critch had wanted his man sniffing around the *Gryphon's* systems. No wonder Demes hung out on the bridge rather than near the cargo bay. Reyne's guess was that this run was as much about Critch learning about the *Gryphon* and her crew as it was getting torrent recruiters delivered to Sol Base.

"I'm receiving a distress signal from Sol Base," Throttle announced.

"Put it on speakers," Reyne ordered.

Sol Base is in a state of medical emergency and requires immediate assistance. An unknown airborne agent has been detected at the station and is spreading outward. Genetic makeup of the agent is included in this message. This message will repeat.

"I'm linking with the station's cams now," Demes said in a rush.

As the message repeated, the view screen switched from the ship's forward path to various video feeds from the surface of Sol Base. Every feed was the same. Bodies of humans, animals, and birds lay strewn across the ground, all covered in a gray dust. Food carts and vehicles sat still. Everything was a muted gray, except for the large view screens that still played vibrant

114

advertisements. It was though life had stopped in a single second, all suffocated within a cloud of death.

Throttle's lips parted. "Oh, no."

Reyne's heart froze. "They've been hit by the blight."

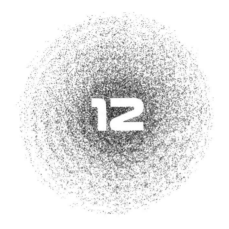

DEADLY PURSUITS

"**G**et us out of here, Throttle. Make it fast," Reyne ordered.

"Good idea," she said numbly.

"The CUF will be all over Sol Base soon, if they're not there already," he added. "And I guarantee any runners in the area will be docked and checked."

"Where do we go?" she asked.

"The Coast will be the safest place," Demes offered.

"He's right. Set a course for Nova Colony," Reyne said.

"Oh, shit," she said. "Too late. We've been flagged by a CUF ship."

"On the speakers," he commanded.

"*Fringe hauler Playa-Seven-Five-Five-One-Bravo, this is the Collective Unified Forces frigate* Nautilus. *You are hereby ordered to dock at port Five. You have five minutes to comply. If you show any signs of noncompliance, you will be fired upon. Respond within sixty seconds, and convey ship logs and crew list."*

"What do we do now?" Throttle asked.

Reyne's lips thinned. "We do what runners do. We run."

Demes let out a whoop.

Throttle's eyes widened. "We can't outrun a frigate."

Reyne shook his head. "Chances are, the *Nautilus* has most of her docks full with runners right now. They can't make jump speed without first releasing or battening down any ships in their docks."

She frantically worked at her panel while Reyne transmitted static back to the *Nautilus*. "There, that ought to have them scratching their heads for a minute or two." He then broadcast to the entire ship. "Strap in and hold on. Things are going to get downright bumpy."

Demes watched Reyne for a moment, and his lips curled up. "You might not make a bad pirate after all."

"I'm a torrent, not a pirate," the runner snapped back. "And figure out a way to jam that damn tracker."

"I'm closing the solar sails now," Throttle said. "And powering up the Flux."

Reyne pulled up the grids around Darios and found the location of the *Nautilus*. It was one of five frigates over Sol Base. Fortunately, nothing the size of a warship.

"The *Nautilus* is dispatching drones," Demes called out.

With no time to get Sixx on the bridge, Reyne had to turn to Demes. "Are you familiar with Class Five photon guns?"

Demes grinned. "Of course."

"You take forward guns, I'll take aft. Do not fire until I give the order. We can't fire unless we are out of all other options. The instant we show we have firepower, they'll send the whole damn fleet after us."

"Can I use the phase cannon?"

"Why does everyone want to use the damn cannon?" he muttered, before adding. "No, stick with the guns."

"Throttle, tell me you'll have us to jump speed before the drones get within range," Reyne said."

"Only a few more seconds. Powering up jump shields now."

"Only a few more seconds, and the drones will be in range," Demes said.

Reyne ignored the *Nautilus'* hails and watched the drones approach on the grid. "They're eight-fifty clicks out. Hurry, Throttle."

"Double-checking coordinates now."

"You're *double-checking?*" Demes asked. "There are drones flying over here to blast us with an EMP."

"You'd rather we fly into an asteroid or star swarm?" she snapped back. "There. Got it."

Reyne's heart pounded. "Four hundred clicks out."

Throttle furiously worked the controls. "Okay. Retract the guns. I'm hitting jump in three, two, one. *Go!*"

The gun bay lights flashed green at the same time the *Gryphon* hummed and shot forward. Sound and vibration merged into one. Reyne found himself plastered against his seat, unable to inhale.

Seconds later, everything stabilized. He immediately began running scans for any chasers. Seeing nothing, Reyne relaxed.

"Throttle, I'd like to have wild sex with you right now," Demes said.

"Hey," Reyne snapped around. "That's my daughter you're talking to."

"Sorry," he said, not sounding the least bit apologetic.

"Throttle, I'd like to take you on a date to my room right now."

Throttle laughed. "I can't believe we outran a warship."

Reyne breathed deeply. "And I'm glad we pulled it off. We have fifteen torrents in the cargo bay, a fully armed gunship, and I imagine Demes here is wanted on all six planets."

"True. I am a wanted man," the young pirate concurred.

Reyne contemplated for a moment. "Demes, you're a tech."

"Yeah."

"Can you get an untraceable message out to all the fringe stations?"

"Sure."

He walked over to Demes and pulled up images of the package he'd pulled from the Myrad hauler. "We need to tell them what's happened at Sol Base, and that the same thing could happen to them. Tell them the blight will come in a package that looks something like this and could be delivered from Genics Corp or any of its subsidiaries." He pointed to the image.

"How do you know all this?" Demes asked.

"We were hired to deliver the blight intended for Ice Port."

"Oh."

Reyne left the bridge and made rounds to check on everyone and everything. Fortunately the only injury was a sprained wrist on a torrent who hadn't strapped himself down in time for the jump. Reyne left him with Doc and returned to the bridge.

As he entered, Demes announced, "I'm finished. A message has been sent to all fringe stations as well as Nova Colony."

Reyne took a deep breath. "Well done. Let's hope it reaches them all in time for them to ramp up security at their docks."

Throttle wheeled backward. "We'll drop out of jump speed in three hours. I'm going to grab a quick bite."

Demes raised his hand. "Grab me some grub while you're at

it, sweets."

She mock-saluted him as she wheeled off the bridge.

Reyne leaned back and watched the stars shoot by.

"Um." Demes broke the silence. "I have some good news and bad news."

Reyne turned. "What's the bad news?"

"The CUF has put out immediate cease-and-desist orders to all fringe runners. Looks like every runner has been put on their terrorist watch list."

"That's no surprise. It's not like they can pin the blame on citizens," Reyne said drily. "And the good news?"

"I lied. It's all bad news. I can't jam the tracker from here. Someone's going to have to go outside to do it."

"Which we can't do at jump speed." Reyne rubbed his temples. "We'll get it as soon as we dock. In the meantime, I need you to send an encrypted message to Critch. Tell him the run's been cancelled. We're heading back, with cargo still on board."

Demes began typing. "Sending it now. And..." Demes dramatically tapped the panel. "Message sent."

Demes leaned back. "You know, I don't think he likes you very much."

"No, he doesn't. I think he'd like to kill me."

"I think you're right." He hesitated before continuing. "Why'd you do it?"

"I didn't."

Demes chuckled. "Critch said you'd say that." Demes shuffled. "Incoming response from Critch."

"What does it say?"

"More bad news. Seems like many runners had the same idea, to head to the Coast. The CUF has sent an armada to block entry to the Coast. Sounds like they're taking the 'shoot first, ask questions later' approach. He said coming to the Coast is a bad idea."

"Shit." Reyne punched in the controls to drop them out of jump speed so he could change course.

"What are you going to do?"

"We're heading to Ice Port."

"Is that safe?"

"No, but I know somewhere we can hide."

"Send a message to Vym," Reyne said. "Tell her she's about to get her hands dirty."

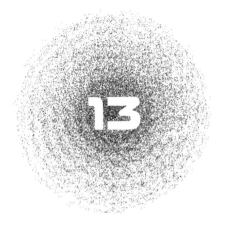

13

TOXIC COMPLICATIONS

Heid

"Sol Base has fallen to the blight," Heid said to Sebin.

"Sol Base?" Sebin's eyes grew wide. "But, cutting off the food supply cripples everyone, including Myr."

"Mason believes they chose Sol Base after the Myr moon attack for that reason. No one would believe Myr is behind something so horrendous. All eyes will be turned on fanatics so that when Myr offers the fungicide in exchange for full control of Darios, no one will try to stop them."

"But, the entire Collective depends on Darios for food."

"And so Myr will win without having to fight a single battle."

He shook his head sadly. "We'll be forced to give in to Myr's demands, or starve."

She clenched her eyes shut.

Sebin wrapped his arms around her, and she looked up to see the concern in his gaze. He ran a hand down her cheek. "You're not in this fight alone. You're never alone."

She forced a weak smile. "You're right. Darios may be lost, but the Collective isn't lost yet."

"We'll find a way," he said. "We've worked too hard and too long for peace to not believe it can happen. We won't fail. We *can't* fail."

She found a weight lifted inside her as his confidence filled her.

"You saw the message," he continued. "Mason has been meeting with Mariner and Aeronaut. They'll figure out something."

"Let's hope they figure out something soon." She took a step back. "I've been unable to reach Seamstress. Communications are being jammed by CUF drones around Ice Port."

He frowned. "Who would quarantine Ice Port?"

She grimaced, as though even saying the name brought a sour taste to her lips. "None other than Corps General Ausyar himself."

He stood aghast at the mention of the much-feared Myrad who was the head of the entire CUF fleet. "Why?"

She nodded grimly. "It seems Myr has chosen the least valuable of the fringe worlds as a convenient scapegoat for the blight. Those colonists have always been the most vocal and fanatical of the fringe. Because of their reputation, coupled with the fact that Playa has never been in the black, financially speaking, Mason believes Myr is setting the stage to cut Playa free from the new Collective."

"Those colonists will never survive without imports from the other worlds."

Heid continued. "It gets far worse for us, I'm afraid. Ausyar is announcing tonight that he's pulling the entire fleet together. All Alluvian senior officers are being retired or reassigned."

Sebin's jaw dropped. "That's impossible. That's not within his power. Our people will never stand for it. Parliament would never reach the two-thirds majority vote needed to allow him to do such a thing."

"You're wrong. It seems Parliament has already granted Ausyar's increase in power. It's safe to say Parliament is no longer a viable entity, and the CUF is now serving Myr's interests. Even now Mason is preaching a conservative approach. He's been cautioning Alluvia to not be hasty in its response to Ausyar's demands."

"Because he doesn't want to see Alluvians die," he said.

She smirked. "Or perhaps he's working with Ausyar to clear the playing field."

"Why would he do such a thing?"

"He's always craved power."

Sebin frowned. "He's a Founder. He would never go against the cause for his personal gain."

"Hm."

"You don't believe that?"

She forced a smile. "You know me. I'm a lifelong skeptic."

He smiled back. "Yes. I do know you." His smile faded. "What will happen to you under Ausyar's changes?"

"The *Arcadia* remains under my command until we connect with the fleet in three days, at which time I relinquish command to First Officer Franklin Laciam."

He clenched his fists. "This is bullshit. We can't stand for this."

"Unfortunately, Mason and I rarely see eye to eye. He's made it clear that I continue serving the CUF as directed by Ausyar. He believes that if I refuse to give up my command, I could undermine his efforts and unravel the few remaining threads holding the Collective together."

"But if you lose the *Arcadia*…"

Heid crossed her arms over her chest. "There's no way in hell I'm giving up the *Arcadia*."

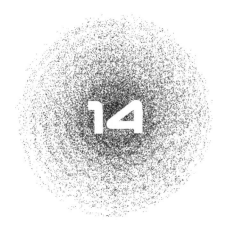

HAUNTED VISIONS

"I have some more bad news," Demes said as they neared Playa's orbit.

"Do you ever have good news?" Reyne asked.

"Plenty of times. Just not when it comes to you."

Reyne sighed. "What have you got?"

"The message never got through to Vym. The CUF's quarantined Ice Port. Oh hey, I do have some good news."

"And that would be?"

"No CUF ships are in orbit. Looks like a patroller dropped off a drone blockade and left. But, there are dozens of the little buggers out there."

"You call that good news?"

Demes shrugged. "Drones are easy to sneak by. They sense

power readings. All we have to do is power down everything and sail right on by them."

"One problem with that," Reyne said. "We still have a tracker transmitting outside the ship. Even if we powered down, it will still transmit. If the drones pick up that reading, they'll turn their EMP blasters on us."

"Uh oh," Demes said, no longer paying any attention to either Reyne or Throttle. "We've got bigger problems than the drones. A warship is dropping out of jump speed. They're flagging us now."

"Ignore them," Reyne said. "Wait, which ship is it?"

"It's the *Trinity*. The CUF's very finest."

"Definitely ignore them."

"Like there's a CUF warship you'd want to talk to?" Demes asked.

Reyne scrambled to pull up the ship's location on his panel. "Throttle, how much juice do we have?"

"Not enough to enter jump speed again."

"I was afraid of that. Looks like we're heading down to the surface. Throttle, keep jump shields up and take us down the approach path as fast as you can."

"Are you crazy? The drones will blast us with EMPs," Demes said. "We'll be dead in the water if we try to fly past them with power."

"I have a hunch they won't," Reyne said. "Throttle, remember flying down Tulan Canyon?"

"Sure, why?"

"I need you to bring us right over the space dock, then keep us low as you take us down the canyon. We need the *Trinity* to think we've docked at Ice Port."

Throttle snapped around. "The canyon? I—yeah, I can do that, but the *Gryphon* is a spaceship, not an airplane. She'll fly like a rock once we hit the atmo."

"I know. You won't have to fly in the atmo for long. I'm entering the canyon landing coordinates now."

Her eyes grew even wider. "We can't land in the canyon. We need a long runway or at least landing grapples. We'll crash."

"Just focus on getting us to the canyon," Reyne said. "I'll guide you from there."

"I'm with Throttle," Demes said. "If we don't die in a fiery crash at the space docks—which in all likelihood is going to happen—without a launch pad to help us break gravity, the *Gryphon* is just a big hunk of metal sitting on the surface of a shithole planet that I'd prefer not to live out my days on."

"Hey, Playa is my home," Reyne countered.

"We're coming up on the drones now," Throttle interrupted.

"The *Trinity* is arming her photon guns," Demes said.

Reyne watched as they cut in between a wide blanket of drones. The drones transmitted instructions—his instrument panel was aglow with warnings, but no EMPs came—and Throttle continued forward.

The *Trinity* fired a warning shot across the *Gryphon*'s bow.

"Shit!" Throttle snapped around to see the blast.

"Keep going," Reyne said.

"They're going to kill us," Demes said. "We should use the phase cannon to—"

"Don't you touch that cannon." Reyne wagged a finger at Demes. "What is it with everyone and the cannon?"

A second shot fired, this one even closer, and Reyne found himself gripping the panel. "Just keep going, Throttle."

Once they made it past the drones, they broke through the atmosphere. If the *Trinity* fired now, it risked hitting the surface, though Reyne wasn't convinced the CUF would care. It wasn't until they'd traveled a few more seconds that he allowed himself to relax.

Throttle let out a breath. "We did it."

"I can't believe we're still alive," Demes said. "You, Reyne, are the craziest man I've ever met. We just flew right through a drone blockade like a Sunday walk."

Reyne grimaced. "The drones are here to prevent anyone from *leaving* Ice Port. They aren't stopping anyone from landing."

"How'd you know that?" Throttle asked.

"Just a hunch. And I'm guessing we do not want to be in Ice Port right now."

"You ignored the *Trinity*," Demes said, and used his hands for embellishment. "The *Trinity*. You do realize that we're all dead men, don't you? They'll never let us get by with this."

"Speak for yourself, pirate," Throttle said, before adding, "We're running out of time to land at the docks."

Reyne looked at her. "You learned to fly in Playa's atmo. You can do this." He grabbed the comm and broadcast to the ship. "Hold on tight. We're on approach for landing."

He turned back to Throttle. "Remember, make it close," Reyne said. "Don't break from approach until you get below the cloud cover. The drones are jamming all communications, but their onboard cameras will be running. We need the drones to record us on final approach so that the *Trinity* thinks we're at Ice Port along with whomever else they're after. We don't want them to send down chasers."

"We're breaking through the clouds now," Throttle said as the *Gryphon* entered Playa's low, heavy cloud layer. The ship rocked and bucked as Throttle fought the winds.

They popped below the clouds. The space dock was directly

below and coming up fast. He held on and grunted as Throttle banked the ship in a high-g turn to glide near parallel to the surface below. They flew over the fringe station, kicking up snow and flying too fast to make out any distinct features.

"Remember the old cave I never let you check out in the hovercraft?" Reyne asked.

"Yeah."

"Now's your chance."

"This isn't a hovercraft," she countered.

Reyne continued. "As soon as that cave comes into view, line up for landing. Be sure to touch down just beyond the entrance. You'll have only ten thousand feet of runway ahead of you. You'll need to have the *Gryphon* slowed down enough for a short landing."

She sucked in a breath. "The winds aren't going to be any help today."

"You can do this landing in your sleep," he added, and meant every word.

She chortled.

He kept analyzing their speed and rate of descent. As soon as they were within one hundred miles of the Tulan Canyon, he brought down the landing gear. "Slow down. We're coming in too fast. I'll drop the flaps."

"Not quite yet," she said. "We'll need the speed once we hit the canyon."

As soon as they reached the valley, Reyne pointed at the black dot in the distance. "There's the cave."

"It's a lot smaller than I remembered," she said. "Okay, drop the flaps now."

He hit the switch, and the ship lurched at the sudden loss of speed.

Throttle talked through her landing checklist. When she'd finished, she blew out a breath. "Here we go."

Right before they reached the cave entrance, Throttle slipped the ship to bleed speed. She straightened the ship out just as it crossed into the darkness. The ship's landing lights were all that lit up the cave, revealing a runway.

She settled the ship down onto its landing gear, which made a metallic cry as the rilon skids came into contact with the surface. The air brakes sounded, and Reyne found himself nearly thrown from his seat as the ship abruptly slowed, coming to a stop three-quarters down the underground runway.

Throttle lifted her hands from the panel as though the controls burned her. "I can't believe I just did that."

"I can't believe it, either," Demes concurred.

Reyne grinned. "I knew you could do it."

Throttle spun to face Reyne. "Why didn't you tell me about this place?"

"Because this is one of those places that legally abiding folks are better off not knowing about," Demes answered for Reyne. "Strange. I had no idea Playa had a smugglers' dock."

"It wasn't built for smugglers," Reyne corrected. "It was the first torrent base ever built, and is, to the best of my knowledge, the last remaining one. That is, assuming the space dock is still operational."

"I'm surprised Critch never flew the *Honorless* into here."

"This base was built before he joined the torrents, when the Uprising was just the Playans against the Collective."

Reyne grabbed the comm and broadcast to the ship. "This is your captain speaking. Welcome to Playa. The home of weak gravity, cold temperatures, and strong winds that take pleasure in sucking you into the abyss if you're not careful. I need you to stay on the ship until we work out the local situation."

Reyne turned to Demes. "Head down to electrical and grab Boden. He'll help you bundle up for Playa's temperatures. I need you two outside to get that damn tracker off this ship and thoroughly destroyed."

"Sure thing, cap." Demes stood with a look of utter distaste before trudging off the bridge.

"Why is he being helpful?" Throttle asked. "Demes, I mean."

Reyne's jaw tightened. "My guess is Critch is paying him quite well to cozy up and learn everything he can about us to relay back."

"We should leave him here."

"His tech skills might come in handy. Still, you'd best keep an eye on him."

"That is something I can do," she said, sounding enthused at the idea. "So, what do we do now?"

"We wait," Reyne said. "Once the CUF finishes searching Ice Port for whomever they're looking for, they'll leave. The *Trinity* isn't going to waste time around Playa too long." *I hope.*

"Think they're here for us?" she asked.

He shook his head. "I don't see the CUF blockading an entire fringe station for a single runner. There's something bigger going on, and I need to find out what it is."

He opened up the frequencies, but all he heard was dead silence.

"Uh oh," Throttle said. "We've got incoming."

Reyne looked out the view screen to see a hovercraft landing not far from them. When it stopped under the *Gryphon*'s landing lights, Reyne could make out the ship.

He grabbed his comm. "Sixx, I need you with me on the surface now. We've got company."

"Friend or foe?"

"Sometimes I wonder."

"Who is it out there?"

"Vym."

A few minutes later, Reyne and Sixx were bundled up in thick coats, wearing gravity belts and an arsenal of guns and knives. As they climbed down from the ship, the newcomers stepped out. It was impossible to make out which was Vym, due to the thick insulation covering them from head to toe, but Reyne guessed she was the shortest of the group.

Sure enough, the most petite member stepped forward and motioned to the base's entrance.

He grabbed the handle and pushed. Ice cracked and fell off as the door opened. He and Sixx stepped inside. Sixx spun to keep an eye on the others, while Reyne searched for a light switch. Vym found the switch first, and a greenish hue filled the base's control room. Heat leached down from the radiant heaters in the ceilings and began to thaw the frozen room.

Vym flung off her hood, revealing a glowering woman. "Aramis Reyne, what the hell are you doing on Playa?"

"I missed the weather."

"You shouldn't have come here. Playa is not safe. The CUF has decided I am the leader of some imaginary bioterrorist organization that seems to include everyone from Ice Port."

"Listen, I didn't exactly have many options. Every runner is on their watch list, and the CUF are attacking anyone who tries to flee to the Coast."

She sighed. "Well, you were smart to dock here instead of at Ice Port—assuming they didn't see your Ice Port flyover act."

"They didn't," Reyne said, confident.

"You'll be safe here, and the launch pad is fully operational so you can get back into the air after you wait out this mess. Just be careful not to be seen, and don't head into Ice Port. If they're after me, they'll come after anyone and everyone who's ever worked for me. In fact, I'm surprised they haven't dispatched chasers to the surface already."

Reyne watched her. "Why'd they single you out, Vym?"

Her lips thinned. "It seems I've pissed off the wrong people one too many times."

He sighed. "Why is it that when it comes to you, all I get is headaches and problems? First the package, then the guns, then the tracker. What next?"

She seemed taken aback by his words. "You know I would have absolutely nothing to do with that horrible blight. As for the guns, I want all torrent ships weaponized. We need to be ready for the Uprising. I would've told you, but I wanted you to meet with Critch first."

"You should've told me. And the tracker?"

She shrugged, her brows raised. "That wasn't my doing. I think you need to ask a particular CUF commandant about that."

Reyne watched her for a moment before accepting her response. "Tell me, what's your part in all this?"

"My part?" Her normally direct gaze skipped to the wall. "I'm simply the stationmaster of Ice Port, the fringe station that has always been the bane of the Collective."

"I'm not talking about that job."

She pursed her lips. "Everything I do—everything I've ever done—is to unite the worlds of the Collective, with colonists treated equally along with citizens. I've been forced to make compromises in the past, but I've taken a stand. I give you my word, my heart beats only for the Uprising. And there are those who will go after me because of that."

A quake rattled the control room, soon following by the sound of thunder.

Everyone shot furtive glances around.

"I didn't know Playa had quakes," Sixx said.

"It doesn't," Reyne replied, his heart freezing within his chest. "That's the sound of a phase cannon."

"That doesn't make sense." Vym frowned. "The *Arcadia* would never fire upon Ice Port."

"The *Arcadia*'s not out there," Reyne said. "It's the *Trinity*."

Her eyes grew wide as she gasped. "It's not her." She threw on her hood. "That changes everything."

"Wait," Reyne called out. "We can form an offensive and buy time for Playans to escape. How many ships with phase cannons do you have at Ice Port?"

She lowered her head. "Counting the *Gryphon*? One. I sent them all to the Coast, along with nearly all my torrents, as soon as I learned of the attack at Sol Base."

"*Shit*," Reyne muttered as he racked his brain for ideas.

"However, I have a very large phase cannon set up within the station," she added. "And, I have no problem firing upon a warship to protect my people if it comes to that." She held up a finger. "Give me your word that you will not head out there and take on the *Trinity*. One small gunship will make no difference in whatever outcome Ausyar has planned for today."

Reyne watched her, his chest pounding.

"I need you to promise me," she said. "The Uprising needs you. Critch needs you, whether he'll admit to it or not. Don't throw away your life, and the lives of your crew, today. You know there's nothing that can be done against a warship."

After taking another breath, he spoke quietly. "You have my word."

"Thank you." She gave a tight nod. "I need to hurry. Ausyar has made his next move, and it's to take me out of the fight. Let us pray my surrender will be enough to appease his plans. I fear it may be the only way to save Ice Port." She rushed to the door, then stopped and turned to Reyne. "I need you to do one more thing for me."

"Name it."

She pulled out a small tablet and began typing. "With the jammers, I can't get a message out. I asked you to meet with Critch. Now, I must ask you to meet with Commandant Heid from the *Arcadia*. Give this device to her when you meet with her. It has to be handed directly to her, not to her officers. It's proof that I trust you, and that she can trust you. You and Critch will need her help in the Uprising."

Reyne laughed. "You want me to work with the CUF?"

"I have no time to argue. Our people are being slaughtered out there!" She forced him to take the tablet. "Without support from the Alluvians, the Uprising will fail." She turned and ran from Reyne, her posse trailing her.

Reyne and Sixx stood there in startled silence.

After a long moment of silence, Sixx asked, "What just happened?"

Reyne gave a long, slow shake of his head. "I think my home is being attacked, and there's not a viggin' thing I can do about it."

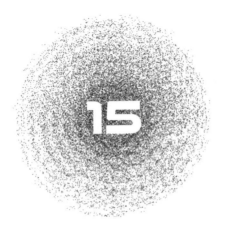

FROZEN SORROW

The first thing Reyne did after Vym left was relocate the torrents from the cargo bay to the base's control room, where the temperature had warmed enough to survivable conditions. At first relieved to leave the cramped hold, they soon began asking questions when they felt the cannon blasts rumble through the base.

He stared down the runway, in the direction of the bombardment taking place more than one hundred miles away. He'd heard—and felt—the deeper, heavier sound of Vym's phase cannon returning a shot, followed by a rush of blasts from the warship. Then, not another shot was fired from the ground. She'd never stood a chance.

The horrific awe of his home being destroyed blistered his

nerves like plastic over flames. Embers of anger burned within his heart, and he craved to jump in the *Gryphon* and fly right into the *Trinity's* bridge. But Vym had been right. The drones would cripple his ship the moment he cleared the atmosphere, and the warship would blow him to bits…and then keep blasting away at the city.

Sixx eyed Reyne before taking charge of the room. "We could be here for some time. You may as well get comfortable. I need a couple volunteers to get the heat going in the rest of this place."

Three torrents raised their hands, and Sixx nodded in recognition. "Once the temp is bearable, go in pairs and tally supplies. See what we have to work with here."

Reyne blinked his eyes as he fought to bring himself back to reality. "Start two levels down," He said. "There used to be a large stockroom down there."

Chatter erupted from the fifteen shivering torrents, and Reyne turned and headed outside, slamming the door on the cacophony of questions and demands. After climbing aboard the *Gryphon*, he locked the door to keep all non-crewmembers out.

Boden and Demes came walking down the hall. Boden tossed a small object to Reyne. "The tracker's been taken care of."

Reyne examined the small black device, which looked like it had been hit with a hammer. He tossed it back. "Good job."

"What's going on out there?" Demes asked. "I've never heard phase cannons before. It sounds like one hell of a battle."

Reyne shook his head and swallowed. "It's not a battle. It's a massacre."

Demes' eyes widened, while Boden sadly shook his head.

Reyne looked upward, as though he could see the *Trinity* through the thousand feet of rock they sat under. "Ausyar announced that Ice Port was housing the terrorists responsible for the blight."

Boden guffawed. "What? No one would believe Playans would harm another colony. Genics Corp was behind the blight. I'd bet my life on it."

Reyne squeezed his fists and breathed deeply, trying not to think about what was happening to Ice Port. "And you'd be right," he said finally. "But they're arrogant enough to believe no one will figure that out if they pin the blame on Playa."

"Citizens suck," Demes said. "Wouldn't it be great if we broadcast everything we know to the entire Collective?"

"Yes, it would," Reyne mused.

"Too bad it's impossible," Demes tacked on. "The only Collective-wide broadcast points are on Alluvia and Myr. I've tried to hack into them a couple times—for fun, you know—but had no luck. There's no hacking into them without tapping into the hard lines."

"Hm," Reyne said as he pondered Demes' words.

Boden and Demes started to walk away.

After a moment, Reyne called out, "Hold up, guys."

They stopped and turned.

Reyne nodded first to his mechanic. "Boden, I need you to work on refueling the *Gryphon*. Grab Sixx to help you. I want us ready to lift off as soon as the CUF leaves."

"There's juice here?" he asked.

"Juice, and a ready launch pad. When you're done, meet me in the commons. We're going to have a crew meeting."

Once he left, Reyne turned to Demes. "How good a tech are you?"

"Good enough to make the crew of the *Honorless*."

Reyne pulled out the tablet. No matter how he worked through the details in his head, the value of whatever Vym was hiding on the device far outweighed the risk of what the pirate would do with it, though Reyne planned to keep a very careful eye on the tech.

He took a deep breath and handed the tablet to Demes, who examined it. "I need you to hack into this tablet and copy all the information on it while leaving it completely intact. No signs of being hacked. Can you do that?"

Demes grinned. "Of course I can."

"Come get me the moment you get it copied. I need it before the crew meeting."

"Am I invited?"

"You're one of the crew, aren't you?"

"Then I'll be sure to have it to you before then." Demes rushed off like an excited boy with a new game.

Reyne headed to the bridge to find Throttle staring down the dark runway.

"They're all dying, aren't they?" she asked.

Reyne spotted the tears running down her cheeks. He took a seat and leaned heavily on his elbows. "Yeah, I think so."

"Because of us?" Her question was soft, tentative.

Reyne leveled his gaze upon her. "No," he answered firmly. "None of this is because of us. This is because the powers that control the Collective are playing gods. Darios fell because it's the most valuable fringe planet. Playa is falling because it's the least valuable."

"I don't understand."

"I don't understand it all yet myself. But I do know that whatever is happening was planned long before we ever found that damn package." He took a deep breath. "Get some rest. You'll need it. I'll wake you when Boden and Sixx return."

She didn't say anything else as she rolled off the bridge and down the hallway.

He sat there and stared out the window, every cannon blast echoing in his heart. He had been born in Ice Port, and had spent the first seventeen years of his life there.

His heart swelled every time he returned home from a run.

Home.

He began to wonder if he'd have any home left after the bombing.

The slaughter raged for hours, and Reyne kept himself busy contemplating Vym's words and the relationship she'd had with the CUF officer.

Demes entered the bridge and handed the tablet, along with a computer coin, to Reyne.

"I was able to ghost it and get you a copy, but the data is still encrypted. I can't break it without my tools on board the *Honorless*. If I can get to my tools, I can break the encryption."

"Then, I guess we need to get you to the *Honorless*," Reyne said, before shooting the pirate a wry look. "Listen, Demes. I don't entirely hate you, so I'll make this clear. I know you're working for Critch every minute of every day, and I know that you'll see he gets a copy of this the instant the jammers clear out of Playa's airspace. If he's serious about making this Uprising work, he needs to see it, too. However, if I find out you've decrypted this tablet and given that data to Critch and not me, I'll drift you. Got that?"

Demes nodded tightly.

The port door opened, and Sixx and Boden entered, bringing a cold breeze with them.

"The ship's refueled and the launch pad is booting up. I'm charging the tug now."

Sixx gave a dramatic shiver. "It's colder than an Alluvian

wench out there."

Boden's brows rose at the mention of his home world.

"A Myrad wench?" Sixx offered.

"Wimps," Reyne said. "We're in a cavern. There's hardly any wind in here. Hell, I've gone for jogs outside in colder weather than this."

"That's because you're a Playan, and everyone knows Playans are abominable snowmen," Sixx muttered.

Reyne gave him a droll stare before hitting the comm to broadcast to the entire ship. "Crew meeting in the commons now."

The group of four headed to the commons. Once Sixx pulled off his coat, he frowned at Demes. "What are you doing here?"

"Crew meeting. I'm a crewmember."

"You're not one of the crew. Go hang out with your buddies in the base." Sixx jerked his thumb toward outside.

Demes shot Sixx an overly wide grin. "Tell them, cap."

Sixx turned to Reyne, who shrugged. "Demes is serving as our tech until we get him back to his pals on the *Honorless*."

Sixx shook his head, turned to the cabinet, and pulled out a bottle of whiskey.

"I'll have a drink of that," Demes said.

Sixx ignored him and took a long swallow. He sat down, then warned, "You can't trust a pirate, Reyne."

"You were working with pirates when I met you, Sixx," Reyne said.

"That's why I know you can't trust them," Sixx replied.

"All right," Reyne said, after Doc and Throttle arrived, "it's time to talk."

Reyne began. "Ever since the Genics Corp contract, we've been set up, lied to, threatened, and shot at. That changes now."

He held up the tablet. "I believe this holds the secret to the success of the Uprising, as well as retribution for Ice Port and Sol Base."

Utter silence.

Then Boden pounded his fist on the table. "Whatever your plan is, I'm in."

Reyne held up his hand. "Hold on. You don't know where I'm going with this yet." He paused. "We know the CUF is fractured. Vym's working with at least one CUF warship commander. In fact, she asked me to meet with a particular dromadier officer. And I told her I would."

The room broke out in an uproar.

Doc crossed her arms. "We don't work with the CUF."

Reyne tamped down the air with his hands. "I already said I'd do it, but I admit it'd be a lot easier if I didn't have to go it alone."

"If you think it's the right thing to do, then I'm in," Throttle said.

"I trust your instincts," Sixx said. "We go where you go. Especially if it's dangerous."

"I'm in," Demes said.

"I already said I was in," Boden grumbled.

"You know I'm always with you," Doc said after things quieted down. "But I don't like the sounds of this."

Sixx pulled out the raindrop pendant he wore. "In case you've forgotten, we already signed up. We're all in for the long haul."

Reyne scanned the faces in the room. Warmth filled his chest as he realized he had the bravest, most loyal crew in the universe. "Okay, then. I guess our next step is to figure out a way to meet with this commandant without getting blown to bits in the process."

"That sounds like an interesting challenge," Sixx said.

"But, hold up," Reyne continued. "We're not going anywhere until we've scraped every bit of intel on that tablet. That's where our handy tech comes into play. Demes here has made a copy of the data, but it's encrypted. So, as soon as the CUF clears out of Playa, we're going to bring the *Honorless* down here, where he can decrypt the files for us."

"How's the *Honorless* going to get here?" Demes asked. "The Coast is sitting behind a CUF armada right now."

Reyne chuckled. "If Critch can't get past a few ships, I've thoroughly overestimated him."

"Didn't I just say you can't trust a pirate?" Sixx asked. "I'm surprised our boy here hasn't decrypted and sold the data already. What's going to keep Critch from killing all of us to keep from contacting this CUF officer?"

"Because Critch wears one of these, too." Reyne tugged out his necklace. "If Vym is out of the picture, he's going to need all the help he can get, even if it means working with both the traitor of Terra and a CUF warship commander."

"What if he changes his mind?" Sixx asked.

Reyne threw a quick glance at Demes. "Then one of us will die, because I won't let anyone get in the way of Ice Port's retribution."

TRUTH IN WORDS

The bombing didn't stop until long after dark, deep into the dead hours. Reyne tried to ignore the phase cannons by keeping busy, but every blast made his breath catch and his heart ache. When the bombardment finally faded, he stood and waited for more. For never-ending minutes, he waited. When hope filled him that the hellfire raining down on Ice Port was finally over, he hustled to the bridge.

Throttle was napping. Demes was busy working, and Reyne worried what secrets the tech was sifting through now, but he brushed past the pirate and to his captain's chair. Immediately, he scanned the Ice Port channels for chatter, but the smothering silence meant that the drones were still in place.

And so the waiting game began.

Three days later, the drones finally pulled out from Playa's orbit, and the static replaced the silence on all channels. Unfortunately, there was nothing but static. No calls for help, no search crews, nothing. Reyne repeatedly tried to reach Vym, with no success. He sent a message to Kason, who he hoped had stayed on Alluvia after United Day, but had still to receive a response.

The only good news was that Demes was able to get word to Critch, who would reach Ice Port in less than two days at jump speed.

And so the waiting game continued.

When the *Honorless* landed at Tulan Base, it filled up the expanse. For a moment, Reyne considered the possibility that the ship would never make it through the cavern entrance, but the all-black ship sailed through with a few feet to spare on each side. It taxied and parked alongside the *Gryphon*, dwarfing the smaller gray ship.

Demes jumped from the station he sat at in the control room to stand alongside Reyne and watch the ship power down. Reyne could sense the excitement rolling off the young pirate. "Go on, get those files decrypted."

Demes jogged outside toward the *Honorless*, meeting Critch and several crewmembers as they emerged. They stopped and spoke before Demes continued to the pirate ship.

Reyne waited until Critch reached the building, and opened the door. "Welcome to Tulan Base."

Critch stepped inside and looked around, and Reyne could tell the man was trying to figure out how he hadn't known that a base this size existed. He shot a look at Reyne. "You could've killed Demes and kept this place all to yourself."

"I could have, but that wouldn't fit in my plans."

"I assume the torrents I left in your care are still breathing?"

Reyne nodded. "They've been helping get this place up and running. Most of them are decent workers. Right now, they're in the lower levels, freshening up the living quarters. They like to stay where it's warmer."

"They're used to worlds that have ten times the temperatures of Playa," Critch said. "It sounds like you're setting up to play house here. While I'll admit it would make an excellent smuggler's dock, what exactly do you plan to do with this base?"

Reyne motioned around him. "Welcome to the Uprising's Playa base of operations."

If Critch's thoughts matched his expression, he didn't believe Reyne. "You believe in the Uprising now?"

"Always have."

Critch watched him for a moment. "Why do I get the feeling you didn't bring me all the way here just so Demes could use his gear?"

"You're right, though I won't know if your trip was worth it until Demes is done decrypting the files. We have some time to burn." Reyne nodded in the direction of the *Honorless*. "I'm guessing a ship that size has at least one hovercraft for getting around the surface."

"You haven't been to Ice Port yet," the pirate said, a hollow intonation to his voice.

Reyne swallowed. "We wanted to look for survivors, but we don't have any ground transport. That's one thing sorely lacking in this base."

Critch shook his head. "Don't bother. There aren't any

149

survivors. We scanned the surface from orbit."

"Most of Ice Port is below ground. You wouldn't pick up heat signatures."

The pirate's lips thinned. He may have frowned, but his features were hard to make out through the scars. "It wouldn't make a difference."

Reyne stood firm.

He sighed. "No one drives my lander except me."

"I'll have my crew show your men around while we're gone," Reyne said. "They'll help you refuel. After that, they'll put your crew to work. There's plenty of stuff around here that still needs done."

Critch grunted, turned around, and headed out the door.

Reyne followed him to the *Honorless*, up its ramp, and on board. He unsnapped his holster, ready to draw his gun the moment the man tried something. Once he entered the ship, his step faltered. The *Honorless* wasn't just a pirate ship. It was a state-of-the-art spacecraft that looked every bit ready to go to war. The hallways were lined with weapons and gear. "I take it you don't get stopped by CUF patrols often."

Critch kept walking. "They're easy to avoid if you know what to look for. Even stealth can be tracked with the right sensors." He opened a thick door and headed down metal stairs.

Docked within the belly of the ship sat a hovercraft, easily as large as Vym's. It was set up differently, though. Instead of rows of seats, the back was a large flatbed, making it ideal for smuggling.

Critch climbed into the pilot's seat and buckled in. Reyne had barely climbed onto his seat and shut the passenger door when the engine started and the craft lifted off the floor. Critch hit a button, and a ramp door on the *Honorless* opened. The pirate wasted no time in taking the hovercraft down the ramp and onto the runway.

Reyne held on and buckled in. They didn't speak as they burst out from the base and into daylight. Reyne looked over to see the pirate glowering. "You hate me that bad, huh."

Critch turned a hard eye on Reyne. "I don't hate you. I see you as a risk to the Uprising. The same way that bioterrorist attack was a blight on Sol Base, Aramis Reyne is a blight on the fringe. You are a reminder of how a single man was able to take down the Uprising."

Reyne turned away. He'd received various levels of animosity across the fringe for the past two decades. Most, he could brush off. But Critch had been his best friend at one time. A man he'd taken under his wing because he'd seen a reflection of his own passion in that man's eyes. Critch's candor was like a broken sword tip burrowed deep in Reyne's heart.

"I hated you once," Critch added. "When I learned that you gave up our location, and I had to watch thousands of men and women get slaughtered. Eventually, I realized you taught me a valuable lesson. You taught me that no one could ever be trusted, no matter how close they are to you. I have to hand it to you, Reyne. You were a damn good actor. You had me fooled that you believed in the Uprising."

"I believed in it as much as you did. I still do."

Critch chuckled in a way that made it clear he didn't believe Reyne one bit. "I should be thanking you. That lesson helped make me the richest pirate in the fringe."

Reyne pursed his lips. "I don't want to waste my energy looking over my shoulder all the time because I can't trust you. I'd rather spend my energy on something productive. The Collective has treated colonists like scum for too long. I plan to change that, even if I have to fly right through the space barrier and bring the fight to Myr's doorsteps. You and I made a good team once, and I know that it will take both of us, united, to give this new Uprising a chance. I'm asking for a second chance to work together so we can see that the Uprising is done right this time around."

Critch chortled. "I'm a pirate. We don't give first chances, let alone second chances." He pondered his next words. "But I'll give your proposal some consideration."

"You do that," Reyne said. He could make out Ice Port on the horizon, and he leaned forward. The horizon had changed. Where the massive space docks had climbed into the clouds, a pile of twisted metal and stone lay.

Ice Port had few structures above ground, due to its extreme weather, but there were no signs of those buildings now. Even the slopes of the caves and caverns that sheltered the city's stores and homes lay collapsed into the ground. "No wonder they bombed the colony for so long."

"They wanted to be thorough," Critch said. "Viggin' CUF."

As they approached the city, Reyne could make out no sign of civilization from the rubble. No stationhouse, no streets, no entrances to the cavernous underground. Anyone who survived the bombing would've died from exposure by now.

Critch slowed down, but the scenery never changed. The utter destruction was worse than anything Reyne had ever seen during the first Uprising. The CUF had wiped Ice Port completely off Playa.

Reyne found it hard to breathe through the heaviness settling in his chest. "Let's head back."

Demes was waiting for them on the *Honorless* when they returned to Tulan Base.

"Tell me you got it," Reyne said curtly.

Demes glanced at Critch.

"No," Reyne said, his hand on his holster. "You're showing both of us the data. Now."

Demes' eyes widened, and he shot another glance to Critch.

"You heard the man," Critch grumbled. "Show us."

The young pirate led them to his bunk. Technology components were scattered all about the floor. He sat down at his cluttered desk. "There's a lot of data here, and I'm not sure how useful it is. I've decrypted it all, but much of it is in code-speak. Messages to and from some group Stationmaster Patel was involved with. They called themselves the Founders. They all went by strange names. She went by the name Seamstress."

Reyne furrowed his brow in confusion. He turned to Critch to see the pirate just as confused. "That's what Vym was hiding?"

"It can't be tied with the original group. They disappeared centuries ago," Critch said.

Reyne leaned forward. "Demes, are you sure that's what they called themselves?"

"Yeah, very sure. The most recent message is from the day of the Ice Port attack."

"I always had my suspicions," Reyne said. "It would explain a lot of things."

Critch took a deep breath. "Well, Reyne. It appears we've both been played." He then turned to Demes, who was watching the captains with an inquisitive expression. "The Founders was an organization even older than the Collective. They were wealthy Alluvians and Myrads who fancied themselves puppeteers, pulling strings to shape the Collective in any way they saw fit.

After the War, when the CUF was formed, they were hunted down and killed. Evidently they weren't all killed."

Reyne mused, "If they still exist, would they be our allies or our enemies?"

Critch motioned to Demes. "What's the data say?"

"Well, you'd better pull up chairs," Demes said. "It'll take a while.

Four hours later, Reyne and Critch stood in the pirate's quarters, having left Demes with instructions to begin running searches to see if he could track down the identities of other Founders.

Critch opened a bottle of bourbon, poured a glass half full, and took a seat.

Reyne took in the Spartan quarters while Critch drank the expensive alcohol, noticing the sharp contrast between the two extremes.

"Now I understand where Vym was coming from," Reyne said. "We have to stop Myr, or else we're looking at a full-scale war."

Critch looked up from his glass. "We don't stand a chance against Myr's warships. They'll slaughter anyone foolish enough to try."

"If we don't stop Myr, they'll take control of the fringe stations," Reyne said. "Whoever controls the fringe controls the Collective. The Uprising has always been about gaining equal rights in Parliament. But it's bigger than that now."

"It's about survival now," Critch said. "Thanks to Vym's data, we know Myr is sitting on a fungicide that can kill the blight. If they continue on the path they've already started down, they can clear out the fringe stations and bring in stationmasters loyal to Myr."

Reyne nodded grimly. "Vym seemed to think Myr planned to try out the blight on Ice Port. When that backfired, they went to Plan B on Sol Base and involved the CUF. The only safe place for us now may be Playa and the Space Coast, but both depend on food and supplies from the other colonies. Myr may as well own Sol Base now, and who knows what they have in store for Spate and Terra."

"Stopping the blight has to be our first priority." Critch said. "As long as Myr has the blight, they hold all the cards."

"We need to get our hands on the fungicide," Reyne said, then he rubbed his temples. "I can't get it through my head that the Founders exist—and that they still think they can control the Collective."

"They'd make a powerful ally," Critch said. "But, reading Vym's messages, it's clear they see us fringe only as pawns. We'd never be able to trust them."

"Agreed. You saw the messages. Vym was going against her fellow Founders to stir up a new Uprising. But if Demes can track down their names, we'll at least have information we can leverage." Reyne sighed. "Unfortunately, I don't see how we can go against Myr without help from them or the Alluvians. Vym was right. We have to get her tablet to the *Arcadia*."

Critch downed his drink and refilled his glass. "Exactly how do you propose we do that? My ship was designed for avoiding warships, not becoming a bull's-eye in front of one."

"We won't have to. I'm sure Demes can figure out how to send a message from Seamstress to Baker to arrange a meeting."

The man's eyes narrowed as he considered the idea. "Where do you propose we meet him? Here?"

"At Tulan Base? Hell, no. This is the last place I want anyone associated with the CUF to know about. I was thinking that Nova Colony would be neutral territory."

Critch barked out a laugh. "You expect a CUF commandant to make it to the center of the Space Coast without getting killed?"

"Yes."

"You realize that every person living on Nova Colony hates the Collective with a burning passion."

"I do."

The pirate thought for a long moment and took a drink. "I'll let Demes know. If this Baker doesn't get himself killed on the way to the meeting, it could be an interesting conversation."

Reyne found himself smiling.

"What?"

Reyne looked up. "I finally realized something."

"What's that?"

"The *Gryphon* and her crew are all dead. We were killed by the *Trinity* during the bombing of Ice Port."

"How is that good news?"

Reyne's grin widened. "Because they'll never be expecting us when we rise from the dead and strike back."

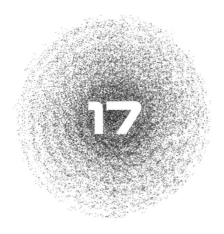

FADED LIAISONS

Heid

Heid lounged in her quarters as the *Arcadia* made its slow way to meet up with the *Trinity* along with the rest of the CUF fleet docked between Alluvia and Myr. She could've been there days ago, but chose instead to set a long course at sub speed. Ausyar had ordered all warships to convene in three days—she had to get creative to come up with plausible reasons for the *Arcadia's* delay.

She needed the time to think.

Her comm chimed again. The fourth time in under an hour. She didn't need to look to know it was from her first officer. She ignored the ping, already knowing exactly what the request would be. Laciam was growing anxious and hounded the commandant to move the *Arcadia* to jump speed, but the Myrad wasn't commandant…yet.

Once the *Arcadia* reached the rest of the fleet, Heid would lose her command, giving Ausyar another warship to use against anyone who chose to oppose his bid for power. If she refused, it meant becoming a mutineer to the CUF as well as to the Founders, both of which had meant everything to her.

Not anymore.

Mason had made his intentions clear the night of Sebin's initiation. She wasn't to disobey Ausyar's orders, because her sedition could force Alluvia to choose between protecting one of their own—a senior dromadier officer—or allowing Ausyar to hunt down the *Arcadia* and kill Heid and her crew. Mason had the gall to call her foolish for arguing with him.

However, Myr had also made their intentions clear the moment they created the blight. It had been pure luck when Mariner intercepted word of Myr's plan to use it at Ice Port to quell dissension. The Three Founders had believed that, by unleashing that same package at the same Genics Corp facility in which it was created, Myr would rethink their strategy and back down. Instead, the attack had the opposite effect. Myr pushed up their plans to disrupt all imports from the fringe stations and take control of Parliament.

Even now, after the destruction of Sol Base and Ice Port, Mason refused to act outright. He wanted the Founders to stay in the shadows, guiding change with a twist of an arm here or an assassination there. The War—their greatest achievement—had brought Myr and Alluvia together. When they'd orchestrated the first Uprising in an attempt to bring peace across the Collective, they'd discovered the fringe brought too many players to control, which led to mistakes being made. The Founders had very nearly failed in preventing the fringe from upsetting the balance of power.

Heid had been a young girl during the Uprising, and had few memories of the battles and events. Everything she learned came from Mason, and she was an excellent student. She understood the need for shadow games. Unlike him, she also knew the time for shadow games was long past.

She tried to convince Mason that the only way to peace—true peace—was equality across the Collective, but he never listened to anything she had to say.

She wasn't the only one. Aeronaut had voiced Seamstress' plan, which included forming a new Uprising. While Aeronaut was ever the diplomat, Heid—as Baker—was vocal. Despite her attempts to persuade her father, Mason remained strongly against Seamstress' actions. Heid wondered what role Mason had played in Ice Port's undoing. After all, Mason had proven on multiple occasions that he had no qualms sacrificing lives if it served his purpose.

She wasn't blind. She knew Mason—and possibly the Founders as a whole—no longer had the Collective's well-being at heart. Over the past twenty years she'd seen egos swell and ambitions rise. She'd watched Mason manipulate the Founders, filling the ranks with those who followed him without question. No new colonists had been inducted into their ranks in over twenty years. Hell, that was the only reason she was brought into their ranks. As Mason's daughter, he assumed her loyalty was absolute.

Her loyalty was absolute...*to the Collective*.

While Mason's loyalty was only to himself. She had no doubt he fantasized about ruling the Collective. She also had no doubt that Myr's current actions were feeding into Mason's dark, selfish plans. Knowing she shared his bloodline was a constant dagger to her soul. Mason was a betrayal to everything she and the original Jacob Mason stood for.

She had a decision to make. She could continue to faithfully follow Mason, like she'd done her entire life. Or, she could follow the message she'd received from Seamstress to see where it led.

She read the encrypted message for the hundredth time.

Baker —

I'm interested in ordering a cake for my daughter's birthday party. Would like to see your catalog. Please join me for dinner at Nova Colony at 28720319.2530. My treat.

— Seamstress

Heid chuckled, though she felt no humor in her predicament. Aeronaut couldn't contact Heid directly, since she reported to Mason and he oversaw the colonies. And so she'd exchanged plenty of personal messages from Seamstress in the past. The old Founder had been trying relentlessly to recruit Baker — and thus, the *Arcadia* — into her Uprising, mistakenly convinced that if Baker joined her cause, Mason and the Alluvian branch would then follow.

As for the latest message, she knew there was no way it came from Seamstress. For one thing, she suspected Vym Patel was dead. From what she'd heard about the *Trinity*'s attack on Ice Port, there would be few, if any, survivors. The second and more telling sign was that this message had too much style for Seamstress' usual bluntness.

That "she" wanted to meet in person was a third red flag. Founders in different branches only met in person for ceremonies. Meetings put each other at risk in case one Founder's cover was compromised.

Then, there was the location for the meeting. Nova Colony was outside Collective control, and there was no Founder stationed there. Aeronaut had tried multiple times, but had never succeeded in identifying a candidate who Mason or Mariner approved.

Heid could only assume Seamstress had handed her tablet off to someone, which was against every Founder protocol. Even then, no one should've been able to access the message system. Someone had managed to hack through the encryption walls—an impossible task, making Heid all the more curious.

Who was behind the message? Were they using intel they had acquired to wipe out the Founders one by one? Was Baker first on their list? Or, did they have something else planned?

She didn't contact Mason to see if anyone else had received a similar invitation. She knew Mason would order her to disregard the message, then get involved, destroying any chance she had at finding answers.

She smiled even as nervous chills flitted across her skin. She had made her decision. She was sick of being played by Mason. Her response was brief.

Seamstress —
Dinner sounds lovely. See you then.
— Baker

She took a deep breath, slid the tablet into her pocket, and headed straight to the bridge. As soon as she entered, Laciam jumped to his feet. "Commandant, I've been wanting to talk with you."

"One moment." She walked over to the navigator. "Nolin, set

a course to fringe sector seven-seven-seven-three-zero-five. On our way there, locate a fringe ship for a standard dock check."

"Yes, sir."

"What are you doing?" Laciam fumed. "We're under orders to immediately return to the fleet. You're intentionally delaying our trip. If you change course, you're disobeying a direct order from the corps general."

"Watch your tone, First Officer," Heid responded calmly, despite her simmering anger. "I will continue to carry out my duties as a commandant in the Collective Unified Forces until we reach the fleet. Feel free to lodge a complaint with Adjutant Reinhardt, who will see that it gets posted. Until then, I expect you to do your damn job."

"Yes, sir," Laciam said stiffly.

"You're dismissed."

He headed off the bridge without another word, and she knew he was walking straight to his quarters to draft an exceptionally detailed complaint, or—more likely—continue a draft he began hours ago. She knew she would have to deal with Laciam soon, and Ausyar's directive after that. First, she needed to meet this Seamstress, and she needed a fringe ship to do it.

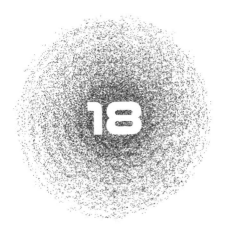

DISTANT DREAMS

Reyne pounded on the door to Critch's quarters in Tulan base.

"Hold on, for chrissakes," came a voice from the other side.

After the sound of shuffling, the pirate opened the door.

"Pack up," Reyne said without any sort of greeting. "Baker replied. The meeting's on. The *Gryphon* is launching within the hour."

"The *Honorless* will lead the way." Critch slammed the door shut.

Reyne scowled at the closed door before heading to the control room, where he left instructions for the torrents who were remaining on the base. He then pinged Sixx on his comm. "Wake up, sunshine. Get to the ship for immediate departure."

Sixx mumbled something Reyne couldn't make out, but

assumed was a verbal nod. He wasn't about to go looking for the man. Sixx had slept with at least two of the torrents already, and who knew where he'd slept last night. Evidently, now that they weren't all cooped up on the ship together, Sixx found them far less annoying.

Throttle, Boden, and Doc had all stayed in their bunks on the *Gryphon*, none yet trusting Critch's crew or the torrents at Tulan Base. Reyne broadcast to the ship as soon as he stepped on board. "Heads up, crew. Prep the ship for departure. We're heading to the Coast."

The first person to enter the hallway was one of Critch's crew, hopping as he pulled on his boots. A man whose name Reyne couldn't remember, not that he tried to. The pirate brushed past Reyne.

"You better hurry," Reyne said. "Your ride is powering up as we speak."

Doc's door was left open, and Reyne peeked inside to find her tugging on clothes, her hair a disheveled mess. His brow rose. "Wild night, huh?"

She gave a weak smile and pulled her hair into a ponytail. "Pirates," she said, as if that single word was explanation enough.

He headed down the hallway. Since Sixx was inside the base, Reyne knew no one besides Doc had had a "sleepover" on the ship. Despite Demes' flirtations, Throttle seemed to only have eyes for Boden, who only had eyes for sweet soy.

The man was currently in between bouts with his addiction, making him bearable to be around and a talented mechanic. When he was on the soy, that was another story. He'd lead Throttle on one minute and crush her heart the next. The guy was a bastard when he was high. After the last binge, Reyne had given him an ultimatum. *Stay clean or get off the ship.* Fortunately Boden had stayed clean so far, but Reyne wasn't confident it would last.

Reyne hoped Boden stayed clean, because he had no idea where he'd find another mechanic willing to work for Aramis Reyne, the fringe's most notorious traitor.

Sixx rushed onto the ship, the circles under his eyes conveying how little sleep the man had got the night before. "It's too damn cold out there," he said through shivers.

"Where's your coat?" Reyne asked.

Sixx gave an exasperated sigh. "Kristen was sleeping on it. I didn't want to wake her."

"Who's Kristen?"

"She's the one with purple hair."

"Ah." Not that Reyne cared. "Get back to the cargo hold to make sure everything's battened down for takeoff."

"Sure thing, boss." Sixx headed down the hallway in the opposite direction to Reyne, who headed toward the bridge. Throttle wheeled out of her quarters at the same time Reyne reached her door.

"So, we're going to the Coast again?" she asked.

Reyne couldn't miss the anticipation in her eyes. "Yes. We'll be flying back with the *Honorless*."

"Ooh, maybe we can fly formation," she said, and wheeled quickly ahead of him.

His heart panged with sorrow for her. A girl with a passion for adventure imprisoned in a broken body. When she was young, he'd told her he'd get her spine fixed. However, neural repair was expensive, and credits were hard to come by. First, it was a cracked propulsion system. Then, it was a snapped solar sail. Big expense after big expense popped up, and Reyne had never managed to buy the one thing he wanted Throttle to have most in the universe.

She never complained, though. If anything, not having the use of her legs made her work harder to improve her flying skills. She had become the best pilot Reyne had ever known. With her skill, she could've been making thousands of credits a month piloting a Collective ship. He'd even hinted at that more than once. But she made it clear. She would never serve the Collective.

She dreamed of flying in a new Uprising.

Little could he have guessed she'd get her chance.

From the bridge, he could see the *Honorless* had already initiated its launch sequence. A row of ten lights on the launch pad was down seven lights already. The engines of the larger ship reverberated through the *Gryphon*, which sat next in queue for takeoff.

The launch pad sat at the bottom of a volcano that had burned out long before Playa's surface froze. Reyne assumed Vym had been the caretaker of this base, keeping it functional and even upgrading the technology over the years. She must've used this base regularly to warrant such a cost. He wondered if she'd used the base purely for her personal, less-than-legal activities, or if she'd had grander plans for it—for the torrents or the Founders. He supposed he'd now never learn that answer.

When the last light blinked out on the countdown sequence, the slingshot launcher threw the *Honorless* upward at ten-plus Gs, and the ship's engines roared. The slingshot was an old technology that was reliable but torturous to use. Most crews blacked out on takeoff from these launch pads, having to rely completely on autopilots. Critch, Reyne suspected, had his eyes wide open and hands at the controls the entire time.

As soon as the *Honorless* was away, Reyne keyed in control of the launch pad system.

"Pre-launch completed," Throttle said. "I'm punching in

coordinates to the Coast now."

Reyne nodded. He pinged Boden. "How are we on engines?"

"Green light."

"Good." He then announced to the ship, "Buckle in. We're up for launch."

Reyne initiated the launch sequence. A conveyor belt transferred the *Gryphon* onto the launch pad as gears locked into place. All ten lights lit up on the countdown, dropping down to nine lights almost immediately.

"The ship is yours," Reyne said to Throttle.

"Powering up nav engines," Throttle said.

The small engines purred, and Reyne checked the sensors. "All green."

The countdown went down to eight lights.

"Powering up Flux engine," she said.

Reyne checked the sensors once again. "Green."

The countdown went down to seven lights.

"Cycling propulsion system."

"Green."

Six lights.

"Approving flight plan," she said.

Five lights.

"Running final checks on life support."

"Green," Reyne said.

Four lights.

"Running final checks on electrical."

"Green."

Three lights.

"Running final checks on mechanical."

"Green."

Two lights.

"Running final checks on all gears."

"Solar sails green. Landing green," Reyne said.

One light.

"Approved for launch. Party time."

The final light went off, and Throttle initiated the launch. All high-g launches required autopilot enabled as backup, but it never kicked on when Throttle was at the controls. With everything entered into the system, the *Gryphon* shot straight upward. Reyne grunted to retain consciousness as his body slammed against the back of his seat, his arthritic joints sending out small jolts of pain. Blackness tunneled his vision, and he fought to watch his panel to make sure no critical systems went red.

Within seconds, all pressure disappeared, and he could breathe easily.

"We're free of the atmo," Throttle said, breathing heavily.

"Well done." Reyne took a moment to run full system checks. "Everything's green. We're ready for jump speed." A flash of light came from the *Honorless'* engines as it went to jump speed right before them. His eyes narrowed and he nodded toward the now disappeared ship. "Catch up to the *Honorless.* Don't let them get too much of a lead."

"Believe me, I won't," she said. "I'm running pre-jump sequence—oh...It's all gone."

Reyne glanced over to see Throttle staring at the view screen. She had the aft monitors on screen, showing Playa's surface. While the clouds hid much of the surface, he could see everything was as still and lifeless as he'd seen on his hovercraft trip with Critch.

He clenched his teeth. "Don't worry. We'll make sure Ice Port gets her payback."

THREE CAPTAINS

Throttle kept the *Honorless* within visual sight all the way back to Nova Colony's docks. Of course, Critch could've easily outrun them if he'd wanted—he had twice the power—but he hadn't, likely because Reyne still held the tablet and the only way to contact the CUF commandant.

After they docked, everyone except Sixx remained on board in case Baker brought trouble along. Sixx accompanied Reyne as protection against both the CUF officer and Critch's people, who seemed to populate the entire Colony.

"We'll hold the meeting in my office," Critch said, hardly giving them a glance.

"Nice guy," Sixx said drily to Reyne after the pirate and several of his crew walked ahead.

Reyne nodded, and they followed Critch into the Uneven Bar and out the back door, through the kitchen, down a wide hallway with crates stacked against both walls, and finally to another door.

Critch entered a long code on the wall panel. The lock clicked, and the door swung open. He strolled inside, followed by three of his crew—including the one who'd left Doc's bunk in a rush the morning they left Tulan Base—and lastly, Reyne and Sixx.

As soon as they entered, Sixx took up a position between Reyne and Critch's crew. If the crew tried anything, Reyne would almost feel sorry for what Sixx would do to them. Almost.

Reyne turned his attention to take in the simple room. The first time he'd been here, he'd had a hellish headache and hadn't expected to leave Nova Colony in one piece. Now, he could appreciate the setup. The room was large—spacious enough for the entire crew of the *Honorless* to sit at the stone table that took up half the space. The other half was open, containing only a rilon desk. A single painting decorated the wall, and Reyne instantly recognized the black-rocked Terran landscape where Critch had been born.

The pirate took a seat in the luxurious leather chair and powered on the panel that covered much of the desk's surface. "I have a direct line to the docks," he said. "We'll know the moment this 'Baker' arrives. If you'd prefer to pass the time at the bar—"

"I'll stay here." Reyne took a seat across from Critch. "That way, you won't forget to notify me when our friend lands."

Critch's eyes narrowed slightly, but he didn't say anything. He hit a comm on the side of the desk. "Send in a meal for six."

"Right away, boss," came an immediate response.

Critch threw a quick glance around the room. "Make yourselves comfortable. We could be here for a while."

Reyne watched Critch ignore him for the ten minutes it took

before several attractive waitresses delivered six trays. He followed them as they placed them on the large table. His mouth watered at his tray of mashed philoseed, cavote pudding, and... "Real meat? How'd you manage to get that out here on the Coast?"

Critch took a seat, grabbed a fork and knife, and began cutting into his steak. "We have a farm in Nova Colony. It raises both goats and chickens. It's been quite productive." Then he tacked on, "And highly profitable."

Reyne went for the meat first. "Critch, you crusty ole pirate, you may have a few surprises in you yet."

The six of them ate in silence, with only the sound of silverware on plates. Reyne didn't mind one bit. The last time he had meat was during the Uprising back on Terra. He and Critch had come across a farm that had been bombed by the CUF, and they'd rounded up the injured animals and feasted like kings that night.

Things had changed a lot since then. Yet, it seemed they were coming full circle.

Not long after they finished, the waitresses returned for the trays. Critch had returned to his desk, and became intrigued by something on the screen. He tapped his comm. "Intercept whoever leaves that ship, and bring them to me. And keep a close eye on that ship. If it does anything even remotely suspicious, puncture its hull."

"Yes, sir."

Reyne's brows rose, wondering if Critch had given similar instructions regarding the *Gryphon*.

The pirate leaned back in his chair. "The *Ocelot* is on my payroll. She's supposed to be picking up a shipment of blue tea on Spate right about now."

"I take it that ship isn't one to just drop by the Coast unexpectedly," Reyne said.

"Never."

Reyne leaned forward to watch. Everything was upside down from his vantage point, but he could still see clearly. Several of Nova Colony's police force marched to the *Ocelot*. The single person in a suit who walked down the ramp was quickly surrounded, and the herd moved to the pressurization chamber. Critch swiped his hand across the panel, bringing a video of the chamber into view.

Once the moisture cloud dissipated, the newcomer removed his helmet.

Critch motioned to the screen. "I know the captain of the *Ocelot*, and Miko has never been that good looking."

"That's Heid," Reyne observed.

"He's a she?"

Reyne nodded. He continued to watch Commandant Heid be escorted into Nova Colony. Critch switched videos again, and they watched her walk into Uneven Bar, where everyone turned to look.

"I know that feeling," Reyne muttered.

No one attacked Heid, likely because no one knew she was a CUF officer; all they could know was she was too clean-cut to be a Coaster, and surrounded by police. She didn't wear a chimesuit, and Reyne suspected she was wearing a spacesuit from the *Ocelot*'s crew. When she arrived Critch's door, Reyne turned to see her enter.

"Leave us," Critch ordered. The police leader nodded, and he and his posse departed.

Heid stood there. Recognition lit her features. "Why am I not surprised to see you, Captain Reyne?"

"You shouldn't be. After all, you put a tracker on my ship."

Her brows shot up in surprise before she regained her composure. "I like to keep an eye on potential allies."

"Spying is not a good way to build a relationship," Reyne said. "Neither is bombing fringe stations."

Her lips thinned. "That was an unfortunate incident that should never have happened. You have my sincerest condolences."

"Condolences won't bring back the thirty thousand lives taken at Ice Port," Reyne snapped.

"No, they won't," she said, her voice softening. "But, I suspect you didn't invite me here to talk about the attack."

"We didn't," Critch inserted before leaning back. "I'm impressed you made it here alive, Commandant. I wonder if I can say the same about the captain and crew of the ship you came in on."

She lifted her chin. "I command a CUF warship. How hard do you think it is for me to get hold of a fringe ship?" When Critch continued to stare, she continued. "You have my word, Captain Miko and his crew are alive and well, and enjoying the fine amenities the *Arcadia* has to offer in return for my use of the *Ocelot*."

She cocked her head as she took in both men and smiled. "So tell me, why have I been invited to a reunion of old torrent marshals?"

Reyne glanced at Critch before turning back to her. "I take it you know this fine gentleman. I'd like to formally introduce Critch, captain of the *Honorless*."

"Critch, pirate and smuggler, with at least six death sentences on your head." Heid gave Critch an appraising gaze. "However, you were once known as Drake Fender, infamous torrent marshal

---

of the Uprising, who served with the even more infamous torrent marshal, Aramis Reyne. Somehow, I have a feeling our little meeting has more to do about rebellion than smuggling."

Reyne cleared his throat and motioned to Heid. "Critch, have the pleasure of the company of Commandant Gabriela Heid, captain of the CUF warship *Arcadia*, who also seems to go by the codename Baker."

Critch leaned forward. "I thought you'd be older."

"And I thought you'd be prettier," she snapped back.

Reyne leaned back with enjoyment. "I see you two are going to get along splendidly."

Critch turned to their crewmembers still in the room. "Leave us."

Sixx eyed Reyne, who nodded, and he followed the pirates out.

"Now, let's get down to business," Critch said.

Heid began. "If you have her tablet, that means she keyed it to not self-destruct when it was taken more than ten feet away from her. That confirms my suspicions that she's dead or no longer a viable asset to the Founders. That, plus, you knew enough to call me Baker, which means you already know far too much for your own good."

"You know, Critch, I think that sounds an awful lot like a threat," Reyne mused.

"I agree. I don't like threats."

"Not a threat, but a warning," she said. "There are those who would kill you for what you've discovered."

"Many have tried to kill me in the past," Critch said. "None have succeeded."

"Yet. None have succeeded *yet*," she cautioned. "The Founders have many resources. You need to be careful."

Reyne spoke. "And I suppose it's safe to assume your friends will know about us soon if they don't already."

She held up her hands. "They won't learn from me, assuming we reach some sort of arrangement."

"Exactly what sort of arrangement do you propose?" Critch asked.

"I propose an arrangement where we don't work at killing each other." She strolled over to the desk and took a seat in the chair next to Reyne. She didn't speak for a long moment, as though contemplating her next words. "The Collective is in jeopardy. If we act now, the colonists can become citizens. If we fail to act, the Collective will implode, and many lives will be lost."

"The Collective imploding could be the best thing for the fringe," Critch said.

"Look at Sol Base and Ice Port," she countered. "The fringe will lose more lives than Myr and Alluvia."

Critch's eyes narrowed. "Why do you care what happens to us colonists?"

"Because, contrary to mass media, Alluvia and Myr need the fringe far more than you need them," she replied. "We depend on the fringe for much of our food and raw material. Right now, Myr is making its move to take control of the fringe stations." She paused. "You know this already, or else you wouldn't have bothered to contact me."

Reyne examined the woman. "Why did you release the blight at the Genics Corp lab?"

Her lips thinned. "We had hoped to discourage those behind Myr's ambitions."

"By 'we', you mean the Founders," Reyne mused.

She gave a tight nod. "Unfortunately, it appears to have had the opposite effect."

"Why didn't the Founders do anything to stop the attack on Sol Base? Or the attack on Ice Port?" Critch asked.

"Believe me, we tried," she said. "But, our resources are limited. We can only do so much without going public."

"So you'd rather watch hundreds of thousands of innocents die than take a stand," Reyne said.

Her jaw tightened. "I'm here to take a stand. Otherwise, I'd be on my way back to the fleet as ordered, to turn my ship over to a Myrad captain." She sighed deeply. "We're getting ready to fight a war no one wants a part in. Neither the Alluvians nor the Founders want to get involved. A Myrad controls the CUF, as well as the blight. Against those odds, a single commandant has little power."

She looked at both men. "Ausyar will build an empire unless everyone joins forces and stops him. Vym had the vision. I want to see it through."

Reyne leaned closer. "How can we trust you? How do we know Alluvia won't step over Myr to take over the Collective once we stop Myr?"

She chuckled drily. "Oh, believe me. There are Alluvians lined up to take control of the Collective if Ausyar fails. I love Alluvia, but what I love more is the idea of a Collective where everyone is equal. If I'm not mistaken, the three of us share that same desire. That was the original goal of the Founders, and it's still my goal."

Reyne thought hard and long. "You're here on your own. You're not here representing the Founders."

"The Founders is a group of individuals. Some have different opinions to others."

"So, officially, whose side are they on?" Reyne asked.

She smirked. "Officially, the Founders don't exist."

"Stop with the word games," Critch said. "Feed it to us

straight."

Heid's lips thinned. "Think of the Founders as two sides of a coin. On one side, we can count on the support of certain individuals. There are many good people in the Founders, and I won't betray them. But, on the other side of that coin, we're doomed if certain individuals find out our plan."

"*Our* plan?" Critch echoed, drawing a circle with a finger that encompassed the three of them.

She nodded tightly.

Reyne motioned. "So, tell us about this plan of yours."

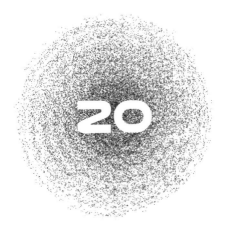

20

IMPOSSIBLE HOPE

"That's all there is to it," Reyne finished.

Every crew member of the *Gryphon* stared at him, slack-jawed.

"That's all," Sixx echoed.

"Yep."

"Let me get this straight," Throttle began. "We're hijacking a Myrad hauler and running straight through the space barrier to land onto Myr. From there, we get our hands on proof of Myr's involvement with the blight, proof that we'll then bring into the heart of Alluvia, where we'll get it to a Collective news reporter, who will then get Alluvia and the fringe all riled up against Myr."

Reyne nodded. "That pretty much sums it up."

"It's impossible," Doc said.

"Which part?" Reyne asked.

"All of it," she answered.

"For starters, we're not pirates," Sixx said. "We've never hijacked a ship together."

"That's why Critch and a few members of his crew will be joining us. They'll lead the hijacking expedition."

"So, we're officially joining ranks with pirates," Boden said.

"Torrents," Reyne corrected. "They're only pirates on their off-days."

Sixx smirked. "Okay. We hijack a Myrad ship. Then, we come up to the space barrier. If any of the Myrads on that ship happen to send out a distress signal during the hijacking, then their codes won't work. The EMP will fry everything in our ship, and we'll die a cold, suffocating death in space."

Reyne nodded. "We'll make sure they never get the chance to make a distress call."

Sixx continued. "Okay then. Myr is a big world. How are we going to know which province this particular Genics Corp building is in?"

"We're counting on our Founder pals for that information."

Doc frowned. "The Founders? They're an urban legend. They don't exist."

"They do exist, and Heid seems to think one of them, located on Myr, is going to help us."

"We're aligning with the CUF now, too?" Boden asked, ire darkening his voice.

"Yes, although I suspect after this, Heid will be considered more torrent than CUF."

"How do you know Critch or Heid won't betray us?" Doc asked.

"Critch watched his family get slaughtered by Myrads and

Alluvians on Terra before the Uprising. He may act like a pirate, but he'll always be a torrent in his heart. As for Heid, she's an idealist. They'll both work with us to see the Uprising happen." Reyne considered the two captains for a moment. "But don't forget for a minute that either one of them would set us up if our deaths fit into their plans. We need to cover our asses every step of the way."

Sixx laughed. "Sounds like one hell of a ménage à trois," he said before letting out a sigh. "Though, I can honestly say I never thought I'd get a chance to pull a heist on Myr."

Reyne smiled. "Sounds enticing, doesn't it?"

"Hell, yeah," Sixx replied. "But, I'd rather skip the part about how we somehow make it onto Alluvia without dying."

"That's where Boden comes into play." Reyne watched the mechanic's head jerk at the mention of his name. "He's an Alluvian resident, and has full rights to land at any time. That's the lowest risk part of the plan."

"*Was* an Alluvian," Boden corrected. "We're all dead, at least on legal records. My access rights would've been cancelled by now."

Reyne shook his head and eyed Boden. "Sorry, pal. You'd been let go from my crew, and so you weren't on our last scalar run. That means you weren't on board when the *Gryphon* landed at Ice Port. Demes has already entered your credentials on Spate for the past month. It appears you've been staying at a brothel in Devil Town on a sweet soy binge. You've run out of money and have already filed for a new visa for landing rights to return home."

The mechanic glowered.

"We had to make it believable in case someone digs into your records," Reyne added before turning back to his crew. "So, Boden will have us land at First City, where Heid has promised

RACHEL AUKES

to hook us up with a reporter friend of hers who will broadcast the story. We'll also bring our little hacker buddy Demes along in case the reporter falls through. Demes will plug into the hard line to the news channel's systems and broadcast the truth across the city and out to the fringe. Alluvia will finally step forward and go head-to-head with Myr, hopefully preventing Myr's hostile takeover or, worse, a Collective war."

Doc shook her head. "This will never work out. It's impossible."

"Well, aren't you a bunch of pessimists?" Reyne asked drily. "Listen, I never said it would be easy, but if we succeed, we can save millions of lives. Make no mistake, this is the Uprising." No one spoke. "Come on, don't you want to be heroes?"

"No," Sixx replied quickly.

"Even if it means every woman in the Collective will want to sleep with you?"

"They already do," Sixx replied.

"Not *every* woman," Throttle added before turning to Reyne. "You know that where you go, I go. I'm in."

"I don't want to be a hero, but I do want to be rich," Sixx said. "Hell, I was in as soon as you mentioned that I'd get to steal from the Myrads."

Boden thumped his fist against the table. "I don't like working with the CUF, but if we succeed, Alluvia will stand up to Myr. That will mean trouble for all citizens, hopefully even bloodshed. They've enslaved colonists for far too long, and they deserve some payback. I'm in."

Doc stared. "This is lunacy."

Reyne eyed her. "Things could get rough out there. We could use a medic who won't crack under pressure."

She stood. "It's a suicide run. We'll all die. I won't be party to

182

that." Doc looked around the table. "You're all crazy. I will not watch you kill yourselves." She stormed out of the room.

Reyne glanced at Throttle, Sixx, and Boden. "Thanks," he said, before standing and following Doc to her quarters.

She'd locked her door, but one of the perks of being captain was having an override code. He punched in several numbers, the door opened, and he stepped inside.

She spun around. Her cheeks were red and her eyes were full of fury. "You're an idiot, Aramis."

Taken aback, he held up his hands. "Whoa, there. I get that you're scared. Hell, I am too, but I'm not doing this out of stupidity. I'm doing this because there are no other options. If we don't stop Myr, the other fringe stations will fall. If we thought things were bad when Alluvia and Myr were keeping each other in check, imagine how bad it will be if Myr gains control. We're second-class folks today, and if Myr wins, we'll all become slaves. Far worse than the tenured, like Boden's family was back on Alluvia."

Her face tightened. "You're going to get yourself killed. I gave everything to save your life once, and now you're throwing it away."

Reyne frowned, confused. "You've saved my life plenty of times, and I'm thankful. But my life isn't worth living if I tuck tail and live it out as a coward."

A tear ran down her cheek. "You're always running toward trouble."

"I only run toward it if it's the right thing to do. I can't change who I am."

She wiped her cheek. "No, you can't."

He wrapped his arms around her and implored softly. "So, will you run with me?"

She sobbed, "Of course," then shooed him away. "Now, go. Leave me alone."

Reyne reluctantly left her quarters, though he felt like he should go back and wipe her tears away and hold her until she quit crying.

He discovered things were no better back in the commons. There, he found Throttle crying. Sixx had an arm wrapped around her, and Boden stared blankly at the wall screen.

"What's wrong?" Reyne asked.

Sixx gave Reyne a long look before turning back to the screen. "Restart Somerville update."

In an unexpected turn of events, an Alluvian citizen has been killed during the Ice Port bombing, meant to eliminate the bioterrorists of the Smithton and Sol Base attacks. Kason Somerville, of the highly respected Somerville and Marion lineage, was found dead by rescue teams at Ice Port. He had holdings on all six worlds, and was believed to be on a routine visit when the attack happened. Corps General Michel Ausyar has offered his sincerest apologies to Somerville's family, and has vowed to do everything in his power to protect citizen lives as they continue investigations into the bioterrorist faction, led by Vym Patel, that has now taken both Myrad and Alluvian lives. This is Lina Tao reporting for DZ-Five, your Collective news source.

"No." Reyne helplessly watched a video of a smiling Kason displayed on the screen. "Damn it. Why didn't he stay on Alluvia?"

"It doesn't make any sense," Boden said. "Why'd he return to Ice Port so soon after United Day? He always stays home for at least two weeks. Even at full jump speed, it doesn't add up."

"Maybe he got stuck at Ice Port for business and never made it home?" Throttle offered before wiping her eyes on her shirt.

Boden shook his head. "I saw him off. I would've heard from

him if something happened."

"I'd bet every credit I own that the CUF bastards killed him because of that package," Sixx said. "Everything hit the shitter as soon as we grabbed that damn box."

"He was a citizen." Throttle sniffled. "They would never kill a citizen."

"He's also one of us," Reyne said, and a cold rock settled into his gut as Sixx's words rang of truth.

Boden pounded the table as he shoved to his feet. "I've seen them do it before. The bastards do what they want and kill anyone who gets in their way."

Reyne watched the mechanic, fists clenched, stomp from the room. He worried that Boden losing his best friend would send the Alluvian on another sweet soy binge. When he turned back, he noticed Sixx and Throttle were watching him.

"They'll kill us, too, if we get in their way," Sixx said.

Reyne took a deep breath before speaking. "Maybe they'll kill us. Maybe not. But I'm damn sure not going to let them get their way without an Uprising."

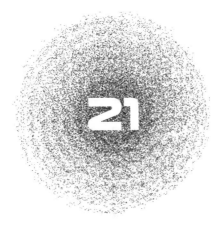

LIBERTY RUN

Heid

Heid had plenty of time to think on her trip back to the *Arcadia*. The *Ocelot* was an old hauler, made for transport and not for speed. By the time she reached her warship, she was antsy for action.

She docked to find Laciam waiting for her outside the decon room.

She gave him a wry grin. "Laciam. I'm half-surprised you didn't try to take over the *Arcadia* while I was away."

"I should have. When Sebin said you left the ship with orders to cut all engines while you took a joyride in some fringe junker, I knew you had crossed the line."

Heid's brow rose. "It's not your place to understand my

decisions, just as it's not your place to question my orders. Plus, the *Arcadia* isn't yours yet. Until we reach the fleet, you will address me as Commandant or Sir. Do I make myself understood?"

"Yes, *sir*."

"Refuel and restock the *Ocelot*, and escort her crew back to their ship. They're free to go."

"Yes, *sir*."

As he strode away, she heard him mutter, "Alluvian bitch. You just wait."

She tapped a simple command on her comm—*Liberty 0747*—and sent it to select crewmembers serving on the *Arcadia*.

As commandant, Heid had the authority to select her own crewmembers, and she'd spent all her years aboard the *Arcadia* placing Alluvians loyal to her throughout the ship. They now comprised nearly two-thirds of her crew, with the remaining positions filled by Myrads, conscripted fringe, and Alluvians of whose loyalty she was unsure.

She had thirty minutes, which she used to make rounds through the hallways, making sure to be seen by her crew. Sebin met her outside the bridge.

She glanced down at her comm to see the time. One minute to go.

He nodded, and she gave a simple nod in return. Words weren't necessary, as this exercise had been planned long ago. Adrenaline rushed through her as she stepped onto the bridge.

Laciam glanced up, but didn't acknowledge her.

"Nolin," Heid called out to her navigator. "Set a course for Terra."

Laciam jumped to his feet. "You can't do that!"

"Watch your tone, First Officer," she warned.

He glared. "This madness has gone too far. You've spaced out. I'm declaring you unfit for duty. Something I should've done as soon as the corps general's orders came in. Guards, arrest the commandant."

Heid made eye contact with the two guards stationed on the bridge. They moved to Laciam and grabbed him instead.

She faced Laciam. "Guards, escort the first officer to the brig."

"What?" he cried out, his blue face darkening a hue. "You can't arrest me. This is my ship!"

"If he gives you trouble, kill him," she added, hoping he'd do exactly that, which would leave one fewer loose end for her to clean up.

Unfortunately, he stood still as her dromadiers disarmed him and led him away.

Laciam called out as the guards shoved him off the bridge, "You'll be shot for this, Heid!"

When the door closed, she turned to the five remaining crewmembers on the bridge. Four were loyal, one—a fringe tech assistant—was an unknown. Rather than speak to her directly, she broadcast to the entire ship. "Crew of the *Arcadia*. We have journeyed across the Collective together, and I ask you now to take another journey with me. The CUF has been usurped by a man who dreams of an empire. The CUF no longer serves the best interests of the Collective, and the entire Collective—not just Alluvia and Myr—need our help.

"The blight was the first slash at disharmony, though our leaders failed us all long before the tragic loss of Sol Base. Then came Ice Port, an innocent victim, used purely as a scapegoat for Myr's imperialism. In truth, the terrorists are much closer to the heart of the Collective than the colony farthest in the fringe." She paused. "The blight, the discord, and the violence come from

189

Corps General Ausyar, who has militarized Myr's government. He envisions a Myr Collective, just as the CUF is now under his control."

She scanned the faces on the bridge before continuing. "I refuse to let the Collective fall. As of now, I relinquish my CUF rank as commandant. I am taking the *Arcadia* as the flagship for the future. I will lead the Collective into a battle—not as a commandant or as a citizen—but as a captain in a Collective made of equals. If you choose to follow me, you will be marked down as mutineers, but history will mark you down as heroes. I will not—I cannot—command you to follow me on this new journey. If you follow me, I promise you danger and risk, but I also promise you that you will be saving lives across the six Collective worlds by choosing to fight for the Collective rather than for Ausyar's empire.

"I give you the choice. Anyone who does not wish to remain on the *Arcadia* to fight for the new Collective must let Sebin Reinhardt know within the next hour. Those not joining the cause for the Collective will be confined to quarters for the protection of the crew, and in two days we will drop them off at Rebus Station on Terra, where they can be picked up by a CUF patrol. Effective immediately, all communications leaving this ship will be blocked. Your one hour begins now. Choose wisely."

Heid lowered her head and focused on breathing in and out.

"Sir?"

She looked up to find the conscript standing before her. "Yes, Sylvian?"

"Did you mean it?" she asked. "That you plan to fight for the fringe?"

Heid nodded. "I fight for the idea of an equal Collective, and it's the fringe that most needs our help right now."

The young woman stood taller. "I'm from Sol Base. I lost everyone I know to the blight. You can count on me, sir."

Heid smiled, finding validation for her plans in the young woman's words. "Thank you, Sylvian." She paused. "Oh, and you do not need to address me with any formal title. As of now, I have no association with the Collective Unified Forces."

"You're still our captain regardless of the insignia you wear," Sebin said, with pride in his voice.

"Aye, Captain," said Nolin the navigator, followed by assent from the remaining bridge crew.

"Thank you." She clapped her hands together. "Put us into stealth mode, and let's get to work decoupling the *Arcadia*'s systems from fleet control. We now fly under our own flag."

HYPOXIC HIJACKINGS

Throttle glared at Reyne, her arms crossed. "Like hell you're leaving me behind."

Reyne set down his beer. "I need someone to stay with the *Gryphon*. We need Boden for landing on Alluvia, and Doc in case someone gets hurt, and Sixx—"

"Because he can walk," she interrupted.

"No," Reyne said calmly. "I was going to say because he was a professional thief, and we're breaking into someone's house."

Critch butted in. "Listen, Throttle. The truth hurts, but we'll be on the planet surface and without a ship. What is a cripple going to do in a place where there are no cripples? Everyone will be looking at you, and we'll be forced to scrub the mission."

She slowly rolled over to where Critch sat as he was speaking.

When he finished, she punched him. "You're a bastard."

"He is a bastard," Reyne said, but noticed that the pirate didn't raise a hand to strike her back. "But he's right, in that this is a mission that will take place on the ground. If it was taking place in the air, you'd be the first on my team."

Critch rubbed his cheek. "Nice right hook." He finished off his beer, kicked off from his chair, grabbed her hand, and slapped a key onto her palm. "I bet Reyne doesn't pay worth a shit, so stay in my guest quarters. Any food and necessities can go onto my account. No one will mess with you at Nova Colony. Have fun, but don't get carried away."

"This is bullshit," she muttered, staring at the key. She glared at Critch. "And you're still a bastard."

"I know."

Reyne forced a smile and squeezed her shoulder. "I wish it didn't have to be this way. I know it's not fair, but we'll be back before you know it." He paused. "You watch yourself around here."

She glanced up. Where Reyne expected to see tears, he saw anger instead. "You're lucky I don't punch you, too."

"And I'd deserve it."

She lifted her chin. "I don't like it, but I get why you're leaving me behind. You can't always treat me like a little girl."

He swallowed. "I know." He kissed her forehead, turned in a rush, and walked out of the Uneven Bar before he said something stupid, like make a promise he couldn't keep.

He fastened his helmet and stepped into the airlock that separated the docks from Nova Colony. Critch joined him, and they stood in silence as the chamber depressurized. As soon as the door opened, Reyne grabbed a zip line and flew down to the docks. He refused to look at the *Gryphon* and headed straight to the *Honorless*. He didn't slow his momentum until he reached its port door, not stopping until he hit the inner door. Critch followed and shut the door behind them. Pressurization took no more than a couple seconds, and Reyne tugged off his helmet and stepped inside. He started down the hallway to meet his crew.

Critch kept pace alongside Reyne. "I know why you're leaving her behind."

"Oh yeah?"

"You're leaving her behind because you don't think you're coming back, and you want her to live. For what it's worth, I would've done the same thing. She's young. She deserves to have a few more years." They walked in silence for a while. "If you don't make it, I'll fix her legs."

Reyne stopped. "Why?"

The pirate shrugged. "She's an innocent." He kept walking. "Plus, she'd make a solid addition to one of my crews."

"Like hell," Reyne said and caught up. "Besides, what makes you think you'll get out of this alive?"

Critch grunted. "I'm too pretty to die."

"Too ornery is more like it," Reyne muttered and entered the commons. The room was large and comfortable, and had luxuries that put the *Gryphon*'s central meeting room to shame. The rest of the team was already waiting for them—Sixx, Doc, and Boden from Reyne's crew, and three from Critch's crew, while the remainder of the *Honorless*' crew was busy preparing for launch. Reyne recognized the trio. Demes, of course. Chutt, the craggy pirate whom Doc had slept with. And Birk, one of the quieter— and better behaved—men on Critch's crew.

Critch leaned onto the table and looked across the faces in the room. "We're heading out in ten minutes. I'll make this quick. It could take days or it could take weeks to find a ship we can use, which means we'll have plenty of time to work out the details of the plan. For now, make yourselves comfortable. Once we clear the Coast, you'll all be given jobs to do."

A male voice came over the speakers. "*Strap in for takeoff.*"

The pirate captain smacked his hands together. "Let's get ourselves a Myrad ship."

Eight days later.

"Crew alert. We're tracking a potential bogey."

Sixx groaned. "That's what they said the last three times."

Reyne nodded and left Sixx to continue cleaning the weapons. He headed to the bridge, hoping this would be the time. Critch was in charge of getting them a ship, and Reyne had to trust the pirate's judgment.

The first ship they came across was a brand new passenger ship. Too many people to deal with. The second, a Myrad patrol ship. Far too dangerous to hijack. The third was almost right. It was an older hauler, but Demes had been unsuccessful in hacking through its surprisingly secure firewall.

When Reyne reached the bridge, Demes looked pleased.

"This is it. I know it," the young pirate said. "It's an old Eagle II. No firewalls. I'll be tapped into her in no time."

Critch scowled. "Eagles are heavy and slow. Made of more carbon fiber than rilon. It's going to make for a long trip."

"Aw, sounds like we'll get plenty of quality time together," Reyne said.

"Hm." Critch glanced back to see Reyne approach before turning his attention back to Demes. "Can you hack her?"

"Hold on...just one more...got it. I'm in. I've got her systems.

Looking for the air filtration…there you are. I'm locking them out and adjusting the oxygen levels now. There. Child's play." He turned around with a wide grin. "They should be hypoxic in under twelve minutes."

Reyne cocked his head, impressed at the pirates' ingenuity. "I'd always assumed you killed the crews of the ships you hijacked."

"Hypoxia is subtle and far less risky. Very few crews catch on in time to don suits. Those that figure it out are the ones we have to watch out for." Critch turned back to Demes. "How many?"

"Let's see," Demes said. "Looks like eleven crew are logged in."

Critch grabbed the comm. "To your stations. We're hunting Eagle." He clapped the pilot's shoulder. "Take good care of her, Gabe. I'll be back for her soon."

"Like always," the man said.

Critch gave Reyne a quick nod, and he headed off the bridge and toward the airlock. Reyne kept pace, and Demes followed.

Doc and Chutt emerged from his bunk, both looking a bit flushed and messy. Then again, the pirate always looked messy.

Reyne scowled, and Critch shot Chutt a hard glare, making it clear he wasn't any happier about the pair's extracurricular activities during a mission than Reyne was. Reyne understood why Doc was doing it. This mission was stressing her out, and she used sex as a coping mechanism. However, it was an unwritten rule that no one screwed around — literally — on the job.

When they reached the door to the airlock, Reyne grabbed his suit and started to slide a leg in.

Critch stopped him. "Here, use this instead." He handed Reyne two tiny oxygen bottles with nose gears. "Suits are too clumsy."

Reyne fastened his bottle around his collar. He handed the remaining one to Sixx.

"Exactly as we planned," Reyne said. "Boden, Doc, and Demes hang back until we clear the ship."

"You and Sixx can also wait until we clear it," Critch said to Reyne. "My crew has experience at this. You don't."

Reyne shook his head. "We can manage."

"Never thought I'd add 'hijacking a citizen ship' to my resume," Sixx said.

"You might find that you enjoy it," Critch said.

The *Honorless* attached to the other ship, sending shockwaves through the airlock, and Critch placed a hand on the wall to brace himself. The screeching sound of rilon against rilon sent shivers through Reyne.

Chutt had grabbed Doc when she nearly fell. "They didn't take evasive maneuvers. A good sign," he said.

Time dripped by as Birk managed the airlock controls, maneuvering the airlock outward from the side of the ship and lining it up against the porthole. Reyne gripped his photon gun, ready for action. When the light finally flicked green, Birk opened the airlock and placed an electronic unit on the Myrad ship's port. After several seconds of blinking red and yellow lights, it flashed green.

Critch looked across everyone before pulling up his oxygen tank breather tube. Reyne quickly followed his lead. Critch opened the door and jumped inside. Birk and Chutt followed him, while Reyne and Sixx covered the rear. Reyne took a deep breath before crossing over to the other ship.

Once inside, they ran first to the bridge, and Reyne knew that would be to ensure no one got any bright ideas and tried to pull away while the *Honorless* was still attached. The pirates moved with efficiency, reminding Reyne of fighting alongside Critch in the Uprising, and he realized that a pirate's life wasn't much different from a soldier's life.

Reyne's pace slowed as he finally understood why Critch had become a pirate. Being a pirate was the only way Critch could keep fighting the Collective without an Uprising.

Reyne moved when Sixx nudged him, and he jogged to the bridge, his arthritic knees causing him to wince. They needn't have hurried. The eight crewmembers on the bridge were in various slumped positions. Chutt, Birk, and Critch were pulling them from their seats and laying them out in a row on the floor. Most were unresponsive, though a couple were still conscious but out of it. Birk slapped a sleeping patch onto each crewmember's neck.

Reyne and Sixx chipped in and helped lay out the crew. As they laid them out, they counted three Myrads, all with the telltale blue skin of those who lived on the silver-rich planet. The remaining were tenured, obvious by the large, electronic ID cuffs that covered a third of their forearms. The cuffs were a shiny silver, to make their status clear from a distance. They would also have implants in case they broke the bracelets and ran. Those who attempted and were caught were punished—often by having their voice boxes fried.

The tenured colonists who signed up to work for citizens on Myr and Alluvia in return for their children's citizenship often learned too late that citizenship rules had many obscure loopholes. Most children—even those born on Myr or Alluvia—never became citizens. The practice to tenure humans made Reyne sick, and it had been just one of the many reasons he'd so zealously fought for the Uprising.

"Eight down. Three to go," Critch said. "Chutt and Sixx, move these eight to the airlock. Birk, check the bunks. Reyne and I will check the rest of the ship."

Reyne stayed at Critch's side, covering their left and back as they moved down the hallway. This ship was a far cry from the *Honorless* or the *Gryphon*. Whereas those ships were kept pristinely clean and organized, this ship hadn't aged well. Rubber marks marred the dented floors, and dust grew thick in corners. Boxes of food sat, unsecured, against the walls.

They bypassed the bunks to find a single crewmember in the commons area. A Myrad, puffy from sweet soy addiction, lay sprawled onto the table. Critch checked the man's pulse. "Dead." He tapped his comm. "One located in the commons."

"By the looks of him, he had Myrad medicine to thank for keeping him alive," Reyne said.

Critch nodded. "The bastard would've died years ago if he were fringe." He pulled the man back, and the body crumpled to the floor with a heavy thud.

"Located two incapacitated blokes in their bunks," Birk reported.

"That should be all of them. Birk, run a final sweep of the ship," Critch commanded.

"Wilco," came Birk's easy response.

Critch picked up the half-full glass of wine that had been sitting on the table.

"How often do you find stowaways?" Reyne asked.

"Hardly ever. The ones we do are generally hiding from the crew and more than happy to make our acquaintance." He sniffed the contents of the glass, shrugged, and took a drink.

"Blue-skins and tenured have been cleared from the bridge," Chutt reported.

"Received," Critch replied before downing the rest of the wine.

Reyne walked around the table and began to check out the cabinets. Roughly half the cabinets were unlocked, and contained the same rations Reyne stocked on the *Gryphon*. They were cheap, but covered all the basic nutrients.

"Here."

Reyne turned to see Critch rifling through the dead man's pockets. He pulled out an ID card and tossed it. Reyne caught it and swiped it over one of the locked cabinets. It opened, revealing contents of meats, cheeses, breads, wines, and chocolate.

"A Myrad would never stoop to eating fringe swill," Critch said.

Reyne found himself grinning as he grabbed a chocolate bar and cut open the plastic. He waved it in the general direction of the dead man. "Thanks, buddy." He took a bite and savored it. This was the second time in his life he'd had chocolate. The first time was when he was five and Vym had tossed him a bar after he smuggled a message from her to a local storekeeper.

"All clear. No more tangos," Birk reported in.

"Good."

"You know, if you ever get tired of Birk, I could use him on my crew," Reyne said before taking another bite.

"You can't afford him."

"How much do you pay him?"

"More than you make running."

Reyne shrugged. "Maybe. But, being a runner is a whole lot safer than being a pirate."

"From what I hear, running hasn't worked out that great for you lately."

"Not lately."

Critch looked away from Reyne and scowled down at the body. "Why do I always find the fat ones?" he muttered.

Reyne sighed as he gingerly rewrapped the chocolate bar and slid it into his pocket, then wiped his hands on his pants. "I'll take the head; you take the feet."

"No complaint there."

Reyne walked over and slid his hands under the man's damp armpits. He grimaced before lifting the body with a grunt. They carried the body to the airlock and moved it onto the *Honorless*, where Doc, Boden, and Demes waited.

Doc, who'd been bent over one of the other crewmembers, moved to check the newcomer. She frowned. "He's dead."

Critch ignored her. "Demes, clean up the air for us." He motioned to everyone. "The ship's been cleared. You can board as soon as the air improves."

One of Critch's crew who was staying on the *Honorless* nodded toward the incapacitated crew. "You want these guys handled in the usual fashion?"

"Yes. Drift the Myrads. Move the tenured into the hold," Critch replied. "When they wake, give them the same option we give all tenured."

Doc gasped. "You can't murder those citizens. They're helpless, innocent."

Critch spun on her. "Those so-called innocents were operating with a crew of slaves. They've made their entire livelihoods off the backs and blood of the fringe. If you want to save them, you can join them in the abyss."

As he spoke, she took steps back, cowering.

Reyne straightened. "He's right, Doc. If they live, they endanger the mission. Our lives are at stake here."

Doc stammered, but wisely kept her mouth shut.

Critch shot a surprised look at Reyne, but said nothing.

Reyne wanted to stick up for Doc, but the truth was, he sided with the pirate on this one. These Myrads had been essentially using slaves. If there hadn't been any tenured on this ship, then maybe he would have considered imprisoning the Myrads. What would he have done with them then? Drop them off at a fringe station so they could run to a CUF patrol and stop any chance Reyne and Critch's combined crew had of reaching Myr unnoticed?

Reyne continued. "Everyone, grab your gear and load up. We've spent enough time lollygagging already."

Everyone quickly dispersed, leaving Critch and Reyne alone with ten sleeping men and one dead man.

"Lollygagging?"

Reyne smiled.

"I never would've taken you for someone to kill unarmed men," he said after a moment.

Reyne sobered. "You never knew me very well." He grabbed his gear and walked away.

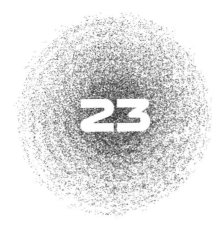

PHANTOM TRICKS

C ritch was right. The Eagle was a slow piece of shit that took over two weeks to cover the same distance the *Gryphon* could've covered in five days at jump speed. Within the first two days, the crews had sorted through all the shipments, finding only fabric and useless electronic parts. The tenured bunks had nothing to offer except trinkets, most of which were hidden under mattresses. The Myrad bunks had luxuries—silver, jewelry and fancy clothes—but nothing of any value to Reyne.

Two captains sharing one ship led to constantly butting heads, which did not make things any easier. Reyne tried to share decisions, but it was hard. He'd been the one in charge for much of his adult life. Critch was even worse—he didn't even try to share command. They finally settled into fifteen-hour shifts, running into each other only at shift change briefings and planning meetings.

Myrad food and wine helped pass the hours, but Reyne worried that the CUF would strike another fringe station while they made their slow way to Myr. They had the Collective news on constantly. Myr hadn't released the blight again, but Ausyar had been busy. The news replayed footage of the CUF taking down fringe "terrorists" and foiling obviously staged bioterrorist attempts. Genics Corp continued to promise that they were working around the clock to create a fungicide.

If their plan was to make everyone fearful and clamor for Myr's help, it was working flawlessly. Every Collective world pledged credits to Genics Corp. Myr had managed to milk people's pocketbooks while pulling on their heartstrings at the same time.

Midway through Reyne's shift on the sixteenth day, Birk pinged him. *"We're within three hours of the space barrier."*

"On my way." He left Boden in the engine room where they'd been running down one of the thousands of gremlins the ship seemed to have.

On the bridge, Reyne found Birk at the controls. "Are we close enough to see radar?" Reyne asked as he took a seat.

The lean pirate sighed. "Not with the outdated software on this beast. I have no idea if we'll see something in five minutes or if it'll be two hours."

Reyne frowned. "We're already cutting it close if we have to change plans. They likely have us located on their systems already." He inhaled. "Let's hope an old Myrad hauler won't raise any red flags." Reyne put his hand on Birk's shoulder. "Ping me as soon as you can see where the CUF patrols are along the barrier."

"Wilco," Birk replied without looking up from his panel.

Reyne headed back to his quarters and went through his gear. He strapped on his holster and sheaths, and checked his weapons. After he was all set, he took a seat and closed his eyes. In three hours they would either be through Myr's EMP space barrier and landing on the planet's surface, or the barrier's electromagnetic pulse would fry the ship's systems and life support, making them sitting ducks to be blown up by CUF patrols—or left to die in their cold Myrad coffin. He wasn't sure which option offered the worse prospects.

When he returned to the bridge, he reviewed the mission schematics that Heid had sent them. He tried not to think about what could go wrong. Instead, he focused on what needed done when they landed on Myr's surface.

At two hours to go, Reyne was ready to bang his head against the panel. The ship's blasted computers still hadn't picked up any traffic, let alone the massive space barrier. It wasn't until ninety-six minutes out that Birk finally picked up hints of the space barrier.

Reyne headed to the commons to grab them some food. On his way back, he pounded on the door to Critch's quarters. "Rise and shine. Ninety minutes out."

He smiled at the string of profanity shouted from the other side of the door.

Critch arrived on the bridge roughly ten minutes later, wearing full gear. "What do we have?" he asked, his voice rough from sleep.

"We're a little over seventy-five minutes out," Reyne said. "We haven't picked up any CUF patrols yet."

Critch grimaced. "This damn ship belongs in a junkyard. If we were on my ship, we'd be close enough to pick up the hair on their asses by now."

Reyne ate as they waited. Critch disappeared briefly, and returned with a meal of his own.

Fifteen minutes later, Birk still hadn't found any signs of CUF ships.

Critch wiped his hands and pushed off the wall to take over Birk's seat as pilot. "Go get ready. I'll take it from here."

As Critch strapped in, Reyne remembered meeting him for the first time. He'd still gone by his real name—Drake Fender—at the time, a talented young pilot ready to take on the universe. Reyne had seen his potential and took him under his wing. The Uprising was a year in, and they discovered hell together. They were brothers-in-arms...until Critch emerged from the Uprising with the belief that Reyne had betrayed everything they'd fought for.

Shaking off the old memories, Reyne broadcast to the ship, "Attention crew. We have one hour until we reach the barrier. Gear up and grab some grub. It might be some time before you eat or sleep once we pass through. Then, get yourselves to your stations. If we get scanned, I don't want them seeing heat signatures of the entire crew all hanging out on the bridge. Everything about us has to look run-of-the-mill."

"I'm picking up something," Critch said finally, frowning.

"What do you have?" Reyne asked.

"Not sure yet." After a long moment, he leaned back. "*Fuck*."

Reyne rushed over to see what the other man was looking at. He frowned. "That can't be."

"That's what I thought, too, but I double-checked. The data's right."

Reyne stared at the view screen, expecting to see everything that was on their radar, even though they were still too far out for the feeble view screen to zoom in on. "It's too late to run. They probably locked onto us hours ago."

"I don't know why they haven't hailed us."

"You think they're onto us?" Reyne asked.

"Don't know."

A chime alerted them to a new notification. Critch checked it first. "Ah, here comes an automated code request from the space barrier."

Reyne inhaled.

"Let's find out if we're going to live beyond the next sixty seconds," Critch said as he fed the ship's authentication codes to the space barrier's system.

The tension throughout the bridge was stifling, and Reyne found his joints complaining.

After a long delay, Critch blew out a breath. "It accepted the code. We're approved to pass through the barrier."

Reyne, too, let out the breath he'd been holding and pointed at the view screen. "The bigger question is, will *they* let us pass?"

Faint dots finally appeared, and slowly grew to form ships. Not CUF patrol ships, but huge warships. From the looks of things, the entire CUF fleet was out there waiting for them.

DIVIDE AND CONQUER

"Why would they be out here?" Critch asked. "The fleet base of operations is in between Myr and Alluvia. They're on the wrong side of Myr."

"Heid said Ausyar was making changes to the fleet," Reyne said. "My guess is this is all his doing."

"You think he moved the fleet farther from Alluvia to make it easier to control?"

Reyne shook his head. "Don't know, but I do know they wouldn't send the entire fleet for a single crew of torrents. They have to be out here for some other reason."

"Let's hope that reason doesn't involve shooting us and screwing up our plans."

Reyne turned to Critch. "Don't slow down, and don't veer off course. We want them to think we're just passing through on a regular run."

"You want to fly?" Critch snapped back.

"Yeah, I do," Reyne answered.

Critch hesitated. "Well, you can't."

Reyne eyed the pirate long and hard before forcing himself to relax. On the *Gryphon*, he'd have access to systems to see everything Critch was seeing. The Eagle, on the other hand, was an obsolete craft. It had few redundancies, including a single panel for piloting and navigating. It made Reyne feel downright helpless.

"Aw, hell," Critch muttered. "We're being hailed."

"Myrad Eagle II hauler Four-Six-Seven-Four-Five, this is the Collective Unified Forces destroyer Vigor. *You are cleared to pass through to Myr. Adjust course to heading seven-eight-four-point-five-point-three-two. This is to have you maintain a safe distance of at least one hundred clicks from the fleet."*

Critch paused for a short moment before sending a response. *"Vigor,* this is Myr-Four-Six-Seven-Four-Five. Message received. Adjusting course to maintain a safe distance. Thank you, and have a nice day."

A response came speedily back. *"Have a good day, and safe travels Myr-Four-Five."*

Reyne chuckled. "Even their old junkers get treated better than colonists."

"Assuming they're not drawing us into a trap," Critch said. "This feels eerily similar to how I nabbed an Alluvian cruiser a few months back."

Reyne frowned. "I wish Demes could be plugged into their systems right about now to see what they're thinking."

"Agreed." Critch rubbed his hands. "Well, we're a Myrad

hauler, and we're going to cruise right past the entire CUF fleet and through that space barrier as if we've done it a hundred times before."

Reyne cocked his head. "I never took you for an optimist."

"All pirates are optimists; otherwise, they'd never leave the docks."

"I thought you were all opportunists."

Critch shrugged. "No difference."

Silence fell on the bridge. Reyne broadcast nothing to the crew in case the CUF was picking up their radios. He knew the crew was nervous, and he considered making rounds to update them, but he couldn't bring himself to stand. Not when the view screen was filled with several dozen warships, frigates, destroyers, gunships, and patrols.

As they approached the fleet, Reyne and Critch shot harried glances at each other. They were easily within shooting range and could be blown into the abyss without a single chance for counter maneuvers. Not that they could make any kind of stand with this ship.

The ships sat in loose groupings. The warships sat together, with the frigates and destroyers separated. Gunships sat closer to the barrier. Patrol ships, work ships, and a mish-mash of smaller ships sat as outliers.

A patrol ship sped toward them, and Reyne leaned forward, gripping his seat.

The spacecraft whizzed past as it angled toward a warship.

Reyne slumped. "Damn, cocky fliers. Reminds me of how you used to fly."

Critch's lip curled up at the corner.

Neither man spoke again until they passed the fleet and entered the space barrier.

The barrier wasn't actually a barrier. It was simply a matrix of EMP buoys in Myr's orbit. It was a fail-safe protective blanket since only CUF ships had protection against EMP fields. Though, as far as Reyne knew, only warships, destroyers, and frigates had the level of protection needed against the high-intensity blasts the buoys emitted.

No one without access codes was landing on Myr.

Flashing lights on the EMP buoys twinkled their locations. "Those things are eerie."

"Yes, they are," Critch said, and Reyne realized he'd voiced his thoughts aloud.

"We're almost through," Critch continued.

After they cleared the barrier, Reyne closed his eyes and breathed. "You won't hear me complaining that we're through that."

Critch cracked his neck. "Not a bad-looking planet. Too bad it's full of citizens."

With the fleet and barrier behind them, Reyne was able to appreciate Myr's beauty. The planet was the first colonized world after Mars and Europa, and he could see why. With a wealth of both land and water, it was a picturesque, temperate world, reminding him of pictures he'd seen of Earth.

Reyne broadcast to the crew, "Heads up. We're clear of the space barrier. Prepare for landing."

Unlike the colonies, Myr had twelve space docks located around the planet. Critch hailed the Smithton docks. They directed him through landing protocols, which he handled as though he were a Myrad captain.

Myr had a thick atmosphere, thicker than all the other planets, and the descent lasted longer and was more turbulent than Reyne had expected. Even still, Critch brought the junker down with finesse.

The space docks they landed at put any fringe station's docks to shame. These docks, built out of silver alloy, were easily ten times the size of Ice Port's docks, and they seemed fifty times as busy. They climbed from the surface like a glistening rainbow, and took up much of the island they occupied. Critch settled the ship down gently onto her base despite her size and clumsy controls.

"Not bad," Reyne said. "Although, I'm sure Throttle would still give you some pointers."

Critch grunted. "If she's anything like you, I'm not surprised."

"Everyone to the commons for final checks," Reyne announced.

By the time Critch had locked the ship down, Doc had finished staining Birk's face with blue dye. He looked as though he'd gone for a swim in blueberry wine—a perfect match to the hue of Myrad skin. Doc then stepped up to Reyne and wiped the stained cloth over his face.

Finished, Doc stepped back to admire her work. "It took me endless hours—and my fingers may be forever stained blue—but it was worth it. You and Birk look perfect."

Boden gave a nod. "You're both too tall, but otherwise you could actually pass as Myrads."

Reyne chuckled drily. "That's something I've never had an interest in being."

"Ditto," Birk added.

Reyne grabbed the long coat he'd found in one of the Myrad's quarters and slipped it on, covering his armament.

Critch was leading the other team, but with his scars, he'd never be able to pass off being a Myrad. So Birk had his face stained and wore a coat like the one Reyne wore, playing the part of a Myrad on Critch's crew. Since Myrads were often outnumbered a dozen to one by tenured, everyone else wore rattier tenured jackets.

Critch slapped his hands together. "Okay, the Genics Corp snatch starts now." He glanced at his watch. "The courtesy time limit to dock without filing paperwork is five hours, which means we need to be wheels-up before sunrise. If any of you aren't back by then, you'll be considered dead or a permanent Myrad fixture. Got it?"

"Okay. Boden and Doc," Reyne began, "under no circumstances will you leave this ship. If you get asked by a dock patrol, make excuses if you have to."

"I still prefer to come with you," Boden grumbled.

"Can't risk it," Reyne said. "You're our ticket to Alluvia. You're staying on this junker, where it's safe."

Doc didn't say anything, and Reyne knew she'd always been more comfortable staying out of harm's way.

"That's not permission to sit on your asses," Critch said. "This ship better be ready to power up within seconds of us getting back on board. It won't take long for them to figure out something is up once we make the snatch."

"The ship will be ready," Boden said quickly.

Reyne grabbed Boden's forearm. "See you soon."

Boden nodded and grabbed Reyne's arm in return. "The sooner the better."

"Hurry back," Doc said, her words hard, yet containing an underlying softness.

Reyne smiled. "I plan on it."

Critch patted Demes' shoulder. "Watch your back out there."

Critch stood for a moment and—surprisingly—grabbed Reyne's forearm. "Take care of my tech."

Reyne nodded and clasped the pirate's arm. "You have my word. I'll look out for him."

Critch stepped back. "Let's do this. Chutt, Birk, let's see what Genics Corp has to offer."

Reyne turned to Demes and Sixx. "Ready to tour a Myrad mansion?"

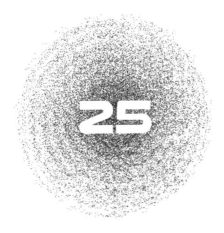

SILVER-COATED PROBLEMS

Critch

The six men separated into their two groups after they left the docks. Critch's team had the more dangerous job, and he wouldn't have it any other way. His team was headed to Genics Corp's Smithton warehouse, where the organization stored its incoming and outgoing inventory near the space docks. Heid's Founder friend believed the fungicide was being stored there.

There were far too many unknowns in this plan for Critch to be comfortable. They had only an address to go on. No map of the place, no intel on security procedures. Hell, he didn't even know if this warehouse had a night shift. The way he saw it, they were running into a potential clusterfuck with their eyes closed and both hands tied behind their backs.

Nonetheless, if anyone could pull off two concurrent heists within the heart of Myr, these two crews could. He, Chutt, and Birk had worked alongside one another in close quarters for years. He trusted them and knew he could count on them to follow his lead.

Critch noticed how stiffly the older man moved now. Nevertheless, he knew Demes would be safe, because he had Sixx there to look after him. Critch had sparred with the runner back on the *Honorless* and found the man had the heart of a pirate. Critch knew he could count on him as long as he paid him well— and he promised to pay him plenty to keep the young tech safe.

He worried more about the risk of Reyne selling them out to the CUF. Critch clenched his fists, thinking about the man he would've gladly given his life for at one time. Vym had asked Critch to give his old mentor another chance. Critch had given his word, but that didn't mean he'd trust the runner.

He pulled up his collar against the damp winds blowing in from the sea. The sidewalks Birk led them down weren't busy at this hour, lowering the risk of someone noticing them as off-worlders. They walked a dozen blocks, past silver skyscrapers that pierced the sky like swords, until they reached the address they were looking for. The narrow, four-story building bore no logo.

"This is the one," Critch said quietly, but loud enough for Birk to hear. Years spent as a pirate had taught him that when someone downplayed their property, they were intentionally trying to avoid attention. That was the property he'd always go for first. It was no different tonight.

Birk gave a quick nod, and led them to the alley between the buildings across the street. Once in the shadows, Critch held up a hand to silence his men while he ran a scan for sensors. Several moments later, he let his hand drop. "Alley's clear."

He nodded toward the Genics Corp building. "They have motion and audio sensors at all windows and doors on the ground level. Looks like they don't want company coming in from the street."

Chutt smiled. "I'd say, let's drop in."

Critch looked up at the roof. "My thoughts exactly."

The trio spent the next two hours breaking into the taller building next door and sneaking through hallways and up elevator shafts to get to its roof. From there, they shot a zip line over to the roof of the Genics Corp warehouse.

As Birk retracted the line, Critch scanned the roof to double-check for sensors. "It's clear."

He walked casually to the roof access door and was surprised to find it unlocked. He almost laughed at the ease of entry. The Myrads were too cocky for their own good. Sure, they had a space barrier, but he was still surprised no one on the surface felt like becoming a thief—or even a vandal—for the hell of it. He imagined Myr's police forces were likely focused entirely on catching runaway tenured.

"Easy pickings," Chutt said from behind Critch.

He turned to face Chutt and Birk. "Warehouse personnel are likely all tenured, so they won't put their lives on the line to protect inventory. Still, there's no need to draw any attention our way."

"No problem," Chutt said, and Birk nodded.

He wagged his finger ahead. "Let's go."

They crept down a short stairwell to the fourth floor. Critch frowned as he took in the layout. As expected, each level had shelves lining its walls, with walkways around them. The problem lay on the other side of the innermost walkway, where a large opening cut straight through the center of the building. A machine on rails ran up and down all four stories as it moved crates from one floor to another. There was little opportunity for them to move around without being in the open.

Critch entered in new search criteria on his wrist scanner, then scanned the building's interior. Dots highlighted the only active sensors—all concentrated in a corner on the second floor. He crawled to the open center, got down on his stomach, and peered over the edge. A few dozen tenured workers, all in white lab coats, were inventorying and moving crates. Another four men wore familiar blue uniforms. Critch flattened himself on the floor and crawled back to Chutt and Birk's position.

"I counted four dromadiers down there."

Chutt scrambled to pull out his gun. "What the hell are they doing here?"

"Doesn't matter. The mission is still on," Critch replied.

"What do we do about them?" Birk asked.

"We take them out first," Critch said. He scanned the warehouse for ideas. His eyes locked onto the massive machine moving up the center of the building.

He smiled.

"I have a plan."

It took Critch, Chutt, and Birk fewer than ten minutes to work out the details of Critch's startlingly simple plan.

On the third floor, they acquired three white lab coats to blend in. Unfortunately, the tenured workers they came across didn't volunteer their jackets as easily as expected, and had to be quietly drifted by breaking their necks.

Once they had their camouflage, Chutt split off from their

group and headed down three flights to the ground floor in search of the janitorial closet, also known as a demolition expert's workshop. Critch and Birk hid for five full minutes before they took the stairs to the second floor to play their parts.

They found it easy to walk around the floor as long as they kept a wide berth from other workers. Walking side-by-side, they performed quick reconnaissance. Two guards stood at the corner where their payload was, while the two other guards made their rounds separately, walking in opposite directions around the floor.

Ready to make their move, Critch nodded to Birk, and they split up. Critch meandered toward their payload while Birk headed for the opposite end of the floor, which was the only spot where the two guards making rounds would pass one another.

Critch looked down so as to not draw attention to his scarred face. He came to a stop before the dromadiers when he saw their boots.

The soldier to his left waved him off. "Move it, chump. This area's off limits."

Critch lifted his face. The two soldiers grimaced. "Damn. What happened to—"

As soon as Critch heard Birk's first shot, he fired both his guns at the same time. The pair of dromadiers fell, dead, shocked looks on their faces. He pulled his guns out from his lab coat. Each pocket now bore a burnt hole.

Someone gasped nearby, and he swung around to find a tenured watching him, her eyes wide.

"You scream, you die," Critch said calmly, leveling his guns on her.

She nodded before taking slow steps back from him. After several paces, she turned and ran.

Critch holstered one of his guns and pinged Chutt. "Now."

"Boom-Boom is on the machine. You have sixty seconds."

"Good," Critch reported. "See you at the RP."

"Ready?" Birk asked as he reached Critch.

Shouts erupted across the floor, and he noticed that more workers had discovered Birk and Critch's handiwork. He yelled out to the tenured workers. "This place is going to blow. You'd better run."

They ran.

Critch motioned to the fungicide. Birk grabbed a crate. An alarm blared. When Critch stepped forward to grab a second crate, his gaze fell on the single metal box stored within a refrigerated unit next to the fungicide. Making a split-second decision, he grabbed that box, and they ran.

They sprinted to catch up with the other workers, blending into the small mob by the time they were out the front door. The first police craft had already arrived. Critch and Birk stayed with the group of workers until the mob slowed to a stop on the street. The two pirates broke off and ran toward the nearby alley.

Someone called out after them, but they kept running. A second later, the shouts were drowned by an explosion. Critch and Birk were thrown to the ground, and a massive wind of heat blew over them. With his ears ringing, and suffering from vertigo, Critch climbed to his feet, then helped Birk to his. They grabbed their cargo and closed the few remaining feet to the alley, where they found Chutt waiting for them.

He bore a wide grin. "Nice boom-boom, eh?"

Critch peeked around the corner to see a pile of burning debris where the warehouse had stood seconds earlier. Bodies lay strewn across the street, and no one was moving. He turned back to Chutt. "You blew up half the viggin' block."

Chutt shrugged. "You said to cover our tracks."

"That you did," Critch concurred.

Birk eyed the box in Critch's arms. "That's not the fungicide."

Critch glanced down. "No, it's not. It's Plan B."

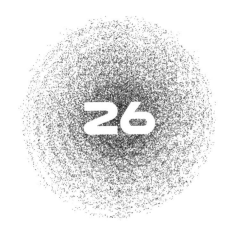

26

THE BEST LAID PLANS

Z ara Wintsel, president of Genics Corp, lived like a queen. The opulence—the sickening wastefulness—made Reyne want to be off Myr and out in the fringe where things made sense. "Let's make this quick," he gritted out. "I want to be on the tram and on our way back to the ship as soon as possible."

"You don't need to twist my arm," Demes said.

"I should've brought a bigger bag," Sixx said, entranced by the fortunes on display everywhere.

Reyne eyed the large duffle. "Your bag is plenty big enough."

He turned his attention back to the mission at hand. If there was evidence of Myr's plans for the Collective, Heid said it would be stored on Dr. Zara Wintsel's personal computer. Heid's friend—one who called herself Mariner—had seen the files for herself and had shared the details with the Founders. Rather than going for the data, the Founders had chosen instead to release the blight at Genics Corp's Moon lab. Unfortunately, the attack did nothing to sway Wintsel and her Myrad co-conspirators from moving ahead with their plans.

Heid suspected that the Founders would assassinate Wintsel and destroy any proof of the Myrad's involvement to help prevent war. With no proof, the conspirators behind Ice Port and Sol Base's destruction would never be punished. And that was something Reyne couldn't abide.

He analyzed the silver-plated mansion that sprawled across the pristine landscape. Fountains and bushy trees dotted the lawn, providing plenty of coverage to approach the house from the back. A smattering of tenured house staff came and went. Four security personnel arrived and made rounds shortly before Wintsel landed, late into the night, in a hovercraft. One of the guards escorted her into her house.

An hour later, several house lights remained on, but Reyne had seen no signs of movement. "How's the security look?" he asked Demes, who lay on the ground between Reyne and Sixx.

Demes ran a scanner as Reyne looked over his shoulder. Dots lit up at the mansion's entrances, but nowhere else. "Piece of cake."

Reyne shook his head. "Let's hope that scanner is accurate." He rose to his feet and stretched. His joints were constantly reminding him how much stronger the gravity on Myr was relative to that on Playa.

"Demes, you stay between me and Sixx," Reyne ordered.

"Oh, come on. I've been through a lot deeper shit before."

"Yeah, but I don't want to listen to Critch's incessant complaining if you get yourself killed," Reyne snapped back.

"Now, follow me."

He took the lead, weaving between fountains and under thick trees to stay in the shadows. It was late, the time Wintsel would be soundly asleep and her guards snoozing on the job.

The trio moved slowly and carefully as they approached the mansion. Reyne, still in lead, peeked around the corner. He counted three windows down to the one that would be the office window. He bit his lip to keep from cursing, and turned to face Demes and Sixx.

"There's a light on," he whispered. "Which means she may or may not be in there. Sixx, I need you to check it out."

Sixx gave a quick nod and moved quickly at a half-crouch toward the window. When he reached it, he flattened against the wall, and gingerly peered around the pane.

As Sixx hurried back, Reyne scanned the yard to make sure they were still alone.

"She's in there all right. She's sitting at her desk reading a book, just on the other side of the window, facing away from us. The room is small and the door is closed."

Reyne grimaced. "Doesn't that woman ever sleep?"

"What's the computer look like?" Demes asked.

"It looks like a computer," Sixx answered.

Demes rolled his eyes. "If it's a tablet, I can grab it and go. If it's a built-in house system, then I can't do that now, can I?"

"Oh. It's a big one."

Reyne noticed Demes' frown. "Demes, how much time do you need to break into her system and copy her files?"

He shrugged. "Depends on her security protocols. Could be thirty seconds. Could be thirty minutes."

"You need to do it in under three minutes."

Demes looked like he wanted to say no, but wisely kept his

mouth shut.

Reyne contemplated for a brief moment. "Sixx, I need you to draw her away from that room to buy time for Demes to hack her system. Think you can figure out a diversion?"

Sixx grinned. "My pleasure."

Reyne clasped Sixx's shoulder. "Be careful."

"Always am."

"You never are," Reyne muttered as the man ran toward the front of the house.

Reyne turned to Demes. "Let's do this." He grabbed his plastic-cutting tools and slid along the outside of the house to the office window, ducking under the two windows before it. He stopped and waited, watching Wintsel for any sign of movement.

He needn't have watched her. A hovercraft alarm pierced the air, and Reyne chuckled at Sixx's flamboyant diversion. He counted to three before glancing through the window, and found Zara Wintsel walking through the door.

He carved a giant circle into the pane. Demes wore sticky gloves and pulled the pane out, keeping it from crashing. Demes crawled through first, and Reyne followed. He landed on the floor with a grunt, rolled to his feet, and quietly shut and locked the door Wintsel had left wide open.

Demes sat at the desk. He set a small black dome over the keyboard. Gray lights flashed across its surface, before turning yellow, then finally green. "I'm in."

A woman's voice emanated from the hallway. "Be sure to report it in, and line up the house staff. I'd bet credits one of them thought they could steal my Selta."

Reyne glanced at Demes. "Hurry. We don't have much time."

The handle jiggled, followed by a woman's frustrated voice. "Guards, why is this door locked?"

"I don't know why, ma'am. Did it lock on its own?" a man responded.

"No, it wouldn't lock on its own, you dolt. You young fools have no concept of how antique handles work." Someone pounded on the door. "Hello? Who's in there? Patrice, if I find out that you've let your filthy daughter roam in my house again, I swear you both will go straight to the Citadel."

"Demes, hurry," Reyne warned.

"Almost seventy percent copied."

"Move to the side, ma'am," the same man who'd spoken before said.

Something slammed into the door and Reyne leaned against the wood, attempting to keep the frame from splitting. As he held the door shut, he took in the shelves lined with priceless crystals. A portrait caught his eye. Zara Wintsel stood in a loving embrace with a CUF officer, who also had blue-hued skin. This wasn't just any officer. This older man bore the insignia of the corps general. Reyne's breath froze in his lungs. "Ausyar," he muttered, and everything suddenly made sense.

"Eighty percent."

Reyne glanced at Demes, who was tapping his fingers on the panel. Movement outside caught his eyes. "Sixx," Reyne said in relief.

Relief was short-lived as another slam against the door rattled Reyne's body.

"We've been compromised," Reyne said aloud, pulling out his gun. "Watch your back."

Sixx nodded and looked from side to side before dropping below Reyne's line of sight.

"I hear you in there!" came the woman's voice. "Guards, open this door right this instant. I'm being robbed!"

"Ninety percent."

The sound of a photon blast fractured the air, but Reyne held the door.

A sharp coldness pierced his left side, and he looked down.

"Son of a bitch." They'd shot the door lock, and the laser-like shot had sliced right through his side. The initial cold sensation morphed into an intense burning.

Something slammed into the door and he flew back, narrowly catching himself before falling.

"Demes, get down," Reyne shouted as the first guard toppled inside.

Reyne shot him point blank. He swung around and fired off continuous shots at the guard on the other side of the doorway. The man stood, shocked for a moment, before collapsing in a heap. Behind that guard, Reyne found Wintsel. "Aw, shit."

She was leaning against the wall, fighting for a breath that would never come. One of Reyne's shots had gone clean through her trachea and carotid artery. She'd be dead in seconds, but still she desperately fought for the last vestiges of life.

"Got it," Demes said, coming to his feet, pocketing his hardware.

Reyne tore his eyes from the dying woman to make sure no one else was coming down the hallway. He turned and clenched his teeth through his inhalation, every breath and movement becoming more painful. Fighting through the agony, he motioned to the window. "Move."

Demes eyed Reyne's wound. "You're shot."

"A clean through-and-through. I'm still in this fight." He followed Demes to the window, concentrating on not touching the open wound. The photon blast would have cauterized the wound, but it could easily become infected without treatment.

Demes tumbled through the window. Reyne followed, with help from Demes and Sixx. Outside, he discovered the two other guards, each dead with headshots.

"Tell me you got the data," Reyne said.

"I got the data, but I won't know if it's worth anything until I look at it," Demes replied.

"Wait. I need to grab some souvenirs," Sixx said.

"No time."

"But all four guards are down," Sixx argued.

"No time," Reyne repeated.

"You're killing me here," Sixx replied. "Fine, but don't you think it was odd she had only four guards for a house the size of a castle?"

"She didn't need more guards," Reyne ground out. "No one in their right mind would trespass on this property. Wintsel was Ausyar's lover."

"Uh oh," Demes said. "And, you killed her."

Sixx's eyes widened. "Oh. That won't go over well."

"No, it won't," Reyne said, knowing full well that he'd just drawn first blood from a vengeful man who could draw on the strength of the entire CUF armada.

An orange glow lit the sky in the distance, and all three men turned.

"Wow, now that's an explosion," Demes said.

"That came from the direction of the docks," Sixx said.

Recognition of the most likely source of that explosion sent shivers across Reyne's skin. "We need to get back to the ship *now*."

Zara Wintsel's hovercraft made quick time back to the ship. The explosion at the Genics Corp warehouse reddened the twilight sky, and Reyne knew they'd be lucky if the docks weren't already under lockdown.

Reyne, the only pilot in the group, had to fly the hovercraft, even though his side was now on fire. He none too gracefully parked the hovercraft outside a café. Demes and Sixx helped him onto the space dock.

Critch, Chutt, and Birk were already walking up the ship's ramp. Reyne and his crew hustled the remaining short distance. Reyne pulled free and headed straight for the bridge, where Critch was already strapped in and powering up the engines.

"Dock Control," Critch transmitted as Reyne took a seat. "This is Eagle II hauler Myr-Four-Six-Seven-Four-Five. We're ready for departure."

"Myr-Four-Five, please hold."

"Shit," Critch muttered as they waited. "They're onto us."

Another response came long seconds later. *"Myr-Four-Five. You are cleared for launch. Moving you onto launch pad Delta Three. We're expecting multiple inbound ships shortly. Be careful out there."*

Critch lifted his brow, and he cocked his head. "Will do, Dock Control. Thank you and have a nice day."

"They must not have been notified yet to go under lockdown," Reyne said.

"This place is seriously lacking security protocols," Critch said. "Releasing the blight on their Moon was one thing, but they felt all cozy and safe behind their space barrier."

Reyne grunted when the ship was jostled over to the launch pad.

Critch noticed. "You need Doc to take a look at that gunshot."

Reyne winced. "Once we're safely out of Myr's airspace."

Critch gave a small nod. "Did you get the data?"

"Yeah. Let's hope Demes finds something useful in it. Did you get the fungicide?"

"Birk and Chutt are stowing it now."

Now that Reyne was no longer on the move, his side began to throb, and darkness crept into his vision. He slumped forward, not finding the strength to lean back.

"Doc, you'd better get up here," Critch said on the intercom.

Reyne vaguely sensed someone moving him. He heard voices, but couldn't make out any words. As he was dragged — or maybe he was floating — he faded into oblivion.

CORRUPTED ILLUSIONS

Critch

Critch watched as Doc and Sixx lugged Reyne to the medical bay, and wondered if the old captain would pull through. Even with the blue stain, Reyne was too pale, and his hair clung to his face.

The pirate waited for the launch countdown to finish. Beyond the launch pad, all he could see was water. He imagined how much easier life on Terra would've been with this much water.

He grimaced. He hated thinking of Terra. He hadn't lived there since the Uprising, and his final days there—the worst days of his life—haunted him still.

They'd been safe and secure at Broken Mountain. They'd even been planning an attack that would've changed the entire course of the Uprising. But then the CUF snuck through the tunnels in the dead of night. The torrents never stood a chance. The CUF never would've found those camouflaged tunnels on their own, and no sensors could've picked them up. That the CUF came through *all* the tunnels at the same time meant one thing. Someone had betrayed the cause.

Coincidentally, Reyne had left the day before with several medics to check on civilian injuries. At the time, Critch had assumed Reyne had been killed. It wasn't until after the attack that he put two and two together.

Reyne was the traitor.

Critch became a hardened leader that day after learning a final, and the most valuable, lesson from his mentor.

Don't trust anyone.

For many years he'd wished for Reyne's head on a platter, for some kind of retribution. Only now, seeing Reyne weak and injured, he found a strange feeling of sympathy toward the traitor.

The panel chimed, signaling the countdown was nearly complete. Glad to focus on the launch, he brushed aside memories that only complicated things, and worked on getting them off Myr and to Alluvia.

Reyne

Reyne woke to a pleasant numbness.

"You're awake."

He turned groggily, and Doc's blurred slender form sharpened into view. "How long have I been out?"

She cupped his face with warm hands. "Three days."

"Too long." He started to sit up, and placed a hand over the tender bruise on his side. He pulled up his shirt to find a bright pink scar buried under a clear, gel-filled shell.

"Be careful." She touched his chest. "I kept you under for your body to mend faster, but you still need time."

"We're clear of Alluvia's space barrier, courtesy of our buddy, Boden. Prepare for landing."

Reyne pushed off the table to his feet and stabilized himself against the spinning room.

"You need to rest," she said, holding him steady.

When the room slowed its spinning, he held an open palm out to her.

She pursed her lips, looking down at his hand and up at his face. After a short battle of wills, she relented. She opened a drawer, tore off a strip of pills, and placed them in his hand.

Her hands went to her hips. "You're a fool if you think you should be moving around. You should stay in bed."

He grabbed an additional strip of pills and wagged it at her before pocketing it, then headed toward the bridge without a word. When he entered, he found Boden at his seat and Critch in the pilot's seat. The mechanic was the first to notice Reyne, and tilted his head in a silent greeting.

Reyne leaned against the back wall. "Did Demes find anything useful in the data?"

Critch threw a glance over his shoulder, giving Reyne a once-over before turning back to his controls. He gave a long, slow nod. "More than a dozen video transcriptions of Dr. Zara Wintsel and Corps General Michel Ausyar planning their takeover of the entire Collective. Seems the pair had the lofty goal of becoming the Collective's first emperor and empress."

"That is a lofty goal," Reyne said.

"They couldn't do all this work in a silo," Critch countered. "They never would've used the blight without the blessing of

Myr's leadership. This is obviously an effort by the entire elite class."

"I wish I could see the looks on the faces of the Alluvian citizens when they see the broadcast," Boden said.

"Speaking of Alluvians, any word from Heid?" Reyne asked.

"Nothing," Critch replied.

"She'll pull through," Reyne replied. "Her Myr intel was good. We can trust her."

Critch focused straight ahead. "We may want to consider a backup plan."

"She'll pull through," Reyne repeated. He hadn't expected much from a CUF officer, but her intel on the Myr heists had been spot-on, and she'd given her word she'd connect them with a news reporter on Alluvia, who would then broadcast any evidence they acquired at Wintsel's residence.

Reyne shot a sympathetic glance to Boden. "If we still don't hear from Heid by the time we land, we might have to head to Boden's to regroup."

"We can't go there. My parents still live there," Boden said quickly.

"We might have no other option," Reyne said. "We can't stay on this ship. It won't take the CUF long to put the pieces together, especially when a Myrad ship is using Alluvian codes. The faster we ditch this junker, the better chance we have."

Critch nodded to the blue world filling the view screen. "We'll be landing soon, but you don't look to be in any condition to leave the ship."

"I'll be fine." Reyne popped a painkiller, pushed off from the wall, and headed toward his quarters to gear up.

By the time he checked his weapons and grabbed some food, Critch had them on the ground in a space dock. Though, on

Alluvia, "ground" wasn't entirely correct.

The space docks, along with every city, were built on massive, floating platforms. The entire planet's surface was covered in water, with giant reed forests reaching up toward the sky. The water was peaceful and gorgeous, and deadly.

When the early colonists arrived from Myr, they brought with them DNA for many of Earth's species. They cloned hundreds of species to provide their food supply, but failed to take into account that mutations to adapt to new climates were inevitable. What had been large, harmless fish used for food on Earth evolved on Alluvia, over the centuries, into deadly predators.

Because of the danger, tenured were used for fishing. Boden's parents had been fishermen, but had managed to buy their freedom. Reyne didn't know the story behind how they acquired enough credits, but he knew that story was the same reason Boden had left and never spoken to them again. With Boden's staunch loyalty to the fringe, Reyne suspected that Boden's parents were the last people they wanted to get involved in their plans.

"We're docked," Critch announced to the ship. *"Grab all your gear. Birk, pack up the fungicide for Sol Base. We'll be finding another ride home."*

"Still no word from Heid?" Reyne asked after they all met at the airlock.

"We're on our own." Critch headed down the ramp. He wore a cloak over his clothes, as did everyone from the ship. Tenured walked freely on Alluvia. The crew took no precautions to disguise themselves, hiding only their weapons, which were outlawed for all non-citizens.

The painkiller had kicked in, and Reyne found himself feeling better than ever, with even his arthritis muted. He strode down the ramp and met Critch at the bottom. Before them stood an ancient-looking, sharp-dressed Alluvian.

"Gentlemen, I am your driver," he said. "I will deliver you to your destination."

Critch eyed Reyne, who looked every bit as surprised as Reyne felt.

Reyne said quietly, "Guess she pulled through after all." He then looked back to the driver and waved his arm. "Lead the way."

The old man led them at a snail's pace through the docks. They walked under a huge glowing sign that read *Welcome to First City.* On the other side, the driver motioned to a white luxury hovercraft before opening the door and stepping inside. Reyne followed, staring at the dozen seats covered in real leather. Bowls of fresh fruit and bite-sized chocolates sat at each seat. He had to remind himself to focus on the mission to keep from tearing into the decadent treats.

He took a seat near the driver, and Critch did the same. The rest of the crew climbed inside, each making sounds of awe and wonderment. Critch rubbed the leather.

"Knowing Alluvians, it's probably human skin," Boden said from behind them.

Reyne and Critch glanced back to see Boden looking all too serious. Reyne returned his gaze to the front, suddenly feeling uncomfortable.

"It's fish skin. He's just messing with us," Critch said softly, though he didn't sound entirely convinced.

While their crew savored the delicacies, Reyne and Critch watched out the windows to see where their strange host was taking them. The ride was shorter than expected, with their driver stopping a mile or so from the docks, in the warehouse district.

The hovercraft settled onto the ground and the driver turned off the engine. "We have arrived." He walked through the craft and opened the door. Reyne shot Critch a quick glance to see the pirate unclicking his holster. Reyne did the same, and led the way.

"Hang in there. This will all be done soon enough," Reyne said to their crew, who had tensed visibly when they stopped.

The driver's short steps made the walk long from the hovercraft into an unmarked warehouse. Reyne took quick glances behind him to see his crew antsy as they scanned the area.

Critch grimaced. "I'm starting to grow a serious dislike for warehouses."

Reyne stopped at the doorway. "Try not to blow this one up."

The pirate shrugged as he stepped around Reyne and inside.

The driver shuffled down an aisle with crates stacked along each side. Critch gaped. "Biome kits, air converters, rations. They could colonize an entire new world with this supply."

"I'm more curious why they're stockpiling," Reyne noted quietly.

The old man motioned to the doorway at the end of the aisle. Reyne swallowed, tension cutting through the painkillers, heightening his senses. The doorway was wide enough that he and Critch stepped through together into the cube-shaped room, where a lone man stood.

"I don't like this," Critch whispered, his gaze darting around. "One door, no windows. This looks more like a cell than a meeting room."

"Agreed," was Reyne's quick response, noticing their driver was nowhere to be found, and the door was now closed. "I'm starting to doubt Heid's good intentions."

Critch shot Reyne a wry look.

"Welcome to Alluvia," the newcomer said, taking a step forward. "You've had quite the journey."

The man stepped directly under the light as he scrutinized the crew. The Alluvian looked to be in his forties—around Critch's age—which meant he was likely older than even Reyne. He wore a business suit and had slick, short hair. There was something familiar about him, though Reyne was confident he'd never seen the man before.

The man continued. "You've brought me information that, if broadcast, would change the Collective forever."

Reyne narrowed his gaze. "Yes, and you're going to help us."

The man smiled. "Of course. But we must be careful. The Collective is in a state of flux. You've all sensed it. Otherwise you wouldn't be risking your lives. However, this is not the first time many of you have risked your lives. I wonder," the stranger began as he slowly paced in front of the crew, "what two torrent marshals, working together again, bodes for our future."

"We're not here for sweet talk," Critch gritted out. "Now, can you get us a reporter—with confirmation that it'll be reported—or not?"

"You were always the headstrong marshal," the man said, avoiding Critch's question. "Following your gut first."

"It's kept me alive this far," Critch said, and Reyne could feel the tension rolling off the pirate. "And it's telling me right now that we've walked into a trap. So, what's to stop me from killing you right here and now?"

The man pursed his lips.

Reyne's blood ran cold as the pieces fell into place. Mason looked familiar because he had the same eyes as Heid, and carried himself much like she did. Or, rather, it would be the other way around, with Heid gaining those traits from her father. He recalled the pleas Vym had written to a Founder on Alluvia, and that Founder's negative responses.

"You're Mason," Reyne blurted out.

The man straightened in surprise.

Critch motioned over his shoulder. "Birk, check that door."

Birk yelled back a couple seconds later. "It's locked, boss."

The man's features smoothed. "You know, there was a time," he began wistfully, "that if a neutral learned of the Founders, it meant his death warrant. Despite that history, here you are today, meeting face-to-face with me, and you're still breathing."

Mason walked in silence for a moment, before stopping. "You see, I was at Broken Mountain the night the Uprising was crushed. I arranged the meeting between the traitor and Corps General Ausyar, though he was a commandant at that time. I didn't intend for Marshal Reyne to be discredited. My intent was for both marshals to perish in the battle, to minimize the risk of the Uprising coming back before we were ready for it." He shook his head. "Unfortunately you both survived, and my concerns are becoming reality. But it's not yet time for the Uprising."

Reyne's blood ran cold, and he pulled out his gun.

Critch spoke first. "Now I know why I didn't like you the second I saw you."

Mason frowned and waved him away. "You think I'm the malcontent here? Everything the Founders do—everything *I* do— is to preserve the Collective. Sometimes hard decisions need made. Innocents, like your friend, Kason Somerville, must sometimes become casualties, or else they may upset the balance."

Reyne found it hard to swallow at hearing confirmation of Kason's murder.

"You bastard. You're a viggin' dead man," Boden said in hard words. "That's a promise."

"Kason never did anything wrong," Reyne said, forcing deep breaths.

"I'll be the first to say Lord Somerville was a gentleman, but he discovered knowledge that he shouldn't have found. I'm tasked with the responsibility of looking at the big picture." He paused for a moment. "I have no choice, much like the traitor had no choice on Broken Mountain. She was forced to choose between the lives of her and her compatriots, or the Uprising. Isn't that right, Aila?"

Reyne sucked in a breath as he spun around to see Doc taking small steps back from the crew. Her crystalline blue eyes watered. When they made eye contact, she didn't look away. He stood, slack-jawed, as he struggled to fit the pieces of a puzzle together that made no sense. Finally, he said the only word he could manage to get out. "You?"

Her lips trembled. "I had no choice," she said in the softest whisper. "They would've killed us."

Doc's teary gaze pleaded with him. He stared, finding himself unable to process what he now knew to be true.

For twenty years, he'd craved to kill the traitor of Terra—not for ruining his life, but for the murder of thousands of torrents at Broken Mountain.

For twenty years, he'd worked alongside the traitor of Terra, and had shared his bed with her.

With a wince, he snapped around to face Mason. He took a deep breath to calm his nerves, then raised his pistol. "Enough. You lured us here and have been biding your time ever since. It's clear you want us dead, so what are you waiting for?"

The man cocked his head. "I concede that you are correct. It's a simple fact that I cannot have players on the board who are unwilling to perform their roles. You're just pawns that should've been cleared from the board twenty years ago. That oversight will be fixed momentarily. Accept my apologies. It's nothing personal."

"Oh, it's personal all right," Critch said just before he fired at Mason.

Mason jumped, startled.

Critch's jaw dropped. "Son of a bitch."

The shot never hit Mason. Instead, a transparent, bullet-proof pane stood between the Founder and the crew.

The man shook his head. "Always the headstrong one."

Critch fired another shot. Reyne fired one off, too, because he was royally pissed off.

"Watch yourselves," Mason said. "I could kill any one of you with a single press of a button."

Reyne frowned and searched the walls until he'd found what he'd missed before. Two holes in the ceiling, and he could make out the glint of a barrel in one. He faced Mason. "You going to slaughter us?"

"Now, now," Mason said. "That wouldn't serve my needs. Corps General Ausyar will be here any minute to arrest you. He'll see that you're all publicly executed. A video of that execution—the final vestiges of the bioterrorists—will be played throughout the Collective. With your deaths, the Collective will be in balance again." He held up a finger. "Though I should warn you, the corps general developed quite a grudge against you, Captain Reyne, when he learned you had killed his beloved. Still, I do appreciate that you tidied up that loose end. Now, it's time for me to tidy up mine."

He craned his neck to peer around Critch to look at Demes. "You're the talented young tech, are you not?"

"What of it?" Demes asked.

Reyne furrowed his brow, trying to figure out what Mason had up his sleeve.

Critch took a step forward, while motioning for Demes to stay back. "Leave him out of this."

"Ah, but I can't. I ran a scan for data chips as you walked into this room, and that man is carrying the information you came here to broadcast." He tapped a couple of buttons on the remote control he carried, and a massive photon blast shot from the ceiling. Reyne protected his eyes from the scalding heat. When the heat dissipated, he looked to find a charred, blackened body, more ash than flesh.

"Demes," Critch murmured, and snapped around to face Mason.

Mason patted the air with his hands in a placating gesture. "I apologize for the primitive manner of execution, but I can't risk anyone accessing the data he carried."

Critch took a deep breath. He walked forward and tapped on the clear pane with his pistol. "How airtight is this room, Mason?"

The man narrowed his gaze. "What do you mean?"

The pirate smiled. "When we first got here, you ran a scan for data chips. But you didn't run a scan for biological agents, did you?" He pulled out a test tube and dangled it.

Mason's face blanched. "What are you doing with that?"

"As you said, I'm the headstrong one. So, tell me, if you shoot me and I drop this vial, what's going to happen?"

Mason didn't answer.

Critch continued. "I'm betting your little guns aimed at me aren't enough to kill every spore before it's airborne. I'm guessing this blight will take out me, you, hell, all of First City."

"You're bluffing. The blight is produced on the moon. You couldn't have gotten ahold of any."

"You willing to bet your life on that?"

Mason swallowed. "There are millions of innocents here. You

can't possibly—"

"Innocents are always the first casualties of war," Critch snapped back.

The pirate threw a quick glance at Reyne before turning back to Mason. "You're going to let us walk right out that door, and you're not going to alert the authorities or do anything else to draw attention to us. You know why? Because before I leave this shithole of a planet, I plan to stash a vial of blight in the middle of First City. And it'll be in a trap that I can set off on any whim. Do I make myself clear?"

Mason's chest heaved, and his face turned a plum red. He held up his remote.

Reyne held his breath and waited for the blast.

Instead, the lock behind him clicked, and the door opened.

"I'll let you buy yourselves minutes today," Mason said. "But the CUF will hunt you to the ends of the universe."

"Let them hunt us," Critch said. "I guarantee they won't catch us before I take your head."

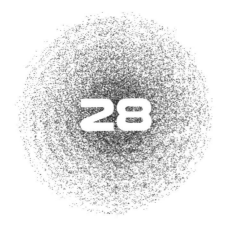

STARING INTO THE ABYSS

Heid

Heid replayed the news segment again. She rubbed her burning eyes, inhaled, and tapped her comm. "Sebin, report to my quarters."

"On my way."

She was on her feet and standing by the time he arrived a minute later.

When he saw her, he frowned. "Is everything all right?"

"No. Everything's not all right." She replayed the news segment onto her wall panel. The volume was muted, but the pictures of the fugitives on Alluvia told the story. She recognized the profiles. Not all of them, but she'd recognize the scarred face of Critch anywhere.

She shot Sebin a hard look. "They made it to Alluvia. Yet, I never received any responses to my messages to them."

His brow knit together. "I don't understand."

"They never received my messages." She shook her head. "You betrayed me, Painter."

He pointed to himself. "What? Me? You should know I would never betray you."

"You contacted Mason."

His eyes widened. "I didn't contact him. He contacted me—"

"You were not to contact Mason!" Her fists shook. She calmed herself down with a deep breath, exhaling slowly. "I gave you explicit instructions to *not* engage Mason under any circumstances. He could not know what we were doing."

"But, he reached out to me right after the torrents left Myr, and said he was helping us out from the ground on Alluvia."

"He lied," she said bluntly. She rubbed her eyes and took a deep breath. "It's not your fault. I should've known he'd put his claws into your head."

"No," Sebin replied, incredulous. "He—"

"Played you, just like he plays everyone, and now a future we've sacrificed everything for is in jeopardy, all because of your naivety. Only Mason would have the authority to block my messages." She pointed to the screen. "Those torrents were counting on my help when they reached Alluvia, and I failed them. Now they're all dead, or soon will be."

She pulled out her gun and aimed it at Sebin. She needed to hold the gun with both her hands to keep it steady.

"Don't," he said.

"People are dying because of us...because I trusted you," she added in a tiny voice she didn't recognize.

He gazed into her eyes for a long moment. He didn't click his heels as he'd always done in the past. Instead, he spoke softly. "I love you."

Her lips trembled. Then she clenched her jaw and shot him through the heart.

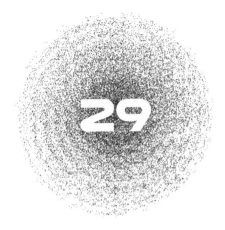

THE STUFF OF NIGHTMARES

Reyne, Critch and the others ran through the warehouse and out the front door. They saw Mason climb into the hovercraft that they'd arrived in and peel away, leaving them with no escape vehicle. In the distance, the hum of multiple hovercrafts was drawing near.

Sixx chose a direction and led them around the building and away from the street side.

The other side of the building wasn't much better. Reyne grimaced against the pain in his side.

"I could use a hovercraft right about now," Critch said.

"We'll take the water," Boden said.

Reyne shot a surprised glance at his mechanic.

"The water?" Sixx asked. "I thought it was full of sea

monsters."

"The catfish hunt mostly at night. Trust me. Some tenured runaways even live under the platforms. We only have to swim down twenty feet or so."

"Twenty feet?" Reyne asked, eying the water with trepidation.

Critch scowled. "I grew up on Terra. What in the eversea would make you think I could swim?"

"I grew up in Ice Port," Reyne said. "I'd never even seen a real lake until I left Playa."

Boden rolled his eyes. "Can none of you swim?"

"Of course I can," Sixx said.

"I can swim," Chutt added.

"I swam a little when I was a child," Doc said.

"I can doggie paddle," Birk said.

"That doesn't count," Boden countered.

Critch shook his head. "Three out of seven, not great odds."

"I can take two of you down with me," Boden said. "I can come back for two more unless Sixx and Chutt can each take one."

"Why not," Sixx offered. "If I'm going to drown down there, I'd rather not drown alone."

"I'll take Doc," Chutt said quickly.

She sighed against the pirate and mouthed the words, *thank you*. The pirate turned and gave her a hooded gaze.

Boden nodded. "Okay, Sixx, you take Birk. That leaves me with the captains."

They followed the Alluvian to the edge of the platform that ran alongside the row of warehouses. Hovercraft engines and voices barking commands came closer and closer.

"We need to hurry," Reyne said.

Boden watched the water. His eyes darted around as though searching for something. "This is a good spot. Climb in slowly and grip the ropes along the pontoons. Whatever you do, don't make any splashes. No quick movements. You have to trust me on this."

"I take it splashing is a bad thing."

"Only if you don't want to draw in a school of killer tuna." Boden sat and edged himself over and down the pontoon, entering the water without making the slightest wave. He went under, and Reyne found himself holding his own breath. Boden lifted his head out of the water seconds later. "Everything's clear. Get in."

Reyne took a deep breath. He was seriously, intensely scared. Stepping into a bottomless ocean was terrifying enough. Stepping into a pit of razor-toothed sea monsters was what nightmares were made of. Reyne sat on the edge and lowered himself into the surprisingly tepid water. He felt the safety of Boden's hand on his back, and found the touch calmed his terror. He didn't go in as smoothly as Boden had, but he also didn't make a splash. Once he was in, Critch followed at the same time as Sixx and Chutt entered the water.

Reyne held himself up, afraid to go under the surface, as though he were safe as long as his head was above water. Birk went in next, and Boden helped him down.

The voices shouting commands were getting louder, and Reyne suspected the CUF had discovered that their prey had escaped the warehouse.

Doc sat on the platform. She looked at Reyne. "I'm sorry. I never knew how to tell you. They caught Throttle and me at the farm. They were going to kill you. They—"

"I'll deal with you later," Reyne snapped back. "Get in the water."

She slid in a bit too fast, but Boden caught her before she went all the way under. He helped her grab onto a rope and she remained frozen, eyes wide.

"I'll take the lead," Boden said. "Sixx and Chutt, you follow. Now, don't worry if you lose me. Just keep diving down against the pontoon until you reach the bottom. Use the pontoon to keep pulling yourself down if you have to. Then go under it and head straight up to the surface. Your ears may hurt, but it's not deep enough to do any permanent damage."

The voices grew perilously near.

Boden heard them too, because he rushed over to grab onto Reyne and Critch. "It's like moving in space. I can move faster if you're limp. Trust me, I won't let go of you. Okay? Take the deepest inhale you can, and let yourselves become dead weight. It's okay to let out air on the way, but remember to never inhale under water."

Reyne glanced at Critch, who seemed to be absorbing Boden's every word. When Boden sucked in a breath, they each did the same. Reyne found himself yanked under the surface, and his first instinct was to kick back up. He fought against it and instead imagined himself in the zero-g simulator at the space dock.

He opened his eyes, and found he could see under the surface, though the water distorted things. Pressure built in his ears until it downright hurt, and he instinctively grabbed his nose and cleared them just like he would when diving through the atmo.

Boden continued diving down, and everything darkened. Reyne found himself in awe of the speed at which they sank, but his lungs began to burn. Even with all the time he'd spent in suits and conserving his air, he craved to breathe, and they hadn't even reached the bottom yet. He grew more and more fearful that he'd drown.

A huge dark shape moved past them. Green eyes glowed on a head the size of Reyne's chest. As he reached for his knife, the sea creature came toward them. He was ready to stab at it, only it didn't get close enough and continued on its journey.

Reyne gripped his blade, waiting for an attack. But then the pontoon was suddenly above him, and he scraped under its slimy bottom. Reyne thought Boden had swum fast before. That was nothing compared to the speed at which they shot upward once they cleared the bottom of the pontoon. He'd barely blown out the last of his air when they broke through the surface.

Reyne gasped and pointed with his knife. "Sea monster. Down. Below."

"It was only a cod," Boden replied. "More inquisitive than aggressive, but if you'd cut it, you would've drawn in every blood-eater in the area."

Reyne eyed his blade and then promptly sheathed it.

Boden motioned to the rafters above them. "Pull yourselves up onto the support beams to get clear of the water. Try not to make much noise, because there's less than a foot of platform between us and everyone on the surface. I'll go check on the others."

He took a deep breath and disappeared below the surface.

"I want that man on my crew," Critch said.

"Over my dead body," Reyne muttered. "If we live through this, I'm going to have him teach me how to swim."

"Now who's the optimist?" the other man said before grabbing onto a rafter and lifting himself out of the water.

Critch made it look easy. Reyne grabbed a rafter and made it look damn near impossible. Pain shot through his side as he pulled himself up. He splashed water and froze, expecting the worst.

"Here." The pirate held out a hand, grabbed Reyne's leg and helped him pull himself the rest of the way out of the water.

"I'm still a little off from getting shot," Reyne said as if that explained everything.

Critch, mercifully, didn't offer a rebuttal.

A second later, Sixx and Birk broke the surface, both gasping and sounding even more desperate for air than Reyne had felt.

"Up here," Critch said and then pointed above him. "But do it quiet-like."

Neither wasted any time getting out of the water.

"I think that may have been the worst experience in my life," Sixx said once he was safe on a beam.

Reyne's brow rose. "Worse than that woman on—"

"Worse," Sixx finished.

Boden broke through the surface. "We're good."

Chutt shot up the next moment, and immediately pulled himself up onto the rafters as though the water was acid.

Doc surfaced a second later, gasping. "You bastard!"

"Keep it down," Boden scolded.

"The asshole cut me!"

Reyne glanced at Chutt, who gave her a knowing grin from his perch.

A wave rippled near Doc, and she twisted around. "What was that?"

Boden shoved away from Doc and rushed to pull himself onto the rafters.

Reyne tensed as he watched Doc. "Get out of the water."

"It's too late," Boden whispered. "They're already locked on."

Everyone watched Doc, who was struggling to tread water. "Help me," she pleaded.

If Reyne could swim, he probably would've jumped into the water. Instead, all he could do was watch in dread as a smooth, gray shape broke the surface. Something barreled into the woman with a splash, and she disappeared under the surface, only to reappear a second later, coughing. "Help me!"

Dozens of gray shapes broke the surface then, all headed straight at Doc. Her shriek was drowned out under the roiling water. A frenzy of tails and fins randomly broke the surface. Red blood swirled among the gray.

Reyne watched the relentless attack, clinging to his lifeline.

Many long seconds later, the water calmed. Reyne stared into the dark water, still expecting her to surface any second, but nothing surfaced, and he could make out no movement below. The blood blurred into the dark blue water until no traces remained of Doc or her attackers.

A sense of loss poked at the edges of his heart, but it was subdued. Strange, he thought, since they'd been close for over twenty years. He supposed it was because he'd lost her back in the warehouse. Her lie overshadowed the time they'd shared together. All that time, she'd known how much it tore Reyne up being seen as a traitor, let alone all the punches he'd taken and shitty jobs because of his tarnished reputation. Still she'd said nothing and played along, as though she were being compassionate. Hell, she was just being selfish.

Looking back, it was obvious she'd been the traitor. He'd been too blind to admit it.

He might possibly mourn her death someday.

But that day definitely wasn't today.

Sixx broke the silence. "Please tell me I never have to get in that water again."

"You never have to get in that water again," Boden said, still staring down. After a couple seconds, his attention returned to the crew around him. He pointed up at one-foot-wide beams. "We walk the rest of the way."

Critch looked up. "How the hell do we walk those?"

"Very carefully," Boden replied.

Six hours later, they'd covered a mile, and every joint and muscle in Reyne's body ached. His side felt like someone had embedded a white-hot rod of rilon in it. During the trudge he'd been forced to accept Chutt's assistance a time or two when he slipped and nearly fell into the water. However, he still planned to have words with the pirate if—when—they got out of this mess.

Finally, Boden got them to the topside through a surface hole cover. Once they were standing on solid ground, Critch cocked his head at the cover. "Why the hell didn't we use one of these to get below the platform the first time?"

Boden shrugged. "I didn't see one nearby."

"Call me surprised we're still alive," Sixx said. "Only one thing. We're still stuck in the middle of enemy territory."

Reyne's comm chimed. He read the short message and burst out laughing. "Well, I'll be damned."

Critch frowned. "What's so funny?"

"Boys, we're traveling home in style. We've got to hurry, not to mention we have the little problem of getting from here to the space docks without being seen. I'm guessing our faces are plastered on every screen across Alluvia by now."

"Leave that to me," Critch said, and turned to Chutt. "I think it's time you have a smoke."

Chutt grinned and pulled out a small plastic bag. "Hell yeah."

Five minutes later, Reyne stood in the shadows near the dock entrance, watching Chutt walk casually down the sidewalk.

"It's a little trick I like to call the Fire Feint," Critch said next to Reyne.

Chutt dropped a lit cigarette near a hovercraft. Within

seconds, the craft's smoke alarms sounded, and everyone in the vicinity turned to the noise.

"Now." Critch led their group through the entrance and down the docks, careful to not look up into any cameras.

"Seriously, where do you even find a cigarette nowadays?" Sixx asked Critch.

"Chutt makes them himself. They taste like shit and will burn your throat raw for a week, but they work like a charm."

The ship came into sight, and Reyne found himself grinning from ear to ear.

Critch's jaw dropped. "How the hell did she manage to get the *Gryphon* onto Alluvia?"

Reyne didn't answer. Instead, he hustled on the ramp and to the bridge, where he found Throttle already strapped in.

"Fuck you for leaving me," she said before he had chance to speak. "Strap in. We're running out of time."

He kissed her forehead and squeezed her shoulder before he took a seat. "I can't tell you how good it is to see you."

Critch entered the bridge. "Throttle, I think I want to marry you," he said as he took a seat.

"Take a number," she said, before returning to her pre-launch prep. "Dock Control, this is Phantom cruiser Alluvia-Two-Three-Hilo-Four-Two. Ready for departure."

"Phantom cruiser Four-Two. You are cleared for immediate launch. Moving you onto launch pad Zulu Thirty-one. Have a nice flight."

Throttle smiled sweetly. "Thank you, dock patrol. Have a good day."

She leaned back in her seat, and Reyne cocked his head. "How'd the *Gryphon* get an Alluvian ID?"

"The *Gryphon* was destroyed at Ice Port, remember? My new friend, Gabriela Heid, loaned me the ID. Her father just so happens to have a Phantom III class gunship sitting in his obscenely extensive private collection. She gave me her personal assurance that his ship would not be making any kind of flight plans for the foreseeable future." She turned and winked. "It sounds like his hangar platform suffered a pontoon failure and his entire collection is about five hundred feet below the surface as we speak."

Reyne stared at the docks for a long moment. "So, we're flying out of Alluvia under Mason's banner."

Critch barked out a laugh. "I wish I could see his face when he finds out that he helped us escape."

"Who's Mason?" Throttle asked.

"Long story. We'll fill you in on the way back."

"Where are we headed?" she asked.

"Nova Colony," Critch said.

Reyne looked back at Critch. "Why not Tulan Base?"

The pirate took apart his pistol and pulled out a data coin. "Because we have unfinished business."

30

FULL CIRCLE

R eyne sat in silence in the pirate's office at Nova Colony. A light on the panel blinked when the data coin's contents finished copying onto Critch's system.

"I'm no tech," Critch said. "But I know that if I upload this data to the Net, there are techs out there who will know what to do with it."

They had no guarantees the information would make it to the Collective news. Most citizens would likely never see it. But if enough colonists saw it, the Uprising would have a chance.

"The fungicide should be dropping on Sol Base right about now," Reyne said. "With a show of good faith like that, coupled with the data, the fringe will band together against Myr. I only hope it will be enough to stop Ausyar."

Critch moved to press the upload button.

Reyne grabbed his arm. "Wait."

"What?"

"It's missing one thing." He reached into the neck of his shirt and lifted out the medallion he wore.

Critch's lips curled. "How right you are." After several keystrokes, he flipped the screen so Reyne could see the cover added to the data file. It was a simple gray cover, blank except for a single torrent raindrop on its center.

Reyne leaned back and crossed his arms over his chest. "Now it's ready."

The pirate tapped a button, and the word UPLOADED appeared over the file.

"It's done." Critch leaned back.

"Good thing Demes was smart enough to make copies of the data," Reyne said.

Critch nodded. "Demes was a good tech."

"He was a good pirate," Reyne added.

"He was a good torrent," Critch corrected.

Critch reached into a drawer and pulled out a bottle of bourbon. He then pulled out two glasses and filled them both. He slid a glass over to Reyne. "Here's to two old torrent marshals taking on the universe."

Reyne watched him for a moment. "I knew you'd finally get it through that thick skull of yours that I wasn't a traitor."

Critch winked. "I may be hardheaded, but I also know when I've been wrong."

"Seriously?" Reyne asked. "That's the worst apology I've ever heard."

Critch shrugged. "I don't think I've ever apologized to anyone before."

"I'm not surprised."

They clinked their glasses, and each took a long drink.

"I received a message from Heid," Reyne said. "She wants to join forces."

"I received the same one."

Reyne thought for a moment before speaking. "I think she's earned the right to wear the raindrop."

"You sure about that?"

"What's your gut tell you?" Reyne countered.

Critch took another drink. "That we should meet with her again." He swirled the drink in his glass. "But, if I find out she had anything to do with that Alluvian shitstorm we were thrown in, I won't hesitate to drift her and take her ship."

"I know," Reyne said. "But if she didn't betray us, having an Alluvian captain and her warship on our side speaks volumes to the Collective."

"It sure won't hurt," Critch agreed.

After a contemplative moment, Reyne spoke again. "The blight. Was it real?"

"Yep. Idiots had it in the same type of crate as the one shown on the news."

"Why'd you take it?"

"Because a pirate always prepares for the worst."

"Would you have used it?"

Critch looked over his glass. "What do you think?"

Reyne narrowed his eyes as he examined the other man. "I don't know."

"There's your answer."

"What'd you do with it?"

"Saving it in case we ever need a Plan B."

"Was it only that one vial?"

Critch never answered. After waiting another long moment for an answer, Reyne pursed his lips, and they drank in silence.

Critch drained his glass and set it down. "It's safe to say a new Uprising has begun."

"Uprising?" Reyne's jaw tightened. "No, we just started a war."

COMING SOON:

FRINGE STATION
Book 2 in the Fringe Series

GLOSSARY OF TERMS

ABYSS: Term used to describe people and ships lost in space, presumably or known dead.

CHIMESUIT: Blue, armored space suit worn by dromadiers. Named for the chime-like sounds the suit emits.

CITIZEN: Free person born on Alluvia or Myr.

COMM: References communications sent/received as well as personal communication devices.

COLONIST *aka* Fringe: General population in the fringe. Considered impure and lesser by many citizens.

CUF: Collective Unified Forces (CUF). The Collective's military forces.

DRIFT: Slang term meaning to die or to kill. E.g., "I drifted him with a single shot to the head."

DROMADIER: CUF soldier.

EM FIELD: Short for Electro Magnetic Field. On-ship technology to produce artificial gravity.

EMP: Short for Electro Magnetic Pulse. Weapon employed by the CUF to disable ships.

EVERSEA: A term referencing the space frontier. An Eden.

FOUNDERS: Secret organization of citizens and colonists who steer the Collective's actions using ulterior methods. Believed to have become defunct after the War.

FRINGE: Refers to tributary planets and colonists under Collective control (Darios, Playa, Spate, and Terra) as well as the Space Coast.

FRINGE STATION: A colony's trading outpost with space docks.

JUMP SPEED: fastest speed at which ships can currently travel. Requires jump shields to protect crews from hydrogen radiation poisoning from high, faster-than-light speeds.

LOGGER: Waterlogged "puffy" person addicted to seasoned water, i.e. water seasoned with sweet soy.

PIRATE: Outlaw who raids ships and smuggles contraband.

RILON: Extremely durable yet flexible metal used on most hulls, weapons, and tools.

RUNNER: Interstellar postman and transporter. Fringe runners commonly smuggle blue tea or sweet soy.

SCALAR: References dark matter or space.

SOLAR SAILS: Large flexible sails on ships used for long-term space travel.

STAR SWARM: Tsunami of space garbage/debris pulled into an asteroid's gravitational pull.

STRETCH: Playan colonist with low-g mutations. Extremely tall, with respiratory and heart defects.

SWEET SOY: Highly addictive drug, often mixed with water.

TENURED: Indentured servant. Tenured are often tricked into servitude.

TORRENT: Colonist rebel who fought in the Uprising twenty years before Fringe Runner takes place.

UPRISING: A revolt by the fringe colonists against citizens of Alluvia and Myr for equal rights.

VIG: Derogatory term, referring to a small, smelly rodent.

VOICELESS: Tenured who have had their vocal cords destroyed because they broke laws or attempted to escape servitude.

***The* WAR**: War between Alluvia and Myr. The War ended with a truce and creation of the Collective and the push for colonizing other worlds for resources.

WOMBIE: Mutated, slow-moving, Spaten colonist who have developed a camel-like ability to store water. Have extremely low IQs.

ABOUT THE AUTHOR

Rachel Aukes is the bestselling author of 100 Days in Deadland, which made Suspense Magazine's Best of the Year list. She is also a Wattpad Star, her stories having over four million reads. When not writing, she can be found flying old airplanes across the Midwest countryside.

Connect with Rachel at
www.RachelAukes.com.

Made in the USA
Columbia, SC
12 March 2020